TWIN GAMES

The Heroes of Silver Springs 2

D1564892

Tonya Ramagos

EROTIC ROMANCE

Siren Publishing, Inc.
www.SirenPublishing.com

A SIREN PUBLISHING BOOK
IMPRINT: Erotic Romance

TWIN GAMES: THE HEROES OF SILVER SPRINGS 2
Copyright © 2008 by Tonya Ramagos
ISBN-10: 1-60601-007-7
ISBN-13: 978-1-60601-007-5

First Printing, April 2008

Cover design by Jinger Heaston
All cover art and logo copyright © 2008 by Siren Publishing, Inc.

PUBLISHER
Siren Publishing, Inc.
www.SirenPublishing.com

TWIN GAMES

The Heroes of Silver Springs 2

TONYA RAMAGOS
Copyright © 2008

Prologue

He left her the airport. Angelina Keaton fought to hear through the roar in her ears as the attorney read the last of her uncle's will. Not that the rest mattered to her. Uncle Edward already gave her more than she hoped for, possibly more than she wanted. Shock tangled with the grief in her heart. He knew the debacle of her last business venture, knew she walked away with barely a penny to her name. He knew how she attempted to pull her father's business out of the red after his death, knew she fell on her nose there too. Yet, in his last will and testament, Edward Keaton left her what he had loved most, Keaton Aire.

The attorney, a tall, lanky man with a balding head of gray hair and beady little eyes, completed the reading of the will, and the chatter among family and friends present began. Some would be satisfied, Angelina knew. Those who loved her uncle, those who had been true friends, those who grieved his passing would expect nothing more from his death than what they received. Still, there were others present, she thought, as her gaze scanned the handful of faces in the room that would be angry, feel cheated and scorned. Her cousin Marshall and her sister Tess were definitely among them. And her mother, Angelina feared her mother would be angry as well.

"It's a second chance for you."

A small, frail hand patted Angelina's thigh and she instinctively reached for it, holding it in her own hand. She looked at her mother, into the greenish-brown eyes so much like her own. She wished she could read the thoughts behind those eyes. "Are you mad, Mom?"

"Honey, whatever for?" Silvia Keaton asked, her eyes shining now with genuine question and surprise.

"He didn't leave you—" Anything, Angelina started to say but left the sentence hanging.

"He left me money," Silvia said and turned her hand over to lace her fingers with her daughter's. "I still have my place in this house and I have my gardens. That's all I need, all I want."

Angelina nodded and thought. She spotted her sister talking with her cousin across the room. Neither looked at all happy, she noted. "Tess isn't satisfied," she said with a sigh. "And he left Marshall the house."

Silvia shot her youngest daughter a glance then turned back to Angelina. "Tess is never satisfied," she said with a small, tired smile. "As for your cousin Marshall, he is the last remaining male to the Keaton name, the estate. It's only right that he get the house."

"If he doesn't get his act together he will loose it," Angelina murmured. Tall, dark, and handsome, Marshall Keaton carried the family looks as well as his father and uncle had in life. He also carried a glass of Scotch everywhere he went.

"I'm sure Edward took as many precautions against that as he could."

"The airport, Mom, I'm scared." The admission left a bitter taste in her mouth.

Silvia gave her a comforting smile. "And you will be more successful because of it."

"The store…" Angelina began and shook her head. The airplane hobby store she'd opened right out of college turned out to be her worst nightmare.

"You made some bad decisions." Her mother nodded. "But you learned from those errors in judgment. You were young, still a bit green even with your college degree. You won't make those mistakes this time."

"And the charter business?"

Silvia sighed. "The charter business was your father's doing. None of us suspected how bad off that business had become or how he got it that way. He hid it well. You and your Uncle Edward tried to save it but it was too far gone. No one blames you, sweetheart."

Angelina looked away, stared off into the distance. Whether no one else blamed her or not, it didn't matter. She blamed herself. She returned to Silver Springs with scraped hands and knees from her own failure only to turn those scrapes into gashes when her father's business went belly-up months later.

"Look at me," her mother said with a slight squeeze to her hand. "Your uncle had faith in you. He's given you another chance to have what you want, what you love. Maybe you can open a flight school. I know how much you love to fly and teaching would be a real joy for you."

"I do and it would. Uncle Edward always told me to forget the past and move on," Angelina remembered. "I guess this is his way of making me follow his advice."

"He loved you, loved you like you were his own daughter." Silvia's eyes filled with tears and she pulled a handkerchief from her handbag, dabbed at the tears.

And she, Angelina thought with a gentle squeeze to her mother's hand, had loved him as much as her own father. Not one to cry in public, she said a low curse when tears swam into her own eyes. She managed to get through the news of her uncle's sudden death, to make it through the wake, the funeral, the reading of the will and no tears fell. Yet, now that it was all over, now that the true weight of the loss started to settle along with the fear of her future, of the airport's future, on her shoulders, she wanted nothing more than to lock herself in a room somewhere and cry.

* * * *

He shot quick furtive glances her way but didn't stare at her, didn't study her the way he wanted to. If he looked too much, too close, she or anyone else in the room might see the rage in his eyes. He was doing his best to hold onto that fury. Now wasn't the time. But soon, he promised himself. Soon he would make the bitch pay.

He curled the fingers of his right hand into a fist in the front pocket of his slacks, uncurled them. Oh yes, Angelina Keaton would pay. The bitch had no right to the airport, to the money. It should have been his. All of it— the house, the land, the money, the business—should have been his. But it was the airport he wanted most and her he hated most. He couldn't have the airport. Edward Keaton saw to that in his last will and testament. He would hate to see it close, but it would happen. Angelina Keaton failed at two businesses already, and he would see to it that she lost the third as well. But first he would taunt her, play with her, and use her to gain his revenge. Ah yes, that would be fun indeed. He'd waited years for this but finally the time to play had definitely come.

Chapter 1

Romantic Illusions. Angelina tipped her head back to read the sign in red neon lettering on a soft pink background that hung over the shop door. An apt name, she thought as she entered the shop. Any romance she ever thought she found always turned out to be an illusion. She stopped just inside the door and gave her eyes a moment to adjust from sunlight to florescent. She couldn't say why she ventured into this particular store except that curiosity finally won. Since her return to Silver Springs shortly after her father's death, she'd thought to pay the place a visit. It would be interesting to see how a sex shop thrived in a mid-sized Southern town. More interesting still, she mused, to see the rich and sheltered Veronica Abbott running the place.

Apparently both Veronica and her store were doing well, Angelina decided as her gaze met with racks of lacy lingerie. She saw shelves of candles, oils, books and other things that would require closer inspection to name. Advertisement posters lined the walls but it was the display of powders, glitters and lotions centered around a picture of a naked couple in an embrace next to a claw-foot bathtub that really attracted her attention. The store marked its six-month anniversary three weeks ago and she knew Veronica's marriage to fire department captain Dean Wolcott hit the six-month mark shortly thereafter.

A handful of customers browsed the store's offerings and Angelina couldn't help but gape when she recognized Stella Franklin, Silver Springs biggest gossip, strutting her stuff toward the checkout counter with an armful of silk and lace.

"Quite a picture, isn't it?" a female voice asked softly.

"I'm trying to decide if I should laugh or be intrigued and touched," Angelina said, her gaze still on the older woman. It was sweet, she supposed, and even a bit inspiring that a woman in her sixties could still feel compelled to dress sexily for her husband.

"I'll tell you what's funny. Stella Franklin was one of my biggest critics when I opened this store. She tried to have me shut down, spread all sorts of vicious rumors that my stock was trash and degrading to the women of the community."

"Now she's a customer." Angelina smiled, seeing the humor in the change of events.

"One of my biggest."

Angelina turned. She already figured out without looking that her companion was Veronica Abbott Wolcott but one look proved the woman was not the same repressed, modest girl Angelina remembered from high school. Veronica had let her hair down, both figuratively and literally. Her long blond hair streamed in a free-flowing curtain around an exultant face with blue eyes that shined. She stood nearly three inches taller than Angelina in flat, teal blue shoes that matched the capri pants she wore with a virgin white top. The blouse fit tight against her breasts and stopped just above her tummy to reveal a silver belly-button ring with a dangling teal heart.

"Wow!" Angelina could think of nothing else to say for several long moments. Though she returned to town several months ago and heard many things grind through the town gossip mill about the changes Veronica had undergone over the years, but to see it firsthand left her a bit dumbstruck. "You look wonderful," she finally managed.

"I could say the same about you." Veronica beamed at her. "How are you, Angelina?"

"As soon as I get my tongue off the floor I'll tell you." She laughed and looked around. She wouldn't have guessed Veronica had it in her, the exotic traits and ambition. As kids, they had attended the same school, traveled in many of the same circles, but never became close friends. They had been acquaintances, Angelina thought. Still, one didn't need to be Veronica Abbott's best friend to know how sheltered her parents kept her, how naive she'd always been. "You are the last person I would have expected this from," she said, gesturing at their surroundings.

"You and everyone else. Do you have something in mind for that special someone?" Veronica cocked her head, one eyebrow raised and a slight hint of a smile on her rosy red lips.

"Ha! What someone?" Angelina chuckled and shook her head. "I was just in the neighborhood, as the old cliché goes, and thought I would drop in, browse around a bit."

"Browse all you want. If you have any questions, feel free to ask." She nodded toward the girl behind the checkout counter. "That's Judy, my assistant. She will be glad to help you if you can't find me." A chime sounded and she looked to the door. Instantly, her face transformed from merely friendly to glowing and stupendously happy. "If you would excuse me, that would be my hubby paying me a quick visit." She put a light hand on Angelina's arm, leaned in and said more softly, "If you're in the market for a hottie, the local fire department is burning up with sexy, hard-bodied males." She waggled her brows, grinned and walked away.

Angelina laughed. No, definitely not the Veronica Abbott she remembered. She stamped out the pang of envy settling in her belly as she watched Veronica throw her arms around Dean Wolcott's neck and plant a long wet kiss on his lips. Now that was a combination she would never have considered, the town bad boy married to the modest little rich girl. A cliché, yes, she thought, but it obviously worked well for them.

The chime on the shop door announced another customer and Angelina turned away, began to peruse the stock. She may not have a special someone to buy for but she had herself. She could get something for personal pleasure and stimulation, she decided. After all, who knew better how to please a woman than herself?

* * * *

Sex Games. Jason Graham's lips twitched as he read the cover of the book in her hands. Simple yet spicy and oh-so tempting, he decided of both the book and the woman who held it. Visions of sexy, revealing costumes and other erotic props came to mind, and he felt his cock awaken from the idea. He loved to play sex games. Problem was, he found it difficult to hook up with a woman in Silver Springs that shared his ideas of fun.

"Looking for some ideas on entertainment?" he asked and felt a weird little flutter low in his belly when her gaze lifted and settled on his. Brown eyes with hints of green looked at him from a face both exotic and sultry. Chestnut hair fell in a silky wave of evenly cut stands around that face to her shoulders. She wore a black shirt that fit loose and hung long over a pair of simple jeans. The clothes concealed all true shape and left everything to the imagination. Imagination was something he possessed in abundance and it had kicked into high gear the instant he walked into the store and spotted her.

"Perhaps," she answered and closed the book, her finger inside the pages to hold her place.

Jason took a small step closer. "Do you like to play games?"

"Perhaps," she said again, and a hint of a smile toyed with the edges of her luscious lips. "With the right guy, of course." Her gaze dropped from his, sliding slowly down the length of him before it crept back up. By the time she met his gaze again, he felt breathless and just a bit light-headed. "Are you here to pick up a gift for you wife, girlfriend?"

"Are you fishing?" he asked and hoped he sounded as calm and together as she did. He certainly didn't feel calm and together. More like frazzled and shattering, he thought and tried to remember the last time a woman had such an effect on him.

She laughed, and the sound moved over him like a warm summer breeze. "More like wondering what a guy like you is doing in a place like this." She winced and wrinkled her nose. "That sounded like something out of *101 Cheesy Pick-up Lines*."

Jason propped the toe of his booted foot on a low shelf, resting a hand on a higher shelf above it as he considered her. "Are you trying to pick me up?" Her gaze raked down him again, and his cock stiffened. Dammit, if she didn't stop doing that the only game he would be playing was tug of war with his cock in a cold shower back at the station house. She lifted a finger, traced the fire department emblem on the left pocket of his uniform shirt and he felt an electric bolt shoot from his chest straight to his groin.

* * * *

Touching him proved quickly not to be the best of ideas. Flames, swift and red hot, bolted into her fingertip, traveled up her arm and burning embers rained through her insides. "You're a firefighter," she murmured softly and let her finger graze down that hard wall of chest, the ridged abs before it reached the waistband of the black jeans he wore. She jerked her hand back, a reflex action of surprise at where she'd nearly touched him, wanted to touch him. Her gaze shot up to his face, and she found him looking down at her, his light gray eyes gone dark with desire.

He caught her hand and, gaze locked with hers, brought it back to rest a half inch above the waistband of his jeans. "Firefighter Jason Graham at your service, ma'am," he said in a feigned accent thick with Southern honey. If he'd been wearing a hat he would've tipped it at her, she thought.

"You aren't a true country boy," she said, and because he wouldn't let go of her finger, she ran the tip over the top of his jeans against his stomach, back and forth, back and forth. She had the satisfaction of feeling that tight stomach contract when he sucked in a breath.

"No ma'am, but I can act like one if it's what you want," he offered, and his lips moved into a mischievous tilt.

"You like to play games, don't you, Jason?"

His lips unfolded into a full-blown smile, and he dropped the country-boy act. "I know I wouldn't mind playing a few games with you."

An alarm sounded in Angelina's head, a warning that she could be getting herself into more than she bargained for. Since she hadn't bargained for anything when she walked into Romantic Illusions, she ignored it. She thought she could use a little fun, deserved it after the stress and problems of the last few months. Feeling bold and just a bit defiant, she let her finger slide beneath the waistband of his jeans and pulled. His foot slipped off the shelf as he came to her. "What kind of game did you have in mind?" she asked, her voice low and seductive.

His hands moved to her waist and he leaned in, stopping only a breath away from her lips. "Something involving silk sheets and lace." His lips brushed hers so faintly she wondered if she really felt them touch. "Or we can be more daring and go for blindfolds and leather."

Her mouth was suddenly too dry to speak. She licked her lips, saw his gaze drop to her mouth and had a split second to remember that they stood in the aisle of a store before he kissed her again. His tongue coaxed her to part her lips then slipped inside, tangling with hers. She heard herself make a low groan and moved her hand to his neck, pulling him closer still to deepen the kiss. All thoughts of right or wrong, of where they were and who could be watching went up in smoke as he devoured her mouth. One of his hands snaked beneath the tail of her shirt, cupping her ass, and she felt his lower body push against her, felt his cock hard and ready through the material of his jeans, of hers. He gave her ass a light squeeze, and she heard a plop just before he broke the kiss.

Angelina opened her eyes, blinked to regain her focus, and looked at him. The man was pure panty wetting perfection and all she could think was bed. She wanted this man in bed.

"You dropped the book." His voice was low, heated, and a bit breathless.

It took a minute for his words to penetrate the fog in her head. The book, she remembered, and stepped back, running a shaky hand through her hair. She glanced down at the book, looked back at him and saw the slow, amused grin unfold on his lips. "I guess it's a good thing it's a paperback," she said, her voice surprisingly steady. Strange, she thought, when nothing else about her felt that way. She looked around, saw that they were alone in the aisle and said a quick, silent prayer of thanks before she bent to pick up the book.

The shrill of an alarm split the quiet atmosphere of the shop, and she jerked upright. She understood when Jason began to fumble with a long, black, box-looking thing that hung off his belt. A radio, she realized as a clipped female voice flowed from its speaker, issuing an address and reason for the call.

Jason listened, responded with an authoritative, "Engine 1 en route," and then secured the radio back on his belt. He stepped to Angelina, cupped her cheek in his large, calloused palm. "If you decide you want to play you can find me at the fire station."

"Jason, let's roll," Dean yelled from the other side of the store.

He grazed his thumb over her lips, flashed her a quick smile. "Don't wait too long, okay?" Before she could answer, he hurried away.

Shaken, horny and unsatisfied, Angelina returned the book to the shelf and left the store.

* * * *

You can do this. You can do this.

Bailey Lamont repeated the words to herself like a mantra as the darkness of the hallway threatened to close in. She gripped the handle of the flashlight she carried so tightly her knuckles began to ache.

Take slow, even breaths. It's just a hallway, and you aren't alone.

No. She wasn't alone. Lieutenant Tripp Barrett and firefighter Ryan Magee were with her. Still, even though she sensed their presence, she felt alone. Her heart raced, pounded painfully against her chest, and she jumped when the radio on her turnout pants squawked.

"900 to 932, how's it going in there?" From his position outside, Captain Dean Wolcott used identifying radio call numbers to converse with the Lieutenant.

"All is quiet and darker than a June bug in here, Cap," the Lieutenant answered through his own radio. "We should be almost to the elevators. Got any word on the power situation?"

"Not yet, L.T. Power Company is working on it."

"How are the accident victims?"

"EMTs have them stabilized and prepared for transport."

Bailey focused her attention on the radio conversation and not the blackness that wanted to smother her. The beam of her flashlight gleamed on metal, and she allowed herself to feel a split-second of relief. *Almost over. Almost out.*

Outside. She wished she could have stayed outside to work the accident scene rather than assist in the rescue of the trapped people in the elevator. Two cars with two passengers each decided to play demolition derby on the main strip. One of the cars smashed into a power pole connected to the main grid and took them both down, plunging the street into darkness. Not that it was all that dark outside, she mused and longed for the sunshine and open space of the afternoon. Because inside the Sparkling Waters Hotel it could have been after midnight and one wouldn't know the difference.

She stopped in front of the first elevator, the Lieutenant on her right and Ryan Magee on her left. She startled again when Magee set the heavy box of tools he carried down on the marble floor.

"Bit jumpy today, Lamont?" Ryan asked, and she didn't need light to hear the mix of amusement and mocking in his tone.

Ryan Magee ragged her. As the only female firefighter on B shift, she expected it to a point. But he stayed on her case more than the other guys. All because she refused to sleep with him. How childish, she thought. As an ex-Navy SEAL with a body that proved it, he thought himself God's gift to women. Bailey couldn't wait for the day when a woman proved him otherwise.

"You okay, Lamont?" the Lieutenant asked in his concerned Texas drawl.

No. I'm not okay. I want to get the hell out of here. Why is it I always get stuck on the rescue team when an elevator goes on the blink?

The words, the complaint, were on the tip of her tongue, but she said none of it. She'd done this once before with the Lieutenant, pulled a trapped victim from a stalled elevator. She'd made it through that time. She could do it again. She *would* do it again.

"I'm fine," she snapped. Uneasiness and irritation added a sharp edge to her voice that she couldn't hide. "How many people and which elevator are they in?"

"Dispatch reported three—two females and a male—in the first elevator," Tripp answered. "Elevator is lodged between the third and fourth floors."

Magee reached in front of her, tapping the end of the Halligan —a multipurpose tool consisting of a claw, a blade, and a tapered pick used for twisting, punching or prying— on the closed elevator doors. "Hello," he yelled. "Anybody in there?"

"We're here," what sounded to be one male and two female muffled voices answered in unison.

"Fire department. Hang on. We're going to get you out of there."

"Give me some light over here, Lamont," the Lieutenant said as he began to ready the rope they would use to harness the trapped trio and lift them to safety.

Meanwhile, Ryan set to work on the elevator doors, using the Halligan to pry them open. "L.T., we need something to jam between these doors to hold them open in case the power comes back."

"Use the pike pole."

Ryan wedged the tool between the doors, and then stuck his head inside. "Is everybody okay? Anyone hurt?"

"No one's hurt," one of the females answered.

"I'm scared," a small voice said on a sob. "I want my mommy."

Bailey whipped her head around. Alarm rippled through her. "Lieutenant, you didn't say the male is a child."

"I didn't know," the Lieutenant answered, concern in his voice as well.

At that moment, the radio squawked again. "932, you get to the people in that elevator yet?" The Captain's voice rang through the hallway.

Rather than Tripp abandoning his work on the rope, Bailey pulled her radio from her turnouts and answered the Captain. "933 to 900, we're at the elevator preparing to pull them up. There's a child in there, Captain."

"That's what I wanted to know," Dean replied. "I've got his mother out here with me. His sitter should be in that elevator with him. His name is Timmy. I know the boy."

Timmy. Bailey remembered hearing Dean talk of little Timmy Walker. She knew Dean often acted as a surrogate father to the boy, babysitting, taking him to baseball games and the likes. "Tell his mom that he's fine and we're about to get him out," she said into the radio and hoped her voice sounded reassuring rather than betraying the panic she felt building inside her.

"She should be inside there with the kid," Ryan muttered. He spoke low as though to himself but Bailey heard him. "No doubt he's in there because he came looking for her."

"He's with his sitter," Bailey reminded him in a hushed tone. "And you don't know why they're here at the hotel."

"Sure I do. Isn't it obvious? The Mom left the boy with a sitter so she could come here and get a bit of dick. Probably didn't go home last night, and the sitter brought him along to look for her but the mother already left."

Bailey gaped at him. "Do you even know Timmy Walker or his mother?"

"No but I know women like her and—"

"Hey you two, pipe down. This isn't the time or the place to argue. And keep your opinions to yourself, Magee," the Lieutenant added in a terse voice. He finished with the harness and rope and peered though the opening in the doors. "Looks like the elevator is closer to the third floor. You'll have to go down, Lamont. Open the trap door and slide the rest of the way inside."

She would have to go down. The words echoed in Bailey's head until they became an unintelligible roar in her ears. She'd known it was coming, guessed she would be the one to plunge into the dark elevator shaft and down into an even darker metal, nearly airless box with three frightened people inside. She couldn't do this, she thought. Sure, she'd done it before, but that was before the fear returned in full force, before the dreams came back, before...

She tried to shake it off. Still, her blood turned to ice in her veins. Fear was like a lead weight in the pit of her stomach. The beam of the Lieutenant's flashlight shone to the side of her face, illuminating her in a dim ray of white light without blinding her.

"Bailey, are you sure you're okay?" Tripp's voice was low, full of concern, comforting.

He almost never called her by her first name on a call. Hearing it now proved how worried he was. She felt his voice as though it were a tangible thing in the darkness. It moved over her, brought goose pimples to the surface of her skin, as it surround her, hug her tight.

At that moment, she wanted to be hugged tight. Oh, to be in this man's strong and capable arms, to be carried outside as though she were a damsel in distress and he her rescuer. And what the hell was she thinking? This man was a fellow firefighter, her Lieutenant for heaven's sake. She worked too hard, busted her ass, to be seen as one of the guys in the department, as their equal. No way. No fucking way would she screw that up by coming on to her Lieutenant.

She also wouldn't screw it up by showing weakness or fear. With her newly recovered determination serving as a fire extinguisher to snuff out the raging hot wall of panic, Bailey squared her shoulders and met Tripp's gaze head-on in the dim glow of the flashlight. "I said I am fine. Let's get those people out of there."

Chapter 2

He burned the spaghetti. Jason snarled at the black lumps that floated to the surface of the pot as he stirred. Not just the sauce, he realized when he leaned over to peer into the pot on the other stove burner. He muttered a curse as he twisted the stove knobs off with a quick, irritated flick of his wrist. A man had to be culinary retarded to burn freaking spaghetti.

Or off in la-la land with an incredibly sexy, unbelievably alluring brunette, he thought, and picked up the pot of noodles. He moved to the trash can and upended the pot. He visualized several twenty-dollar bills falling into the trash with the noodles, bills he would give the pizza man for tonight's dinner. Worse, the guys of B shift would rag him to no end for burning dinner.

He glanced at the utilitarian black plastic clock hanging on the wall just inside the kitchen door. Still an hour or so before the men and women—he couldn't forget about B shift's only females, Bailey Lamont and EMT Terri Vega—would gather around the long rectangular table for grub. He could make it, he thought. There was just enough time to hide the evidence of the burnt spaghetti, rush to the grocery store on the corner and pick up fresh fixings. He could get back to the station and have one hell of a pot of spaghetti going inside the hour. He could even throw some garlic bread in the oven since he forgot to pick that up the first time around.

He made quick work of disposing of the sauce and other evidence of the ruined food and fished his keys out of the front pocket of his jeans. He'd only taken two steps toward the kitchen doorway when he heard voices. Shit, he thought, and spun on his heel, turning his back to the door. He heard the Captain enter the kitchen with Lieutenant Tripp Barrett and watched his well-thought-out plan go up in smoke.

"It's claustrophobia. I'm almost sure of it," Tripp said in his lazy Texas drawl. "Today wasn't the first time I've noticed her getting a bit panicky on a call. Remember that one a few months back?"

"Yeah, I remember. We talked about it. Didn't I give you permission to set up a blackout scenario, test her out, so to speak?"

"You did and I planned to." the Lieutenant sighed. "But every time I attempt to schedule the dammed thing something comes up. Thing is, it seems to have gotten worse."

"Have you confronted her about it? Did you say anything to her about it after today's call?" Dean asked. He gave Jason a slight nod in greeting as he passed him on his way to the refrigerator.

Jason watched as Dean pulled a can of soda from the fridge, glanced at the empty stovetop, sniffed the air and walked to the table. Jason turned around in time to catch the Captain smiling as he pulled out a chair at the table and sat down across from the Lieutenant. So much for pulling that one over, he thought but the Lieutenant continued to talk before Jason or the Captain could comment.

"I'm not sure how to bring it up, what to say to her," Tripp admitted on a sigh. "You know Bailey, Cap. She's tried so hard to be one of the guys around here for dammed near a year now. Hell, she never stops trying. And to show a weakness, any weakness at all." He snorted a laugh and shook his head. "Not Bailey Lamont. The dammed woman is too proud and stubborn for that."

"She may be," Dean said and idly spun the soda can on the table. "But if she is claustrophobic and she gets out on a call somewhere, starts to freak out, it isn't only her life she'll be putting in danger."

"Yeah, I know. I'll talk to her, see what I can do." Tripp hesitated, drumming his fingertips on the table. "Thing is, Captain, I'm not sure what to do with her if she is claustrophobic. I mean, how do you help someone like that? Can she even be helped?"

Immediately, Jackson popped into Jason's mind along with memories of a long summer of days spent in small spaces and dark places. "My brother is, was, claustrophobic."

The Lieutenant looked at Jason as though just realizing he was in the room. "You mean your twin brother, the FBI agent?"

"Jackson," Jason nodded. "He's been claustrophobic all our lives."

"He got over it?" Dean asked.

"Not over it as much as learned to control it, I think." Jason walked to the table and hiked a hip on the edge. "He didn't have much choice really, not if he wanted to succeed at the bureau."

"Bailey won't have much choice if she wants to continue being a firefighter either," Tripp said dryly. "She's hiding it right now and doing fairly well, but there may come a time when she'll snap." His gaze sharpened on Jason. "She will also slice up all our dicks and put them in that burnt spaghetti you dumped in the trash if she finds out we had this conversation behind her back."

Jason winced at the reference to the spaghetti. He supposed he fooled no one but himself with the idea to hide his screw up.

"If what I saw a couple of days ago at my wife's store was any indication, I would say Jason has better plans for his dick." Dean leaned back in his chair and grinned around the rim of his soda can.

"Shit," Jason muttered and felt heat rise to his cheeks. He slid off the table and turned his back on the men. Embarrassment wasn't something he often felt and certainly never showed. He didn't know what he expected. He did kiss the brunette in the middle of the store with a handful of customers perusing the aisles. And his Captain was at the front counter, he reminded himself. He walked to the phone that hung on the wall at the end of a row of cabinets. Maybe if he placed the order for the pizzas now he could distract the Captain and Lieutenant.

No such luck, he realized when Tripp asked, "Isn't picking up a woman while on duty against regulations?"

"Looked to me like he was trying to perform CPR," Dean said, and Jason didn't have to turn to know the man was grinning from ear to ear. "Jason, you never told me you wanted to add EMS to your list of qualifications in the department."

Jason groaned and turned to lean against the counter. Might as well get it over with, he thought, and decided to play along. "I've considered it." He shrugged. "I thought I might get in a little early practice. You know, try it out first to see if I would like it." He winced because he knew he said too much.

Both men hooted with laughter.

"Did she look a bit breathless?" Tripp chuckled.

"She did when we left," Dean volunteered.

Breathless, hot, and ready, Jason thought and couldn't suppress a low chuckle of his own when he remembered how she dropped the book. He could still feel her slim body pressed against his, the warmth of her mouth and the way she tasted, sweet with a faint hint of mint. The kiss had been impulsive. Her light touch made him forget where they were, who could be watching. And when her fingers slipped inside his pants his hormones took over. If not for the fire call, he didn't know how far things would have gone. He shot a quick glance at the radio on his side and silently cursed it even as he thanked it for its timing.

"Damn, looks like I need to go hang out in Veronica's store. That place is turning out to be more of a make-out hot spot than Lookout Point." Tripp kicked back in his chair and propped his booted feet on the table. "Does this breathless victim have a name?"

Tripp's question pulled Jason from his thoughts. Hell, he didn't even ask her name. "I—"

"Angelina Keaton," Dean answered for him.

"Isn't she the one who inherited that airport off Old Hwy 90?" Jason blurted. He closed his eyes at the bemused expression on the Captain's and Lieutenant's faces and felt the heat rise to his cheeks once more.

"I thought you knew that," Dean said, tongue in cheek.

Tripp laughed. "You were checking the woman's tonsils in the middle of Romantic Illusions and didn't even ask her name?"

"I…uh…was getting to it," Jason stammered. In truth, her name hadn't fit into the equation. He'd been too busy trying to set up a date so he could get his hands on her to worry about her name.

And didn't it figure? The one woman he found who could possibly share in the same types of enjoyment as he, the one who could end this hellish run of celibacy he'd been on lately had to be rich. And not just rich, she had to be a freaking Keaton. Not that it mattered, he supposed. He wasn't looking for anything long-term and, judging from the way she'd come on to him, neither was she.

"She's had some troubles lately, hasn't she? That airport," Dean qualified. "I've heard a couple of calls over the police scanner in the past month or so."

"What kind of calls? What trouble?" Jason asked. Wealth and pizzas forgotten, he pushed himself off the counter and returned to the table.

Dean shrugged and sipped his soda. "I'm not sure really. Break-ins, theft. If you ask me, someone isn't happy that Edward Keaton left his favorite niece the airport when he died."

"You springing for pizzas for dinner or do we have to dig through the trash can for the charred spaghetti?" Tripp asked. "That is what I smelled when I walked in here, isn't it? Word of advice from the worst cook in the department, when you burn something, take the evidence to the dumpster outside and spray some heavy-duty air freshener."

"Yeah," Jason said absentmindedly and walked back to the phone. "I was getting to that. What do you want?" he asked but his attention, his thoughts, were once again on Angelina. Only this time, he wasn't picturing her naked in his bed, legs spread and a come-get-me smile on her alluring lips. No, this time he saw pictures of violence he didn't want to think about or put name to. Could she be in danger? Were the break-ins at the airport simple random acts of violence or something more? A pang of fear, a feeling as uncommon to him as embarrassment, settled in his veins. It sounded to him like someone else wanted to play games with Angelina Keaton and they weren't the same sort of games he had in mind.

* * * *

"You didn't tell me you were seeing someone." Tess crossed her arms, poked out her bottom lip, and all but stomped her foot at her sister.

"That would be because I'm not seeing anyone," Angelina said and walked past her sister to enter her small office in the airport building. Lost in her own thoughts, she didn't have time for one of Tess's pouting episodes. She had orders to place, paperwork to gather, and a meeting in less than an hour. She toyed with the idea of skipping out on the last. Spending time with some bigwig out of Vegas, a high-level executive by the name of Gilbert Churchill, was sure to give her a headache of momentous proportions. She already decided Mr. Gilbert's church fell off the hill years ago when he selected the gambling industry to make his millions. Anyone in that line of business was the lowest of slime in her eyes.

Gilbert Churchill wanted to buy the airport and seemed incapable of accepting no as an answer. Angelina had no intentions of selling out. Not to anyone, but especially not to Mr. Churchill. The man didn't know it but she blamed the gambling industry for the loss of her father and the subsequent loss of his business. Or would that be the other way around, she wondered. In essence, she lost both at about the same time, the demise of one leading to the downfall of the other. She could only hope that a face-to-face meeting with Mr. Churchill would make him see how serious she was about not selling out.

"Then who's the hunky guy delivering you gifts and flowers?" Tess demanded.

Angelina sighed. She let her shoulder bag fall into the seat of her swivel desk chair as she turned to her sister. Time or not, Tess wouldn't leave her alone until she got the answers she wanted. Persistent bitch, she thought and secretly admired that about her sister. "What are you talking about?"

"Oh, cut the crap, will you? You are so bad at hiding stuff. That's what." With an eye roll of aggravation, she pointed rather melodramatically at the desktop.

With a performance like that, no wonder she failed as an actress in Hollywood, Angelina thought. She scowled, looked over her shoulder and down at the desk. The flowers, she saw, consisted of a single long-stemmed red rose. The rose lay atop what she supposed would be the gifts in question, a small rectangular package wrapped in red paper printed with tiny little handcuffs and fire trucks. She turned as a smile unfolded on her lips. She knew before she picked it up and read the attached card who delivered them. *You forgot this. Are you ready to play?*

"What? Did you forget something at his house?"

"I haven't been to his house." *Yet*, Angelina added silently and picked up the rose, sniffed and allowed herself a moment to relish in its fresh scent. She returned the rose carefully to the desktop and picked up the package. It was covered in what looked to be a child's birthday wrapping paper and she knew why he'd picked it. The fire trucks and especially the handcuffs held a far deeper meaning. It made her smile turn into a goofy grin thinking about what that wrapping paper implied. It was definitely a keepsake, far too cute and fitting to crumple into the trash.

"You know who it's from. I can tell by that idiotic grin on your face. What's 'Are you ready to play?' mean?" Tess demanded. She stepped closer to the desk, put her hands flat on the cherry wood surface and leaned in. "Play what?"

"Baseball," Angelina said absently. Though she still stared at the package, it was Jason's face she saw. His light gray eyes full of desire and need, his pale pink lips tilted in an oh-so sexy grin that made her juices flow faster than a waterfall. She could still taste him, could still smell him, still feel him. Her palm itched to rub over his baby-fine dark buzz cut. Her fingers tingled with the need to resume their exploration into his pants and uncover the treasure concealed within. She wanted to bury her nose in his rock-hard chest, breathe in his scent that was both musky and sweet and all too male.

"Yeah, right." Tess slapped the desktop. "Do you think I'm stupid?"

Angelina looked at her sister and caught the string on her temper just before it snapped. "Some things are meant to be private, Tess," she said and gave herself kudos for sounding so calm.

Tess's long, slender face went from crinkled and angry to soft and friendly in an instant. Like putting on a mask, Angelina thought and knew it was exactly like that. Tess's green eyes could change all the colors of a rainbow depending on her mood, and Tess's moods were many and varied. In less than ten seconds, Angelina watched her sister's eyes go from a dark green outlined in red to the soft green of a baby's jumper. Her lips, painted drop-dead red, could form in as many different shapes. Again, depending on her mood. She wore her chestnut hair short, cut to Hollywood's latest style. It flattered her, Angelina thought, though she preferred the look of long hair. Also in the latest styles of Hollywood, Tess decked herself in a button-down blouse of blue and white sailor stripes with a navy blue skirt that met at mid-thigh, the waist lined with bold brass buttons.

"Not between sisters. We shouldn't have any secrets. Come on, Angel," she cooed. She always shortened Angelina's name to Angel when she wanted something. "Don't keep me in the dark. Sisters are supposed to share everything."

"We've never shared everything, Tess," Angelina said dryly and watched the so- expressive green eyes of her sister go smoky gray in a flash of sorrow before the red of anger returned. It was like looking through one of those View-masters that she played with as a kid, she thought. Only the paper disk that fit in this one had negatives of Tess's expressions. Pull the lever on the side and watch the mood change, pull again and there's another one.

"You're right, Angelina. You never needed to share anything with me." Tess pushed herself off the desk. "You always had everyone else to confide in while I—"

"Had everyone else to confide in too," Angelina finished for her. She'd been wrong. Her sister could be one hell of an actress when she believed in the part.

"Bullshit!" Tess spat. "You've always had it all. Even now, even with Daddy and Uncle Edward dead, you still have it all."

Angelina put the package to the side of the blotter, the anticipation and excitement to open it now sour in her stomach. "And I have a lot more to lose because of it." But she couldn't think of that now, wouldn't dwell on all she lost in the past, all she stood to lose now. One wrong move, that's all it would take. "You had them the same as I did," she said and began to sort through the day's mail.

"Yeah, right." Tess snorted. She turned and started to pace. "The only time I ever had Daddy was when he took me hunting. As for Uncle Edward..." She shook her head. "They always loved you best. Proved it in the end too, didn't they?"

"If you're referring to this place, Uncle Edward left it to me because he knew I love it as much as he did. He knew I wouldn't sell it to the highest bidder." Had faith in me that I could finally keep a business up and running, she added silently.

"You should sell it. Take that Vegas suit for as much as you can and wash your hands of this place before..." She stopped when Angelina's head popped up.

"Go ahead, Tess. Don't hold back to spare my feelings. I should sell it before I run it into the ground like I did my store. Before I lose it to the banks like Dad's charter business."

"That one wasn't your fault," Tess said and lowered her voice, added an ounce of compassion to her tone. "I know that, Angelina. I know about the gambling, the loan sharks. There wasn't much you could do to save it. But do you really want to risk it all again, risk everything for this place? You're already starting to lose, what with the break-in last month. How much did they walk away with? And the damaged tow tractor. How much is that going to cost to fix?"

The perpetrator or perpetrators walked away with several thousand dollars worth of fancy electronics her uncle kept in what was supposed to be a secure room in the terminal. The tow tractor would cost even more to repair or replace. "I'm not selling, and that is the end of it. I'll do whatever I have to do," she vowed and returned her attention to the stack of mail. She laid bills in one stack, sales catalogues in another, tossed fliers and other junk mail in the wastebasket on the floor. A brochure on flight instruction caught her attention for a moment but the sight of the legal size manila envelope with her name scrawled across the front in block letters made her suck in a breath. She felt the color drain from her face even as her pulse began to race.

"And people dare to say that I'm the hardheaded, brainless one in the family," Tess muttered in disgust. "You're going to end up with nothing again. You know that? Angelina, stop ignoring me."

Angelina looked up at the sharp sound Tess' heel made on the tiled floor when she stomped her foot, but she hardly saw her sister through the haze of fear that clouded her vision.

"I really hate it when you..." Tess trailed off, cocked her head, and seemed to study her sister. "What's wrong? Angel, you look like you've seen a ghost."

"No," Angelina said quickly and shook her head. "Nothing is wrong." She snatched up one of the sales catalogues and slapped it on top of the envelope. She would have to tell, of course, inform the police that she received another one. She felt certain she knew what the envelope contained. The others arrived in the same way, in the same kind of envelope with the same block handwriting. No address, no postage, and no fingerprints. Yes, this one would be identical.

Though she'd been a bit spooked by the first envelope, she nearly dismissed it, reasoned it away. Arial photos of Keaton Aire, the surrounding land. A photographer, she'd decided. Someone flew over taking pictures and simply wanted to share. The next set made even less sense at first. Shots of equipment, equipment that were stolen two days later in the break-in. Yet, when she attempted to turn them over to the police after the break-in, she discovered them gone from the locked drawer of her desk. Warning photos, she'd realized too late, photos to torment. There hadn't been any photos when the tow tractor was sabotaged, but she felt certain the same person or people were responsible. What would the pictures in this latest envelope tell her?

She wanted Tess out of the office, wanted to open the envelope without her sister's prying eyes. Before she contacted the police, she needed to see for herself, alone, what the vandal planned to do next. Now that she knew the envelope to be a warning of what to expect, maybe this time the damage could be prevented.

Tess's gaze dropped to the mail Angelina held, narrowed on the dark yellow edge of paper that peeked beneath the catalogue. "It's another one, isn't it?"

Angelina sighed, closed her eyes, and nodded. She wouldn't get a chance to open it in private now.

"Let me see it." Tess stepped around the desk and held out a hand.

More on reflex than design, Angelina took a step back and moved the envelope out of her sister's reach. "You didn't see who brought it?"

"No. All of that stuff was in the outside box. I just brought it into your office when I came in today. The only person I've seen this morning was Mr. Hunky with the rose and the present."

"It's addressed to me." Angelina gulped, licked her lips, and tried to steady her breathing. "I'll open it."

"Shouldn't we call the police?"

Angelina looked at her sister and took in the latest mood change. Worry stirred with fear in Tess's eyes. We. Now, in the face of whatever the envelope held, she spoke of them as a unit, as true sisters, and Angelina felt comforted not to be alone after all. "We will," she said and stayed put this time when Tess moved to stand beside her. "We'll open it first. Then we'll call the police." At Tess' nod, she tossed the catalogue back onto the desk and turned the manila envelope over.

"Wait!" Tess's hand shot out. She gripped Angelina's arm. "Shouldn't you wear gloves or something?"

"I don't have any gloves in here, and it won't matter anyway. You brought in the mail so your prints will be on it, mine are on it, but they won't find any others."

Tess reached across the desk with her free hand and snatched a couple of tissues from the box on the corner. "Probably not," she agreed and held the tissues out for Angelina. "But our fingerprints aren't on whatever is inside. Just in case, okay? He could have slipped up this time."

Angelina stared at her sister. Who would have thought Theresa Keaton could be so smart and cool under pressure? She certainly wouldn't have believed it, and the guilt of that sliced away at a small corner of her heart. "You know all those people who call you hardheaded and brainless?" she said now as she took the tissues. "They're only half right. You're anything but brainless, Tess."

"Thanks." She drew her eyebrows together and added, "I think."

Angelina smiled, but the moment quickly faded as the weight of the envelope in her hands seemed to grow. She knew she imagined that weight, the tangible feel of it at least. She sighed. "Let's do this."

Her fingers were surprisingly steady as she carefully untucked the flap on the envelope. Not glued, not sealed, she thought. No trace of saliva. She made sure to cover her fingers with the tissues as much as possible when she reached inside and pulled out a single photo. She felt Tess move closer still, slip an arm around her waist as she leaned in for a better look.

"What is it?" Tess whispered.

Because she did, because the atmosphere in the office seemed to demand it, Angelina whispered too. "I'm not sure." She stared at the photo bright with colors against black and wrinkled her brows. Lines of yellow, red, and blue crisscrossed over something black and blurred. Words too small to read seemed engraved on small silver plates. She held the picture up to the light and, when that didn't help, began to rotate it in a clockwise direction. "It almost looks like some kind of abstract art."

"It's too out of focus." Tess's voice rang with frustration.

"It's a close-up of something. Too close though, I can't tell wh—" Angelina froze, the picture now turned at a ninety-degree angle. Her pulse roared in her ears. Fear slid through her, wrapped around her heart like a vise and squeezed as realization took hold. "Dear God. Tess, it's a—"

Boom! The force of the explosion rocked the airport terminal.

* * * *

"So it is true. You are taking time off."

"Don't you ever knock?" Jackson Graham snapped shut his briefcase, looked up and his cock screamed in agony. FBI Agent Mallory Stone, his best friend's sister, his sometimes partner and want-to-be lover, stood in the doorway of his office looking like any man's wet dream come true.

Hair the color of autumn leaves spiraled around a heart-shaped face with sea blue eyes and pink glossy lips. She wore a choker of shiny black leather and no adornments. Large silver and black earrings so long they nearly brushed her shoulders dangled from her lobes. Shoulders that were smooth bronze and bare, he noted and fought the urge to loosen his tie. Her top—he supposed it would be considered a top though it appeared to be little more than a scrap of material to him—was strapless, tantalizingly tight and disturbingly short. Perfectly bronze, tightly toned abs led to a siren red miniskirt so mini it made Daisy Dukes seem conservative. What appeared to be six-inch heels in the same siren red completed the ensemble. She looked like a slut, a two dollar hooker, and he felt himself wanting to reach for his wallet and offer her any amount of money to do with his throbbing dick as she pleased.

"Do you have to dress like that at the office?" he asked blandly and picked up a case file from the blotter, flipped it open, and pretended to study it. Anything to keep his eyes off of her and those shapely golden legs that went on for miles.

Jackson heard those legs put into action now. His heart rate increased with each clack of Mallory's heels on the tiled floor as she walked toward him. He felt the heat that radiated from her, heat that grew hotter and seeped into his pores, coursed though his body and straight to his groin when she stepped around the desk. She perched her barely covered, delectable rear end on the edge of the desktop a mere half inch from where his arm rested and leaned in, caught hold of his tie and tugged.

"What's the matter, handsome?" she asked in a low voice that dripped with sex. She was so close, he felt the warmth of her breath, smelled the fresh mint scent of her toothpaste. "Does this outfit make that so conservative brain of yours think provocative thoughts?"

Provocative thoughts? Talk about an understatement! Right now, the images in his head would make one hell of a B-rated porno flick. He thought he might have even seen such a scene once. Not that he indulged in smut films. His twin bother, Jason, did though, and Jackson happened to come by one or two over the years on Jason's television set.

Yes, Jackson thought now. He remembered one. A particular favorite of Jason's called something like Big Busted Executives or The Pleasure Bureau or something equally cheesy. An office scene just as this with a sleazily dressed female—much like Mallory—and a male dressed in compete suit and tie—much like himself. For a moment, his mind cast him and Mallory in those staring roles. With one quick sweep of his arm, he cleared the desk of all clutter. He stood and moved between her already spread legs. Forgetting all niceties, all pretense of tenderness, he crushed his mouth to hers, began to grope her soft curves even as she unfastened his pants. Her hand snaked into his briefs, curled around his cock, and pulled it free. In the swift speed of television film, he was inside her. She fell back on the blotter, hips hanging off the desktop, her ass in his hands as he pounded his dick inside her in vicious, rapid thrusts that had her screaming his name.

"Jackson."

Yes, he knew what she wanted, how to make her scream.

"Jackson?"

He came back to reality with a start. She didn't scream his name, not in reality, but she did say it in that sex-dripped voice that promised everything in his mental porn flick and more. Both slightly embarrassed and disgusted with himself by the vividness of his imagination and the full-blown erection it caused, he reached up and pulled his tie from her grasp, smoothed it down in place. "Aren't there regulations for the bureau that emphatically prohibit such dress in the office?" He sounded like a pompous ass but the last thing he needed was for Mallory Stone to know how powerful an effect she had on him. Though she often made no attempts to conceal her attraction to him, he'd done too well to hide his feelings over the years to fuck up now.

Mallory sighed but, not one to be pushed aside so lightly, didn't drop her come-fuck-me act. Still perched on the edge of the desk, she crossed her legs, studied her red painted nails. The movement had the barely there mini raising another half inch and Jackson felt a circuit in his brain fry. "I'm on assignment," she said now more conversationally. "Undercover."

"More like out of cover dressed like that," Jackson muttered and wondered for a fleeting instant if she wore any panties beneath that so-short shirt. He quickly pushed the thought aside along with the images it conjured.

She grazed one of those fingernails down his cheek, traced the line of his jaw and he dammed near whimpered before he caught himself. "You just don't want to admit how bad this outfit makes you want me."

It wasn't the outfit, or the lack thereof, that made him want her, but he wasn't about to tell her that. She could wear a burlap sack, and he wouldn't want her less. But he couldn't have her. For a myriad of reasons, both professional and personal, he would never have Mallory Stone. "Fraternizing is frowned upon in the bureau. You know that." Oh man, why had he said that? It made it sound as if...

"Frowned upon and discouraged yes, but not forbidden," Mallory said and let her hand drop in the narrow space between her hip and his arm. She curled her fingers around the edge of the wood and sighed. "I also know that you never fail to remind me of that in some way or another."

"I take my job seriously, Mallory."

"As do I. I also take my own happiness seriously, Jackson. I enjoy life. I have fun with it. You should try it sometime," she suggested.

He looked up at her. He didn't allow his gaze to drift to the dark shadow between her ample breasts, didn't allow himself to think of how it would taste to lick her there. "With you, I suppose."

"I've been trying to get you to for years now. You fight a hard battle, Agent Graham."

A battle he felt himself loosing with each passing day. Was it possible she did in fact know the depth of the effect she had on him? Could she have figured out how badly he truly wanted her? The problem with Mallory Stone was that while she offered him probably what would be the best, hottest, most mind-blowing sex of his life, she offered nothing more. She was also his best friend's sister. The combination tightened the noose on any thoughts his brain or his dick might entertain of pursuing anything with her. Jackson watched her grow into a woman, complete the FBI Academy and become one of the best young agents in the bureau. He no longer worried about the cases assigned to her, knew she could handle herself in the line of duty. He no longer saw her as an innocent and, as a result, found himself in the need of reminding time and time again that she was indeed his best friend's sister. No, Mallory Stone was far from innocent, and one leisurely look at her now proved that.

"You headed to Silver Springs?" she asked and hefted herself to sit on the desktop rather than lean against it as she had been. She didn't bother to pull at the skirt, to prevent it from rising farther still, which Jackson noted with a great pain in his already engorged cock, did exactly that.

"Yeah, I'm told I'm way overdue for some time off." He supposed he was, he thought as he calculated that his last semi-vacation happened well over two years ago. And he could've happily gone another two years without a break too. He loved his job, enjoyed the day-to-day pace of it whether out on assignment or stuck behind the desk.

"Well, I've got to agree with Adam on that one," she said of the leader of their team. "So, is Cameron going with you?"

Surprised, Jackson cocked an eyebrow. "Didn't your brother tell you, he's being sent on an assignment on the West Coast? He's all gung-ho about the sunshine and babes in bikinis."

Mallory's lips twitched. "He'll have a blast," she predicted and hopped down off the desk. "It wouldn't hurt for you to take a page out of his book while you're in Silver Springs. They have beaches too, don't they?"

"I've never been much for the beach scene."

"Maybe you should give it a try anyway." She shrugged and walked to the door, hips swaying like a well-oiled metronome. "You're much too uptight lately, Jackson. Get laid while you're gone. Have a quick fling. Maybe it will do us both some good."

Jackson wasn't sure what good his having a fling would do her. What he wanted from Mallory Stone was far more than a fling.

Chapter 3

Flames licked the smoke-filled sky. The poignant fumes of burning chemicals, gasoline, oils, and who-knew-what-else contaminated the air. Jason saw the fire, smelled it, even before Engine 1 made the scene. As Ryan Magee parked the engine and prepared the truck to ready the hose on back, Jason slid his head into his Nomax hood, covered that with his helmet and connected face shield. He already wore full turnouts from the heavy-ass jacket all the way down to his waterproof boots. As he hopped off the truck and circled around the front bumper to the opposite side, he delved his hands in his thick, fire-retardant gloves.

It was all routine, methodical, each step done more out of habit than thought. He was grateful for that because his thoughts were currently with the woman positioned at a safe distance some two hundred yards away. Angelina Keaton stood with one hand clamped over her mouth, the other clinched tightly at her side around something yellowish in color, watching as what appeared to be a shed going up in flames. A part of him longed to go to her, to offer comfort though words to soothe and console had never come easily for him. But right now he had a job to do and, despite the habitualness of it, the act of battling this fire would demand his full attention.

"What have we got, Captain?" he asked as Dean Wolcott approached.

"Looks like the chemical shed exploded."

"Anyone hurt?" Ryan asked as he began to pull tanks of foam from the truck.

"Mechanic was thrown to the ground from the force of the blast," Dean answered. "EMTs have him now. Jason, I want you working with the Lieutenant and Max at the Hazmat truck. Max is charging the foam lines now. You know what to do."

Jason gave the Captain a quick salute and double-timed it to the awaiting Hazmat truck positioned closer to the fire. He grabbed a self-contained breathing apparatus from the jump seat and slipped into it, adjusted the shoulder straps so that the air pack fit to his back as comfortably as possible. "We need to attack this thing from a distance, L.T.," he said to Tripp Barrett, hardly recognizable decked from head to toe in his own set of turnouts, his face mask already covering his mouth and nose. "Shoot the foam into the air, and let it rain down on the fire."

The Lieutenant nodded and motioned for Jason to take the point.

Jason slid the face mask of the SCBA over his mouth and nose. Clean, cool oxygen filled his nostrils. He picked up the hose, nodded to Max Jasper, the Hazmat truck engineer, and moved toward the flames. The remaining firefighters of the Engine Company were battling smaller fires started by flaming debris from the explosion. But Jason was exactly where he wanted to be, tackling this big mother with all the skill and training he possessed. He stopped some fifty yards from the inferno, angled the hose, and opened the nozzle. A heavy mist of cloudy white foam shot into the black smoke above the flames to float gently down like a blanket onto the fire.

Tripp Barrett joined him with another hose, tackling a point adjacent to his. Their foam streams met and crossed in the air. It reminded Jason of the final scene in *Ghostbusters* when the streams from their proton packs crossed, expelling a dangerous ray of blinding light. He felt like a giddy child, adrenaline pumping ferociously through his veins as he watched the flames die a slow but definite death.

* * * *

"Angelina, you got a minute to answer a few questions?"

Angelina shot a glance over her shoulder as Silver Springs Police Detective Samantha Becket approached from behind her. Tall and built like a brick shithouse, the detective made an imposing presence even on the open airport grounds. A presence Angelina really didn't want to feel right now. She said nothing as the detective stopped beside her, choosing instead to watch the firefighters as they gathered their equipment and loaded it back onto the trucks. It had taken them nearly two hours to extinguish the fire and the smaller blazes caused by the explosion. Two hours of torment and despair for Angelina. Who could have put a bomb in the chemical shed and why? Why send her a picture, give her warning if not time to prevent the outcome?

"Who did you piss off, Angelina?" the detective asked in a bland tone.

Though the bluntness of the question surprised her a bit, Angelina didn't look at the other woman. "That seems to be the sixty-four-thousand-dollar question, doesn't it?"

"I can't help but believe that these..." she seemed to search for a word, "...attacks are directed at you."

Duh! You think? Angelina thought nastily. It hurt to know someone hated her so much that they would do such things to harm her. It angered her more that the same someone could show such disregard about harming others in the process.

"First the theft, then the destruction of property, and now this," the detective continued. "They're escalating."

"It was a bomb."

"A b—" Surprise made the detective stammer. She stopped and blew out a breath. "Fire department hasn't determined the cause yet."

"It was a bomb," Angelina said again in the same absent tone. Out of the corner of her eye, she saw the detective nod slightly, noticed a muscle in the woman's jaw clenching.

"Want to tell me how you know it was a bomb?" she asked and sounded a bit on the defensive side.

Angelina guessed she didn't like someone of an unofficial caliber filling in holes in her case for her. Well, that was too dammed bad. She didn't speak but rather held up the envelope in explanation.

"What is this?" Samantha asked and all but snatched it from Angelina's fingers.

"Open it. See for yourself." Angelina finally looked at the detective, watched as the woman removed the photo from the envelope, studied and turned it as Angelina had done hours earlier. She saw when recognition dawned on the other woman's face.

"You kept the picture this time," the detective said after a long moment. When she looked up, her brown eyes were hard, suspicious.

Cop eyes, Angelina thought.

"Why didn't you inform the department of this?"

"I opened it approximately thirty seconds before the explosion."

"Not much warning time, huh?"

Angelina laughed, but there was no humor in the sound. "I suppose that could be my fault. I don't know when it was delivered. Tess brought it into my office this morning, put it on my desk. If I—" She stopped and shook her head. If she'd come to the airport sooner, collected the day's mail earlier...

Samantha Becket returned her attention to the photo, studied it more closely, then slowly shook her head. "I'm no expert on explosives, Angelina, but knowing what I do, it looks to me like you weren't meant to have any more than a few seconds of warning this time."

"What are you talking about?" As the final remains of smoke began to dissipate in the sky, the sunshine became a blinding ray of yellow light. Angelina held one hand over her eyes as a makeshift visor and leveled a glare at the detective.

"Remote detonation," Becket said and met Angelina's gaze. "I could be wrong, but from what I can tell in this picture this bomb was triggered to blow by remote control."

"How can you tell?"

"See this?" the detective pointed at a small, rectangular box attached to the top of the bomb in the photo. "That looks like a remote detonator to me. The bomb squad at the department will be able to say for certain."

"You mean..." Angelina let her words trail off as the implications sank in. The perp had watched her, waited for her to get the envelope, waited to see her reaction, and then triggered the bomb before she could stop it. "But how?"

"Where were you when you opened the envelope?"

"My office, behind my desk. I was arguing with Tess—"

"You had a fight with your sister?" the detective's ears perked up like a dog tracking the scent of a favored bone.

Angelina rolled her eyes and dropped her hand back to her side. "Tess and I are always fighting about something or another, Detective. We're sisters."

"What were you arguing about?" As the detective asked the question, she carefully shuffled the envelope in one gloved hand, reached with her other into her shirt pocket and withdrew a pen and small notepad.

"Come on, Samantha," Angelina moaned, using the woman's name rather than her rank as an officer in hopes she would hear how ridiculous she sounded. "You can't possibly think…"

"What did you and Tess fight about?" the detective asked, her tone now low and stern.

"Some guy she thought I was dating, Uncle Edward, my failures in the past, the airport. Name it, Sam, it probably came up in the argument somewhere."

"Why fight with your sister about your uncle, the airport?" Becket asked, now relentless in her interrogation.

Angelina sighed. She would have rather answered a question about whom Tess thought she was dating. That was an easy one, she thought as Jason Graham came to mind. She looked for him in the handfuls of firefighters, EMTs, and officials still on the scene. She'd known it was him. The second he hopped off the fire engine, even dressed in full turnouts, she'd recognized him. What was it about a man in uniform? She wondered now as her gaze landed on him where he stood some seventy-five yards away talking with another firefighter. There was definitely no sex appeal to a set of baggy, florescent yellow, grimy turnout gear. Nope. Nothing sexy at all. Until you put that uniform on a man like Jason Graham. Then suddenly the sex appeal skyrocketed.

She wished she could talk to him. She didn't know what on earth she would say to the man. Maybe something like: "Hey, I've thought about you pretty much nonstop since you rushed out of Romantic Illusions the other day."

Yeah, clue him in to the fact that you've been obsessing.

If she were going to do that, she might as well go all the way. Say something like: "Hello. How are you? Me? I'll be doing much better once you take me into my office, strip off all my clothes, and fuck my brains out."

Though a novel idea and one she felt certain she would enjoy immensely, it probably wasn't too appropriate right now, she decided. Especially when she had Detective Samantha Becket beside her breathing down her neck.

Angelina tore her gaze and thoughts from Jason as he removed his face helmet and looked her way. "Tess feels a little cheated by Uncle Edward's death," she told the detective. "They were never that close, Tess and Uncle Edward. At least not as close as he and I were." Tears threatened to fill her eyes as she talked about her uncle, but she refused to let them. Maybe later when she could be alone, she would have herself a good cry, release some of the still lingering grief, the newfound anger, and the pain.

"She's jealous because he left you the airport," the detective concluded, her voice flat and devoid of emotion.

Angelina shrugged. "I don't know why. She doesn't give shit one about this place. She's been working here a couple of days a week, a few hours. More to drive me nuts than because she..." She stopped, realized what she was saying and how it must have sounded to the detective.

"Because she?" the detective prompted.

"Look Samantha, Tess has nothing to do with what's been happening around here. Maybe she's a bit angry with Uncle Edward, maybe she feels a bit cheated and a bit jealous. That still doesn't make Tess, my own sister for crying out loud, a burglar or an arsonist."

"Anger and jealousy can make people do all sorts of things," the detective said and fanned the notepad in the air toward in ground. "Look Angelina, no one ever wants to believe anything bad about someone they know—"

"Tess is more than just someone I know," Angelina cut her off, her own anger beginning to rise. "She's my sister, and she has nothing, I repeat, nothing to do with any of this." Furious now, she started to walk away.

"Angelina, I'm not through," the detective called after her.

"You are for now," Angelina shot over her shoulder.

"I still have more questions. The FAA and the FBI will want to talk to you."

That put a hitch in her step. She'd expected the Federal Aviation Administration, had already spoken with them once. The FAA always showed up when a case involved anything dealing with airports. But the FBI? Had the situation really gotten that serious? She looked out at the land in front of her, land scattered with fire trucks, ambulances, police cars and enough men in uniform to start a heat wave, and knew. Yes. It had become that serious.

* * * *

The explosion aroused him. The knowledge that he caused the big boom served as more of an aphrodisiac than the flames. He hadn't known it would feel this way, hadn't expected the rush of power and sheer happiness that coursed through him as he watched the shed burn. It was over far too soon. His excitement died along with the flames. Next time he would make it last. He couldn't set another fire like this one. No. They would be expecting that now.

He looked at Angelina Keaton and wanted to roll with laughter. She would never guess he did this to her precious airport, did this to her. They'd taken everything from him. *But you're paying for it now, aren't you, little bitch?* She would continue to pay too. He wasn't done with her yet. She would continue to pay and so would the other one. Yes, he had plans for both of them. And the finale, ah yes, the grand finale he planned would be the best part of it all.

* * * *

"You've got five minutes," Dean Wolcott told Jason as they put the last of the equipment back on the truck.

"Sir?" Jason asked dumbly.

"Go talk to her. I suspect she could use a friendly ear right now."

Jason looked to Angelina and slowly nodded. She stood alone again, seemingly lost in her own thoughts, her own worries. Maybe he shouldn't bother her, he thought even as he felt himself being pulled toward her. He didn't know what to say, how to offer the comfort she would most likely need right now. But maybe what she needed more was something to take her mind off her troubles. That he could do, he thought confidently as he reached her.

"Fancy meeting you here."

She looked at him and gave him a ghost of that radiantly hot smile he remembered. "Yeah, fancy that."

"The fool doth think he is wise, but the wise man knows himself to be a fool."

"Excuse me?"

Jason chuckled at her confused expression. "Shakespeare. I doubt he meant it in this particular context, but the quote seems apt to me. Whoever is doing this stuff thinks he's wise but he's really a fool. He'll slip up and when he does they'll get him."

"And I'm the wise man who knows herself a fool because I can't figure out who he is or why he's doing these things to me?"

"You think you are, anyway." Jason shrugged. He watched her gaze do that slow slide down his body that drove all the blood in his veins straight to his cock.

"Strange, but you are the last man I would have expected to quote Shakespeare."

"You don't know me well enough yet. Play with me and you'll learn a lot more."

She laughed, and this time her smile was genuine. "If you came over here to distract me, you're doing a good job."

"Offering distractions isn't all I'm good at."

"Conceited much, Mr. Graham?"

He closed the distance between them in one step and dropped his voice though he didn't think there was anyone close enough to hear them. "Convinced, Ms. Keaton. Play with me, and I'll prove it."

"Name the game."

Jason's heart skipped. Any reservations he may have had about starting something with this wealthy heiress to the Keaton fortune swept away in a tidal wave of pure unadulterated lust. No arguments, no hesitation. Oh yes, she was ready to play. He gazed into her eyes, as all of the things he wanted to do to her became clear images in his mind. He knew exactly how to get the opportunity to make those images reality too. Well, almost. "Name the play."

"The play?" she repeated slowly.

"The Shakespeare quote is from one of his plays," he explained, and as he did so he leaned in closer, close enough to brush his lips over the silky smooth skin of her cheek. He didn't touch her even though he desperately wanted to. He knew the Captain watched him and probably several other people were watching him too. To them, his closeness would appear as though he merely leaned in to whisper to her, keep their conversation a secret from prying ears. "Come to my place at eight tonight, tell me the name of the play and the character who said the quote."

"Shakespeare trivia?" she said a little breathlessly. "What are the stakes?"

Jason thought fast. He was making this up as he went. He prayed she didn't know a thing about Shakespeare but even if she did few people would get the play *and* the character's name. "Name them correctly and you can have your way with me. Anything you want at your command."

"And if I can't name them?"

He had to clench his hands into fists to keep from touching her, from giving her a small taste of the things he had in mind to do to her. "You will be at my command."

She nodded slowly, and he could see the acceptance swirl with the excitement that filled her eyes. "Are there any rules to this game?"

"No Internet."

"How do you know I won't cheat?" she asked, her so-expressive green eyes gleaming with mischief.

"I suppose I'll have to trust you."

"I don't have any books on Shakespeare," she confessed.

Jason grinned and knew he would be a lucky man tonight. "Guess you'll have to try the public library."

"The library is closed today. It's always closed on Wednesdays, remember?"

Oh yeah, he remembered.

"But you knew that." She drew her bottom lip between her teeth but it didn't conceal her smile. "How do you know I'm not some Shakespeare Einstein?"

He was betting she didn't know Shakespeare from Mel Gibson but figured in the end he would win either way. "2110 Beachside Terrace," he said and indulged himself in a quick brush of his lips over her flesh before he walked away.

* * * *

Angelina had always considered Shakespeare boring. She'd never been one for poetry, and all the words no one ever really said such as doth, shalt, and thou did nothing more than give her one big migraine. Tonight, however, she thought she might gain a new respect for the late, great playwright. Tess's years of study to be an actress paid off for Angelina but only in part. She managed to find out that the quote for tonight's little game was from the play *As You Like It*. The character to credit, however, remained a mystery. Tess thought it was someone named Toadstool or Toadstone or some shit but seeing the character was a male and a part she would never have played, she didn't know for sure. As far as Angelina knew, Kermit the Frog could have said it in reference to Animal when he attempted to date Miss Piggy.

Oh well, she thought as a colony of butterflies took up residence in the pit of her stomach. At least she knew half the answer. Did that mean she would be granted half the command in Jason's little game, she wondered, and pulled into the driveway of 2110 Beachside Terrace.

She turned off the engine but sat for a moment simply staring out the windshield at the single-story house. Though it appeared small, it looked welcoming, comfortable, inviting. The walls were half red brick, half white siding. White shutters hung on either side of curtain-free windows offering an unobstructed view straight through the house. The front yard wasn't much larger than a postage stamp, she noted as she got out of her car and walked up the driveway toward the front door. There were no statues or fountains like those that glittered in the yards of the Keaton Estate. No gorgeous, colorful flowerbeds or an herb garden like the ones in which her mother spent all her time.

Simple, she thought as she reached the front door. She raised a balled fist, rapped her knuckles on the door three times. Her gaze dropped to the side of the walkway as she waited. A pair of large black boots with a yellow florescent band around the rim sat in grass once green but now speckled with gray and black, presumably debris from the boots. Those boots were the only indication that a firefighter lived inside. Well, the boots and the bumper sticker on the back of the midnight blue pickup truck she'd parked behind, she reminded herself, and chuckled. The bumper sticker read: Want to steam up your kitchen the right way? Invite a fireman for dinner.

The door swung open and Angelina watched the mental picture of her kitchen go up in flames. She bit back a low moan of appreciation before it escaped. Sweet Jesus, he was shirtless. His perfect muscles covered in a thin layer of sweat that glistened in the dim light. He wore a pair of ratty jeans, unbuttoned at the waist with a hole in the right knee. His feet were bare. He looked, Angelina thought and barely managed to keep herself from drooling, like a male model for one of those tough-guy colognes. The kind in the magazine articles that caught a woman's eye and clearly said, 'Buy this cologne for your man, and he will look like me.' Only Jason Graham didn't need any sort of bottled scent to make him a sinful heart attack.

He gazed at her, a slow smile playing with the corners of his mouth as though he knew exactly the thoughts going through her mind. "Password?" His eyes, so light gray they could pass for silver, sparkled with amusement.

For a long moment, Angelina simply stared at him. Her palm itched to skim over his so short dark hair, her fingers aching to trace the smooth features of his face, the ridges of his muscles. Password? What did he mean by that? She wondered. Then it finally hit her. The quote. The game. He would waste no time establishing command. "*As You Like It.*"

Surprise flickered in his eyes. He nodded. Yes, she'd gotten the name of the play correct. "Now, tell me the character and you can have it as you like it."

How fitting, Angelina thought. How had she not caught the play on words before now? She wrinkled her face and answered with the first character that came to mind. "Scooby-Doo?"

He hooted with laughter. "Rell me rady, rour ralf right," he said in his best imitation of the favored cartoon dog.

And just like that, Angelina knew with a certainty the likes of which she'd never felt before that she shouldn't be here. She should run, hide, get as far away from Jason Graham as possible because playing games with this man would be playing games with her heart.

Nonsense, she told herself as she stepped over the threshold. What they would share would be sex, plain and simple, pure and fun between two attracted and consensual adults. Sex that she wanted to start right now.

She trailed a finger across his stomach as she passed him, touched the tip of her fingernail over his bare flesh. She heard him make a low growling sound at that, and as she stepped past him, his hand caught her hair, stopping her in her tracks. He yanked her head back, gazed into her eyes for the briefest of heartbeats, let her see his intentions in his eyes before he smashed his mouth to hers.

So he wanted to play this rough, she thought, her insides fluttering with both delight and exhilaration. She liked it rough but she wouldn't make it easy for him, she decided, as she heard the click of the front door slamming as he kicked it shut. Then he turned her, backed her against that door, as he continued to attempt to consume her with his lips.

She moved her hands between them, pushed against his chest, not hard but enough to get his attention. His eyes opened, but he didn't pull back from the kiss and she saw in his gaze that he understood. She was resisting but not really. She merely wanted to give him the illusion that she didn't want this.

"Open for me," he said against her lips. He licked the outer edge of her lips, nudged and nipped until they parted for him. His tongue plunged into her mouth, demanded and took until she felt breathless and quivering all over.

Rather than fight him anymore, she slid her arms around his shoulders, one hand turning to cup the back of his neck. His knee pushed against her legs, urged them to spread, and when she clenched them tightly together his hands moved to her ass, squeezed until she arched her lower body into him. His hands distracted her and she forgot all about fighting his knee. He drove it between her legs, his thigh coming up to meet her center. She gyrated against him, hips pumping, the roughness of his jeans, of hers, igniting the already growing heat in her pussy.

"Jesus, Angelina," Jason whispered as he tore his mouth from hers. His hands moved over her, skimmed her sides, eased between them and over her breasts. "I hadn't meant to do this yet. I made dinner."

Angelina rested her head on the door behind her, one hand still cupping the back of his neck while the other grazed over his broad shoulder. "I thought I was dinner," she said breathless. The feel of his wide hands on her breasts, cupping, squeezing made her womb feel as though a wild animal clawed inside her.

"You were supposed to be dessert."

"So I'll be the appetizer instead." She slipped a hand between them, found his bulge, stiff and ready behind his zipper. She covered that bulge with her palm and drew a low growl from his throat. "Fuck me, Jason. Right here, right now. I want this," she squeezed, not hard but hard enough, and watched with great satisfaction as his eyes rolled back in his head, closed "Inside me."

His fingers began to fumble with the tiny buttons of her blouse. "Dammit," he growled in aggravation, his eyes opening to stare down at the pesky objects. "How much do you like this shirt?"

"It's one of my favorites." Angelina grinned at him, amused by the irritation in his expression, by the sheer need that radiated from his body.

"Too bad. I'll buy you a new one," he said, and she heard the buttons of her blouse pop and fall to the hardwood floor.

"Jason!" she gasped, but his hands were already covering her breasts once more, working to free them from her bra.

"Shit! Next time wear something easy for me to take off."

She laughed. She couldn't help it. She hadn't given much thought to her clothes. He'd seen her at her worst in a way too large shirt and baggy jeans the first day at Romantic Illusions, and she knew she hadn't looked much better at the airport. Still, he'd wanted her. Why bother to get all dolled up when she wouldn't be wearing it long anyway? Hell, she barely made it inside his house before he started to undress her!

"If you'll move back a bit, I can get my hands behind me and reach the clasp," she told him.

"Too much trouble." Roughly, he pushed his fingers under the edge of her conservative white bra, yanked it up until her breasts hung free. He made a low sound of pure male adoration as he gazed down at her and licked his lips. With one tantalizing finger, he traced the areola of her right breast. "God, you're beautiful."

Angelina watched him as the nerve endings in her breast flamed under his touch, her nipple tightening almost to the point of pain.

"Your tan isn't complete."

She felt embarrassment tinged her cheeks, and she was glad his gaze remained on her breast. She loved the sun, thought she looked her best with tanned skin but rarely had the opportunity to sun nude, and tanning beds bored her to misery. So she had tan lines. Small, narrow ones since her bikini really didn't cover much but strips of white flesh nevertheless. A fact that never bothered her until now.

As if he sensed her sudden discomfort, he glanced at her and gave her one of his boyish grins. "I'm glad. Your nipples are large and so dark against your natural milky complexion. If you were to tan your whole body, it would ruin the contrast." He rolled her nipple between his thumb and forefinger, and she writhed against him, arched her breast into his hand.

"I'm…glad you…like it," she panted. It felt like an electrical wire tied her nipple to her pussy. A wire that sizzled, sparked, and blazed to life at his touch.

"Oh baby, I do," he whispered and leaned in, caught just the tip of her nipple between his teeth, nipped.

"Holy shit!" she cried out and wriggled against the door. He caught her hand between them, pushed it above her head, pinning it to the door as he devoured her breast. Her other hand fell from his neck to his shoulder, nails digging into flesh as he sucked then gently bit and finally licked the low arousing pain away. His attention moved briefly to her other breast and took it with the same feverous hunger.

She couldn't stand it, the fiery ardor that soared through her. Wetness pooled in her center, leaked from her lips to soak her panties. Her clit burned with need, ached to be touched. "Jason, please!"

"My command, remember?" he said against the sensitized flesh of her breast.

"I got half of it right."

"There are no half points, no shared command tonight." His hand released her wrist, slid down her arm, glided down her side and over her hip to the button-fly of her jeans.

She heard him growl and mentally said goodbye to her favorite pair of button-fly jeans as she heard the brass buttons go sailing through the air, felt the stiff material give. "Why didn't you tell me to wear a skirt?"

He chuckled, a quick burst of sound against her flesh. "Do that next time," he said and quickly, efficiently pushed her jeans and panties down around her ankles. She toed off her tennis shoes and stepped out of her clothing as he sank to his knees before her.

* * * *

"Sweet Mother of God," Jason whispered at the sight of her bare mound glistening with her own juices. He didn't know what he'd expected to see beneath the conservative clothing, but the sight that met his eyes certainly wasn't it. Smooth, silky flesh met his gaze, and he wanted to climb inside her, consume her, become one with her.

He touched her, his fingers slipping between her soft folds to part them for his mouth. He heard her quick intake of breath, and it only served to fuel his growing need. He suddenly craved the taste of her more than oxygen. She got in his head. Whatever she did affected him more than the strongest alcohol, made him dizzy with it. She was so sensual, so sexy, so dammed hot she scorched his fingers. Control was like an ice cube melting more and more each time he touched her.

His dick throbbed behind the zipper of his jeans, begging for a release he would not give it. Not yet. He wanted to be inside this sweet, tender flesh, but he would pleasure her first, drive her to point of hormone overload before allowing himself satisfaction. Time seemed to stand still as all that mattered quivered in his hands, writhing against the door.

He felt her hands on him, one resting on his shoulder, the other on the top of his head as he leaned in and took a tentative, sampling lick. She tasted sweet and hot, her ripe flesh smooth under his tongue.

"Jason, please, a bed, a couch, something," she breathed as her fingers tightened on his shoulder, her hand grabbing at his hair but unable to get a grip on the short strands.

So willing, so eager, he thought and felt his balls tighten with a surge of lust so ferocious he nearly lost himself right then and there. She wanted him, needed him. Had a woman ever radiated such desire for him before? She was amazing, open and honest, unabashed with her wishes, with her body's demands. He could drown in this woman, he realized, and felt a quick prickle of fear snake down his spine.

Sex, he reminded himself. A woman like her would never want more than sex from a man like him. Not that he truly wanted anything more from her. It was all a game. A game in which they could both win if only they kept it light, fun, completely carnal. Surely that wouldn't be hard to do. He needed only to think of his past to keep his emotions in line.

"I'll hold you up," he told her, his hands moving to her hips to steady her against the door as he delved his tongue between her folds.

She spread her legs wider, arched her hips, opening herself to him, and he drove his tongue inside the damp heat of her pussy. Her muscles clenched around his tongue as he lapped at her wetness, licked the walls of her vagina. He moved one hand, slipped it between her legs and replaced his tongue with two fingers, driving them deep and fast inside her. The sweet sounds of pleasure she made filled his senses as the hot grip of her sex latched onto his questing fingers. He licked at her swollen clit as his fingers probed inside her, slowly at first, then faster until he heard her breathless pleas for mercy.

"Jason, I want to—"

"You're interrupting my appetizer," he said in a low tone of warning.

She gasped a chuckle. "But I can't—"

"Cum for me, Angelina," he said against her flesh. "I want to taste your come, feel your body as it contracts around my fingers." His lips moved over her clit, caught it in a gentle suction as his tongue circled around it. He bent his fingers inside her, found that sensitive spot and relished in the cry it pulled from her lips. She was close, so close. He moved his fingers inside her, stretched her even as he increased the pressure of his mouth on her clit.

The orgasm burst from her in screams of unintelligible sounds. Her body jerked in his hands, her clit quivering with brutal spasms under his tongue, her inner muscles forming a vice around his fingers. Hot juices filled his hand, and he pulled his fingers from her to drink her wetness.

Her eyes fluttered open as he slowly stood in front of her.

He grinned at her. He couldn't help it. She looked so amazing slumped against the door, naked but for the bra he'd pushed up rather than remove. Remnants of her juices lingered around his mouth and he licked his lips, savored the last tastes of her. "Are you all right?"

She laughed at that, a quick burst of surprised air. "Ask me again when I can breathe."

"Can you stand on your own?"

She blinked at him, seemed to consider for a moment, then nodded.

"Stay here. I'll get you something to wear."

"But I didn't…you didn't… I want to…"

"We'll get to that later," he cut off her protest, trailing a finger down the length of her from neck to belly button before letting his hand fall away. "Tonight's game is far from over, sweetheart."

Chapter 4

The beer tasted like horse piss. Not that Bailey knew firsthand exactly what horse piss tasted like. Still, the comparison seemed apt. She set the bottle on the table and idly peeled at the label as she gazed around the bar. She couldn't say what drew her to the Paradise Lounge tonight. Nor could she say why she felt the need to wallow in a bottle of beer. Especially since wallowing had never been her style, and beer never set easy on her taste buds.

He knew, she thought, and felt an icy dart of fear pierce her stomach. Okay, maybe he didn't know, but she'd been afraid for a while now that Lieutenant Tripp Barrett suspected something was off with her. Still, suspicion could be as detrimental to her place in the department as knowledge.

She'd thought it was going away, her fear of the dark, of enclosed spaces. She'd been on the fire department for over a year now, made it through six weeks of the grueling fire academy before that. She'd been in blackout mazes, smokehouses, worked scenes where visibility was no farther than the beam of her flashlight. She handled them all. Yes, at times she felt that trickle of fear. Yes, her heart rate increased each time. Still, she handled herself, handled the situation, and it hadn't been so bad.

What changed? She wondered aimlessly and picked up the beer bottle, taking a long pull. She winced as the revolting liquid washed down her throat. Why did she want to freak out again when faced with the dark? And what was with the dreams? Why had they returned with a vengeance? She woke in the middle of the night drenched in her own sweat, heart racing out of her chest with little to no recollection of the nightmare that woke her.

"Maybe you should try something that comes in a glass rather than a bottle."

Bailey looked up, focused on the owner of the voice, and her heart stopped. Not out of fear this time but surprise and, dammit, desire. "L.T.," she said and let the surprise sound in her voice even as she ruthlessly stomped out the desire.

"Mind if I join you?" he asked but was already sliding into the booth across from her before she could answer.

"I didn't expect to see you here." Dear God, she didn't *want* to see him here. Not here, not now. Not when she'd been attempting to drown her sorrows in the awful concoction of yeast and bubbles and whatever the hell else beer was made from.

"I could say the same about you." He set a glass of some amber liquid on the table between them and pinned her with one of his steady, unreadable gazes. "Come to think of it, I've never seen you here before."

Because the bar scene was so not her thing, Bailey thought. The Paradise Lounge was the hot spot in Silver Springs for every available, off-duty firefighter, EMT and police official. Everyone but her. She could count on one hand the number of times she came to the lounge, present visit included, and still have fingers left over. The other times she'd been coerced into showing. A birthday party for David Karlston. The L.T. hadn't attended that party for reasons totally unknown to her. A heartbroken EMT, Terri Vega, had needed someone to talk to when she split with her latest fling of the week. And once she'd gotten roped into coming here for after shift drinks with Jason Graham and Ryan Magee. The last had been a huge mistake as Magee spent the evening attempting to convince her how badly she wanted him.

"We've managed to miss each other," she said now and wished with all her body and soul they wouldn't have crossed paths tonight. In her current state of mind, conversation with Tripp Barrett over a couple of drinks in a dimly lit booth in the back of the lounge was the dead last thing she needed.

He looked too dammed good. He'd dressed up. She'd never seen him dressed up before. He wore a short sleeve, button-down shirt, sapphire blue with gray pinstripes. The stripes matched the gray slacks she'd caught a glimpse of as he sat down. She'd never seen him in anything other than a uniform T-shirt or full-fledged turnout gear, and the sight of him in something different, something more classy, sent exquisite sensations of lust straight to her feminine core. Was this how he dressed to pick up women when he went out for a night on the town? The thought had her snatching up her beer bottle and taking yet another long, revolting swallow. She prayed the alcohol would work fast, numb her overactive brain, cause sudden blindness, and strike her stupid. She closed her eyes as she set the bottle down again. She didn't need the alcohol to strike her stupid. Carnal thoughts of herself and Lieutenant Tripp Barrett did that long ago.

"Is there any particular reason you're torturing yourself with that sh— stuff?" He caught himself before he said shit. Of all the men on B shift, most of whom tossed around foul words like papers in the wind, Tripp always watched his language in front of her. He tilted his glass at her beer bottle before taking a sip of his drink.

Bailey glanced at the beer and shrugged. "I didn't know what else to order," she admitted and felt her cheeks grow warm. She didn't know why such an admission embarrassed her. So she wasn't a big drinker. Big deal. At least she could almost guarantee that her liver and kidneys were still in good working order.

"Most women go for something more along the lines of a tequila sunrise or a margarita." When she winced, he chuckled and added, "But you aren't most women."

God, he had a great smile, she thought as she studied him. It lit up his face, brought out the best of his features. Not that he had any bad ones. Maybe he had a few more lines around his hazel eyes and thin mouth than a lot of men. Laughter lines, she decided, lines that enhanced rather than took away from his good looks.

"I usually drink wine, but white wine puts me to sleep and red makes me…" She stopped, inwardly horrified at what she'd nearly revealed. He so didn't need to know what red wine did to her. It made her horny, ready for heart-pounding, sweat-soaking, deliciously sloppy sex.

His smile slowly died as a look of hunger came into his eyes. Or maybe she was imagining that look because no way would the Lieutenant look at her with anything more than friendship in mind. Would he?

No. She was projecting. She'd never been able to read this man. What made her think she could start now?

"Try this." He pushed his glass across the table to her.

Bailey picked up the glass, held it to her nose and sniffed. When the scent failed to register in her alcohol challenged mind, she took a tentative sip. "That's not too bad. Kind of sweet but not in a fruity way. What is it?"

"Southern Comfort with a splash of Coke." He reached for the glass as she slid it back to him, their fingers brushing.

And there it was again, Tripp thought. That quick flicker of something he couldn't quite pin down in her eyes, something that struck him suspiciously like...desire.

Tripp stared at her, watched as her gaze quickly skittered away, as she pulled her hand away as though she'd been burned. A cocktail waitress passed, and Bailey flagged her down, ordered a Southern Comfort for herself and another for him. When the waitress returned moments later, he paid for the drinks, ignoring Bailey's objections.

"You can buy the next round."

She nodded, then picked up her glass and, to his utter astonishment, downed half of it before returning the glass to the table.

Tripp raised a brow and stuck his tongue in his cheek to hold back a smile as he studied her. "You might want to take it easy on that. It tastes good but, Southern Comfort has a way of sneaking up on you if you aren't used to drinking it."

She laughed but it sounded halfhearted, part amusement and part disgust with herself. "I'm not used to drinking anything," she confessed. "At least not anything with alcohol in it. I don't...I don't drink often."

Tripp suspected as much. He knew she'd come here a couple of times with members of B shift but only when the guys laid on the pressure. Even then, he'd been told she'd barely finished one drink the whole time she stayed there.

"Have you eaten anything in the last couple of hours?" At her slow shake of the head, he flagged down the waitress again and placed an order for chicken strips and fries from the adjoining café.

Bailey grimaced at his choice of selections. "That's loaded with carbs and calories."

"Carbs and calories are exactly what you need if you plan to drink more than that." He shot a pointed glance at her glass. "The bread will help absorb some of the alcohol. Besides, what are you worried about calories for? You have a—" Great body, he almost said. Whoa man! He put the mental brakes on his tongue as well as his thoughts. Although she did have a killer body, he silently admitted, she managed to keep her muscles in a delicate balance between rock solid and gently toned. He knew she worked out daily and the result was that of healthy, firm curves.

She looked at him now. Her quizzical expression tangled with, God, could that really be desire in her eyes?

Tripp backpedaled. "You have a job that keeps you active enough, and you work out enough, you shouldn't need to worry about calories."

She laughed again, but this time it sounded as forced as the smile on her face. "Every woman has to worry about calories." She picked up her glass and downed the remaining liquid.

Was she trying to get drunk? He wondered as he watched her. She'd looked away again, seemed to study the slowly growing crowd in the lounge. The volume level would pick up soon as the night crowd gathered for dancing and drinks. A part of him wished he and Bailey were somewhere more private, someplace they could talk without fear of being overheard, someplace they could be alone.

And deep in his gut he knew what a very bad, bad idea that was.

* * * *

"Do we get to pop the buttons off this shirt too?" Angelina asked. Jason had given her one of his shirts. A pale pink button-down that reached nearly to her knees, the sleeves so long she had to roll them several times to reach her elbows. The man actually owned a pink shirt! She'd been flabbergasted by that until she realized a man who practically oozed sex from every pore wouldn't need to worry about such a soft color ruining his masculinity.

Jason chuckled as he slid open the back door of the house. "We'll get to that after dinner." He motioned for her to walk out before him.

Angelina stepped outside and stopped. She shot him a surprised glance over her shoulder. "You have a swimming pool?"

"It's one of the biggest reasons I bought this house." He stepped past her, led her to a small table on one side of a wooden deck that stretched the width of the house.

"But you dammed near live on the beach." Angelina placed her plate on the table as she sat down in the chair he held out for her.

"I've never cared much for the beach." He shrugged and took the seat across from her. "Too much sand. Plus, I prefer my own private place to swim. No need to worry about what is in the water that I would rather avoid."

Angelina propped an elbow on the table and raised a quizzical eyebrow at him. "Don't tell me you're afraid of sharks."

"Sharks, jellyfish." He picked up his fork. "Hell, I'm not real keen on sharing water with any type of fish."

"Wow! A man who can admit he has a weakness. I like that."

"Besides, we would risk the chance of being arrested for indecent exposure, public nudity, and who knows what else with what I have in mind after dinner."

A mischievous gleam passed through his eyes at that and her insides did the tango. "Say goodbye to your shirt," she said and speared a broccoli floret with her fork. He'd grilled steaks, but rather than simply slap a couple of cuts on the rack, he'd done something to them, something that made their flavor out of this world. With them, they had baked potatoes and steamed vegetables. Food they had to reheat after their appetizer at the front door. Still, even nuked in the microwave, the first bites melted in her mouth and nearly sent her on another colossal orgasmic wave of ecstasy. "Oh God, Jason, this is incredible!"

"I'd hoped you would say that about other things I do to you, not what I put in your stomach."

Angelina groaned playfully. "Don't tell me you're one of those types who needs to hear how great you are after sex. Oh baby, that was amazing," she said dramatically. "Oh baby, I've never had it so good."

"Nah, there's no need." He shoved a strip of steak into his mouth and spoke around it. "I already know how good I am."

She started to call him conceited but remembered his response the last time she'd done that. "*Convinced, Ms. Keaton. Play with me and I'll prove it.*" He'd proved it all right, and she couldn't wait for him to prove it again.

"Seriously, where did you learn to cook like this? And what did you do to this steak? It's fabulous!"

"Trade secret." He grinned. "If I told you…"

"You would have to kill me." She rolled her eyes as she finished the sentence for him. "Okay, wiseass."

"My father. He cooked for the Army."

"*The* Army, not an army?" she clarified and laid her fork on the edge of her plate, picked up her wine glass. He'd poured them flutes of chilled red wine from a bottle out of a bucket of ice on the edge of the table.

Jason nodded. "He's retired military."

"The Army doesn't teach you to cook like this."

"He likes to cook, found out it was one of his passions after my mother…left."

His slight hesitation told her there was more to his mother's leaving than he wanted to say. Though curiosity twisted inside her like a rubber band, she let it go for now. Later, she promised herself, she would pry into his past.

"So your father learned to cook and then taught you," she concluded in an attempt to keep the conversation lighthearted.

"Me and my brother." Jason nodded and sipped from his own wine glass.

"You have a brother?" Angelina asked and wondered fleetingly if the brother looked even half as good as Jason.

"He lives in Waterston. Works for the Waterston division of the FBI."

"The FBI?" Angelina couldn't hide the surprise in her voice. She picked up her fork again and waved it in the air above her plate now. "Wait a minute. So your father is retired military, you have a brother…" She stopped and cocked her head to one side. "Older or younger?"

"Uh, older."

"I figured he would be," she said and scooped up a healthy bite of her baked potato.

Jason placed his fork on the table by his plate and idly spun his wine glass in his fingers as he studied her. "Why?"

She shrugged. "Because it takes a while, *years* in some cases, for a person to make a name for themselves in the FBI. You aren't that old yourself. What? Twenty-nine?"

"Thanks." He smiled. "But make it thirty-two."

"Really?" Her eyes widened. "You sure don't look it." She saw the question move into his eyes and bit back a smile, already knowing him well enough to know he wouldn't ask. "I'm twenty-eight. Thanks for not asking."

"Another thing my father taught me, never ask a woman's age."

"Smart man, your father. I'd like to meet him someday."

She wanted to meet his father. Jason never, ever introduced the women he dated to his father. Not because he was embarrassed by his father or anything. No, because his father would embarrass the shit out of him with talk of wedding bells and frilly dresses. His father wanted to see his sons married. Clint Graham's own wife may have turned out to be the prized demon but he was certain his sons would have better luck. He saw such luck in every woman Jason or his brother Jackson dated.

"Anyway, where were we? Oh yeah, it makes sense that your brother would be older."

Jason didn't bother telling her that Jackson was all of four and a half minutes older than him. No need to divulge the fact that they were twins. Even though he doubted she would ever meet his brother.

Despite the fact that he and Jackson were identical from the roots of their buzz-cut heads to the tips of their toenails—save for a small birthmark on Jackson's left thigh that Jason didn't have and the fire helmet tattoo Jason got on the back of his right shoulder not long after joining the department—Jackson tended to be the lady magnet. Something about his cool demeanor, his conservative style, and approach drew women to him like a bee to honey.

"So, you have an Army father, a brother who is an agent with the FBI, and you are a firefighter." She laughed and shook her head. "Talk about covering all of the branches of public service. And all of you can cook like a dream. Go figure."

"My father and Jackson are actually better cooks that I am," Jason admitted. "Jackson took to the whole culinary thing more than me. He does all of the fancy flambé and chop, chop, chops and shit. Me? I still burn boiling water sometimes."

"You do not," she said on a bark of laughter.

"I burned an entire pot of spaghetti sauce and a pot of noodles to boot at the station the other night."

Angelina covered her mouth with her hand, but it did nothing to stop her giggles. "You didn't!"

"Cost me a fortune in pizza delivery," he muttered. His pocket still ached from that. Not because of the money he'd put out on the pizzas for the guys, but because of the pride he'd had to eat right along with his pepperoni and cheese slices. "See, that's how it works around there. One guy is assigned kitchen duty. You either cook or you have to buy takeout for the whole shift. Since I burned what was bought to cook—"

"You had to spring for pizzas."

"Of course, it wouldn't have happened if I hadn't been thinking about you."

He watched as her laughter slowly died, as her smile grew hot and sensual. Yep, that was the smile, the look he'd been unable to get out of his mind that day and every day since.

She picked up her wine glass, tipped it back as though she needed a bit of liquid courage, and stood. His shirt swallowed her. It fell around her soft curves like a sheet. Yet, with the top buttons left undone, the neckline parted to dammed near below her naked breasts and those incredible, shapely legs, he thought she might very well be the sexiest thing he'd ever seen.

Jason stood too, unwilling to let her get even a moment of command tonight. He'd won the game, and he intended to make every last moment of the evening his prize.

They met halfway but when she seemed to expect him to pull her into his arms, he sidestepped her instead, moving quickly to a small stereo that sat to one side of the slider leading into the house.

* * * *

Angelina watched him, anticipation and a keen awareness growing in her veins as he flicked on the radio. He found a station playing a particularly fast, techno-type song and turned to face her. He waggled his brows at her, and she had to laugh.

As the beat of the music hammered in the air, her hips began to sway, her head nodding ever so slightly to the rapid tempo. She liked music like this, free, rapid sounds of drums and keyboards, guitars and synthesized instruments. All they lacked were the florescent high beam streams of light and the crowded dance floor, she thought.

Then again, she amended, as he slowly strolled toward her, being alone with this man in his private backyard promised to offer loads more excitement than any dance floor.

"You know what I want right now?" He stopped several steps away from her and stood with his thumbs hooked in the pockets of his jeans. He looked, she thought, like a full-page spread in the year's sexiest male calendar. His gaze slid down her slowly, as if he could devour her, taste her with his eyes, and tingles exploded beneath the surface of her skin.

"I think I have a pretty good idea," she said and took a small step toward him. The hardwood of the deck felt cool under her bare feet. A light wind ruffled the air, drifted up under the shirt she wore and chilled the naked warmth between her legs. She hadn't bothered to put her underwear or bra back on, had known it would be a waste of time. All through dinner and standing before him now, knowing all that remained between her naked flesh and his work-roughened hands was this thin cotton shirt, put every nerve ending in her body on ecstatic alert.

"Dance for me."

"Dance for?" It took a moment for his words to sink in, for her to understand his meaning. He wanted her to *dance* for him as in sexy, sensual moves as she stripped for him. She stopped and looked around the dimly lit yard. A candle burned on the table where they'd eaten dinner, two more flickered in the nearby window ledge. A streetlight on the corner offered a ray of yellowish light that did little more than create shadows along the fence line.

Privacy fence, she noted. High, made of solid wood, the lumber close together as to leave only the smallest of cracks. Someone would have to want to see really bad to peek in on them. She found the idea of that, of someone watching, not as unsettling as she expected. More like an unexpected turn-on.

The song segued into another similar song but with a bit slower tempo. This one was more exotic, more flowing, and Angelina allowed the sound to seep into her, possess her limbs. She placed her hands on her waist and began to move her hips in a circular movement of grinding seduction in time with the music. As the beat did a slow hesitation, she spread her legs, bent her knees and eased down, touched the ground with her fingertips. The song did a leisurely crescendo, and when she began to stand, she skimmed her palms over her skin all the way up.

Her gaze locked with Jason's, and she had the satisfaction of seeing him gulp as her hands reached her breasts through the material of her borrowed shirt. She cupped them and brushed her fingers over their already taut peaks as she turned her body in a small, graceful circle. She'd taken dance classes when she was a child and put those lessons into practice now, adding her own provocative twists, turns, and touches. She thought of all the television shows she'd seen where women danced for men, of the topless bar she'd once visited in fun with her Uncle Edward. A pole or a bedpost worked well for a prop. Neither was available to her now, but she would improvise.

Her circles brought her closer to Jason, and when she reached him she draped one arm on his shoulder, raised one leg and pushed her lower body against his side. She let her leg slide down his body to the ground and bit back a smile at his quick intake of breath. She gyrated her lower body against him as she began to move behind him, her hand skimming over his collarbone, down his chest. She leaned in, licked her way across the back of his shoulders while her hand explored his chest, found his beaded nipple and gave it a light twist.

"Oh, God." His whispered cry was barely audible. It rolled through her, fueled her already blazing fire, and drew the wetness from her already slick pussy lips.

She rose to her tiptoes and nipped his earlobe. "Fuck me, Jason." She used her gentle grip on his nipple, her other hand on the back of his shoulder, to turn him to face her. His gaze met hers, his eyes flaming hot and dark with need. She released her hold on his nipple and let her finger trail down the hard planes of his abs, his stomach, the enormous bulge in his pants. Her pussy lips contracted, her clit burning in anticipation.

She let her hands fall away from him and took a small step back. His gaze followed her hands as she brought them to the neckline of her shirt, caught the edges of the material in each hand and yanked. Buttons popped, fell away and she reveled in the slow smile that unfolded on his lips. A smile that gained the intensity of molten lava as she shrugged out of the shirt and let it fall to the deck in a pool of cotton at her feet.

Her hands returned to her body, and she caressed one breast, let her other hand skim lower to slip between her legs. Her skin was warm and smooth under her own palms, her own touch arousing and erotic.

"Sweet Jesus, you drive me crazy," he said, his voice cracking with desire.

Angelina laughed, a low and seductive sound, as she spread her legs enough for him to see when she slipped one finger between her slick folds. "Isn't that what you want?"

He made quick work of his jeans, removed them and kicked them to the side. She had a second to note he wore no underwear before he grabbed her, pulled her hard and fast into his arms. His hands immediately found her hips and he lifted her, her legs wrapping around his waist as he entered her.

"Oh my God!" Angelina threw her head back and cried out at the sudden intrusion. She locked her ankles behind his back, her hands holding onto his shoulders, her nails digging into skin. She was wet, ready for him but even so he stretched her. Their position drove him impossibly deep inside her.

"Look at me Angel." His voice was deep, strained. When she managed to raise her head, meet his gaze, he asked, "Can you swim?"

She blinked at him, his question confusing her clouded mind. "Y—yes."

Without pulling his dick from inside her, he carried her to the pool, planted soft kisses on her cheeks, her lips, and her neck along the way. She felt no fear that he might drop her, no fear that he would hurt her in any way. His arms were steady beneath her ass as he slowly descended the steps of the pool.

Angelina braced herself for the chill of the water but found it warm and inviting instead. He stopped when the water reached his shoulders and walked her back against the wall of the pool. She released her grip on his shoulders and splayed her arms along the wall behind her as he eased his dick out of her until only the head remained before he slowly inched his way into her again.

"Jason! No!" She panted as he repeated the same snail-paced movement. Her fingers wrapped around the pool ledge, and she tried to use it for leverage, tried to meet his thrusts with quicker, harder ones of her own. But he held her too close, his hands on her hips and ass too tight. He controlled their pace, and nothing she could do would change that.

"My God, Jason," she breathed, her inner muscles flexing around the thick, hard meat inside her. "You're driving me crazy!"

"Isn't that what you want?"

She wanted to laugh at having her own words turned around on her but couldn't find the strength or the sanity. His thrusts held her firmly against the wall, and he moved one hand, slipping it between them to cup and fondled her breast.

"This isn't going to be enough," he growled as he drove himself inside her one hard, deep, and glorious time before he returned to the slow pace of agony.

She didn't know what he meant, but she suspected he was talking more to himself than to her. She raised her head to look at him, to question him, but he smashed his lips to hers, cutting off any and all words. His tongue invaded her mouth when it opened on a gasp of surprise. And finally, *finally*, he drove his cock into her with a ferocity and speed that didn't slow. He pounded inside her, met the end of her with each harsh inward push. Water sloshed around them, the sound joining with their moans of pleasure and creating a new kind of song all their own. He was no longer gentle, but she didn't want gentle. She wanted out-of-control, animalistic sex.

Pulse points of pleasure slammed through her clit, her vagina, and she knew she was close. He seemed to know it too because he tore his mouth from hers.

"Hold on to me and take a deep breath."

She nodded, did as he asked, and he took them under. The water rushed over her head, drowning out all sound. Her back still firmly against the wall, he spread his legs wider and continued to plunge deeply inside her. The eroticism of being under water, unable to breathe, unable to speak, unable to move, had the orgasm slamming into her. She felt his body stiffen between her thighs as he found his own release.

They broke the surface gasping for air.

* * * *

"What are you doing here, Bailey?"

It surprised her that he would ask. More, the concern in his tone, the soothing comfort that accompanied his words made her throat tight. What could she tell him? A half a beer, three Southern Comfort and Cokes, two chicken strips and a handful of French fries later and she still didn't know why she came to the Paradise Lounge tonight.

She looked away from him and watched as a couple stepped onto the empty dance floor. The night was still early for the heavy party crowd. The kind that made the noise level jump about ten octaves and slammed back drinks in an attempt to see how inebriated they could get before 3 am when the lounge closed. The kind who demanded live music, screeching loud and pulse-pounding fast. For now, for the small, quiet early evening crowd, the jukebox, and soft music sufficed.

Bailey watched wistfully as the man led the woman to the center of the small, polished wood dance floor and gently drew her into his arms. The song that played was slow, a ballad Bailey thought she recognized as something from the 90s era. Bryan Adams maybe? The couple swayed more than danced, held each other so close even oxygen had difficulty moving between their bodies.

She looked away because it was far too easy to picture herself with Tripp on that dance floor. She could all but feel his strong arms around her waist, the length of his tall, hard body against her trim frame. God, but she wanted to feel that for real! She wanted to feel *him*.

"I need to leave," she said briskly and picked up her glass, draining the last sips. She dug in her purse, withdrew a few bills to cover her share of the drinks and tip and tossed them in the center of the table.

"Bailey, wait."

But she was already sliding out of the booth. She pulled the strap of her purse onto her shoulder and walked away. She thought she heard Tripp scramble to his feet behind her, thought she felt his gaze on her back as she hurried out the door of the lounge. She knew he followed her when she heard the telltale sound of his booted feet as they stepped onto the asphalt of the parking lot.

She finally stopped at the edge of the concrete walkway that spanned the front entrance. Palm trees lined the grass between the walk and the asphalt with bushes of some type of flower she couldn't name scattered between the palms. It gave the place a bit of an island look. She thought she wouldn't mind that right about now. A deserted island where she and Tripp could be alone.

No, she told herself. The purpose of the secluded island would be to get away from Lieutenant Tripp Barrett. It would be a place where he couldn't follow her as he did now.

"What happened in there?" He gently grasped her elbow and turned her to face him.

That simple, friendly touch had pulse points of desire shimmying through her all the way to her toes. God, she had to get better control over her responses to this man!

"I just..." Need to get away from you. Want you so badly I can taste you. Long to be in your arms so bad it makes my whole body ache. "I'm just ready to go home, Tripp, ready to go to bed." Something moved through his eyes but it was too quick, too vague to name.

"You shouldn't drive, Bailey."

She loved his Texas drawl, the slow and lazy sound of it even as it dripped with concern for her safety. How many times had she wondered what that voice would sound like in the heat of passion? Did it become more drawn out, more sluggish, when he became aroused? Did it get clipped and begin to fade as he climaxed? That was, of course, supposing he talked during sex. Some men didn't say a word.

Bailey shook her head. Shit, shit, *shit*! It didn't matter if he recited the complete script of the movie *Backdraft* while having sex. She would never know, and she had no right to wonder about it now.

"I wish you would tell me what's going on with you," he said softly, his hand still on her elbow as he gazed at her, seemed to will her to talk to him.

"I can't." Dammit, her voice broke. For quite possibly the first time ever, she actually read his eyes, saw the fear that she would start to cry shine through them like a pair of headlights set to super bright. She looked away and tried to move, but his grip on her elbow tightened enough to stop her. "Let me go, Tripp. Just let me go before..." *Before I do something we will both regret like kiss you, or tell you how badly I want you beside me tonight in the dark holding me and taking away all my fears.*

A single tear escaped. It slid down her cheek, and he raised his free hand to catch it, brush it away with the pad of his thumb. Bailey couldn't help it. She leaned in to his touch. She closed her eyes, inhaled deeply, and when she opened them again he was there. Right there, his lips so close, almost touching hers. Her heart stopped. She was certain of it. She could no longer feel her blood moving through her veins, no longer feel the oxygen moving through her lungs, no longer feel anything but the blessed heat that radiated from his lips.

Then he kissed her and, oh God, it felt better than any kisses she'd ever imagined in her dreams, or hell, even in her walking day fantasies. His lips brushed hers in a feathery caress so soft, so sweet she thought she'd imagined it. But no, this wasn't a case of her imagination working overtime. This was reality, a fantabulous reality where Tripp Barrett's mouth held hers captive, a reality where his tongue licked the outside of her lips requesting entrance, a reality where her lips parted on a soundless gasp.

His tongue swept into her mouth and tangled with hers in a dance so malleable and melodious she thought she might melt in his arms. He pulled her closer, wrapped his wide forearms around her waist as she'd fantasized him doing earlier in the bar and drew her closer still. His body felt solid and long against her, a rigid wall of muscle more powerful than it appeared.

Her own arms found their way around his neck, and her head tilted, deepening the kiss. He tasted so amazingly wonderful, of liquor and soda and man. A man that was Tripp Barrett, her mind slowly registered far too late. Sweet Jesus, what was she doing?

Gasping, Bailey tore her mouth from his, her eyes wide and horrified. Her hands wrestled with his arms on her waist as she frantically tried to scamper away from him.

"Bailey. Jesus, Bailey. Wait." Tripp tried to hold on to her, but he finally let her go, his fear of hurting her evident in his suddenly readable expression.

She saw hurt, pain, confusion and lust in his eyes, and each one of those emotions ripped at her heart. "I'm sorry, Tripp," she whispered and spun on her heel. She said a quick prayer of thanks to whatever God existed when she spotted a taxi pulling into the parking lot. Without a single look back, she left Tripp Barrett, her lieutenant, the man she so wanted to be with tonight and every night for the rest of her life, standing in the parking lot of the Paradise Lounge.

Chapter 5

"I want twenty-four hour surveillance. Three eight-hour shifts," Angelina told the manager of Beechland Security. "Give me your best men. No greenhorns. I need sharp eyes and experience." She listened as the man named off a price that made her gut tighten and her pocketbook shrink. She gulped. You get what you pay for, she thought and, with a few more instructions, she sealed the deal, said goodbye.

"I hoped you would do something like that."

Angelina looked up, startled by her mother's voice. "Mom, I didn't hear you come in."

"You've been on the phone for hours," Silvia Keaton said as she walked to the long, brown leather sofa against one wall. She perched on the edge of one cushion.

"Business calls." Angelina sighed and replaced the receiver in the cradle on the edge of the desk. Reordering supplies, setting up fuel deliveries, lining up a contractor to rebuild the ruined supply shed, and dealing with Mr. Churchill. She groaned inwardly at the memory of that thirty-minute phone call. The man was relentless! And since she'd missed their scheduled meeting because of the catastrophe at the airport that same day, he became more insistent and cantankerous. *We must meet, Ms. Keaton. I have a proposition for you that I know you will not be able to turn down.* What did it take, she wondered, to deter the man from his goal? Apparently even a bomb didn't phase the dumb ass.

"You've hired security for the airport," Silvia said now.

"It needed to be done anyway. Someone really should be on the property twenty-four/seven. Apparently I should have done it a lot sooner." She sighed and pushed a hand through her frazzled hair. "I can't be there all the time." Though she considered taking up residence in her office at the airport until the culprit was caught.

"How long until you can reopen?"

The police shut down all airport operations while they are investigating. Angelina wasn't even allowed access. For now, she was forced to use her father's old office here on the second floor at the Keaton Estate.

"A couple of days at most. I've lined up security to begin day after tomorrow."

"I'm concerned, Angelina," Silvia Keaton blurted. She wrung her hands in her lap as she stared stone-faced at her eldest daughter. "And I don't mind telling you I'm very, *very* scared."

So was she, but no way would she tell her mother that. The explosion, the photographs, the sharp-edged brush with death, the danger she knew in her gut still awaited her just around the corner scared her shitless. Still, she would not give up without a fight. If she learned anything from her past failures, she learned how to fight.

She stood, pushed all thoughts of immediate business matters and Mr. Churchill with his campaign to take her airport out of her mind, and walked around the desk. The faint stale odor of cigars lingered in the air, and she thought briefly of her father. This had been his haven in the Keaton Estate. He'd sat behind this very desk for more years than she could count, possibly all of her life, smoking cigars and piddling with one business matter after another. As a young girl she would come in here to sit on his lap before bedtime and discuss little girl things—Barbie dolls, the tree house she wanted to build in the backyard, what she wanted to be when she grew up. As a woman she would sit in a chair before the desk, drink a glass or two of alcohol and discuss grown-up things—the world economy, the war in whatever country the United States was fighting at that time, poverty, and politics. Yes, she'd spent many hours with her father inside these four walls and on the adjoining balcony as well. Would his scent ever fade? Would his presence?

She took a seat next to her mother on the sofa and wondered how he would handle this. Her father had always known exactly what to do, precisely what to say to ease her mother's fears and doubts. He'd been so good at it, he even managed to hide things that later became detrimental to the financial portfolio and, later, his own life.

But Walter Keaton was gone now, as was Edward—the only other soul ever able to offer her mother true solace. It would be up to Angelina now.

Up to her to hold together her often too fragile mother, to hold together what remained of their part of the Keaton family.

Angelina sighed inwardly. It was simply one more daunting task she wasn't confident she could accomplish, one more weight she didn't know if she could carry. Yet, she knew she would do it. Confident or not, weak or strong, she'd been left without a choice.

When she turned to face her mother on the sofa, Angelina hid all her doubts, all her inhibitions and fears. She put on a comforting smile and reached for her mother's hand. "There's no need for you to be worried or scared, Mom."

"How can you say that?" Silvia Keaton jerked her hand from her daughter's and stood abruptly. "Someone is trying to force you to close that airport, trying to hurt you, and you tell me I shouldn't worry, I shouldn't be afraid!"

Angelina stared at her mother, watched as she paced the beige plush carpeted floor of the office. Silvia Keaton didn't shout, she didn't fall privy to emotional outbursts or temper tantrums. The Silvia Keaton Angelina always called Mom was a quiet, frail woman who would sooner fidget her way into a corner than to stand up and express her true feelings. As Angelina studied her mother, she saw that while she may be fidgeting, her hands quickly gripping and releasing the sides of her floral-printed skirt, she was far from any corner. Angelina wanted to applaud her mother for finally showing some backbone, but instead she kept silent, afraid if she spoke, if she answered her mother's question, she might shatter her mother's resilience.

"You are my daughter, Angelina," Silvia said as if Angelina didn't already know. She put a hand over her heart, as she continued to pace. "I have only two daughters, all I have left in the world, and you tell me not to worry when someone is threatening one daughter's life and the police, the FAA, and the FBI believe it's the other daughter doing the threatening."

Angelina did gape at her mother now. What was she talking about? The police, the FAA, the fucking FBI! She stood on legs that were suddenly shaky and walked to her mother. "Did someone come here to talk to Tess, Mom?"

"That detective." Her mother nodded. "That female cop that's so pretty even though she looks like something that stepped out of the Amazon jungle."

"Samantha Becket," Angelina provided the name. She would have laughed at her mother's description of the tall, robust woman if the conversation hadn't been so serious. "Yeah, she talked to me—questioned me, I should say—the day the bomb went off at the airport. She was the officer on the case when the vandalism and the theft happened too."

"She questioned your sister today, her and some older man that looked like he spent far too many days and probably nights too at the Krispy Kreme."

"Mother!" Shocked and faintly amused, Angelina couldn't hold back her reaction this time. She gasped, pretending to be appalled in hopes of lightening her mother's mood. "Where do you get these descriptions?"

Silvia waved a hand through the air, dismissing the question with a simple, "Your sister's words."

Figures. It sounded like Tess. "And the FBI?" she asked, still in shock over that one. Yet, hadn't Samantha Becket mentioned something about the FBI getting involved too? Would they really spare time for a bit of sabotage at a small town privately owned airport? She didn't know a thing about the FBI, how the agency operated, its cases or its agents but she knew someone who would, she thought as a vivid picture of Jason Graham came to mind.

"Tess said that detective told her that the FBI has been called in, that they will want to talk to you, both of you." Silvia stopped, turned to look at Angelina, her eyes filling with tears. "They think Tess is behind this. How could they think my youngest daughter could do such a thing?"

"They're reaching, Mom. Grasping at straws." Angelina closed the distance between her and her mother, pulled the slim woman into her arms and held her tight. "I told Samantha Becket that Tess and I were arguing when I received the last envelope, that Tess was the one who brought the mail into my airport office." Looks like the detective jumped on that like a dog with her favorite bone, she thought. Questioning Tess, thinking that she could have put the envelope in with the other mail, staged the whole thing so that they were in Angelina's office arguing when the bomb went off.

"Tess wouldn't have anything to do with this." Silvia Keaton pulled back and glared at her daughter with searching eyes. "You know that, don't you?"

"Of course, I know that. But that doesn't change the facts, Mom. Someone is trying to sabotage my airport. Someone wants me out of business. This…guy," she said for lack of a better word. "Is delivering photographs. Warning me of what is about to happen but not allowing me time to prevent it. They're good photographs too. These aren't taken by some amateur."

"Your Uncle Edward was always good with a camera," her mother said softly, reminiscently.

"He was," Angelina agreed. The family had books of photos her uncle had taken of the estate, family functions, the airport, and nearly everything else that passed in front of his camera lens. "But I don't think Uncle Edward is sending me pictures from the grave." Her mother shot her a look, and Angelina bit back a smile at the irritation in her eyes.

"And Marshall. He's good with a camera too. Gosh, Angelina, Tess plays around with cameras herself. If the police find that out…"

"Lots of people dabble with photography, Mom. I remember Dad even toyed around with it for a time. And with the right equipment, nearly anyone can make it look professional," Angelina said quickly, hoping to soothe her mother's fears. "I know Tess isn't involved. What I don't know is, who is." She took a deep breath, hesitated. "Mom, do you have any idea who it could be? Is there anything I should know?"

"I—I don't know what you mean." Silvia Keaton removed herself from Angelina's embrace, turned her back, and wiped tears from her face.

"You were always so close to Uncle Edward," Angelina said. "I thought maybe you might know something, know of someone perhaps who would be unhappy by my inheriting the airport. That's when all of this started. Nothing ever happened while Uncle Edward was alive."

"No, it didn't." Her mother sniffled as she turned back to face her. "Which leads me to believe that it's more directed at you than your uncle or the airport, baby."

"At me!" Though she sounded surprised even to her own ears, it wasn't like she hadn't thought of this herself. But who had she pissed off enough to make them want to hurt her, to hurt the airport, or the people near it?

"That's why I'm so worried about you, Angelina. And then you go out and don't come home last night. You don't call. No one knows where you are or who you're with and…" Silvia stopped, sniffled. "I was so worried something happened to you, that whoever is doing this decided to..." She couldn't say it. Angelina could see it in her expression, the worst of the things her mother felt, feared.

"I'm sorry, Mom. I didn't think. I came home. It was just really, really late. You were already asleep." She shook her head and felt like a real ass for not considering anyone's feelings but her own, not once even thinking that perhaps her mother might worry about her staying out all night in the face of all that had happened lately.

"You're accustomed to coming and going as you please," her mother said. "I know that, and it is how it should be. But with this maniac out there... I just wish that you would at least let me know where you are until all of this is over, until this man is found. Will you do that for me, please?"

"I will." Angelina said but her mother continued to talk over her.

"At the very least, tell me who he is so I'll have some idea of where you are."

"What makes you think I was with a man?" Angelina bit her lower lip to keep from smiling.

Her mother tilted her head, looked at her through eyes that gleamed with playfulness even though they were swollen and red from crying. "Honey, I may be old, but I was a young girl once too. I remember what it was like, remember the signs."

"You are not old," Angelina said, aghast. "And what signs? I haven't seen any signs."

"Take a moment to look in the mirror once in a while, dear daughter. The signs are all over your face. You're beaming. You're happy, full of life, and you have that glow. That's the most difficult sign for a mother to see because on the one hand it makes a mother's heart fill to see such a glow, yet on the other it makes a mother uneasy."

"And what glow would that be?" Angelina asked slowly. She wasn't sure she wanted to hear the answer.

"Sex," her mother said simply. "Great sex, by the looks of it."

Angelina felt her jaw drop. Had she really just heard the three-letter word come from her mother's delicate lips? No. No way. Her mother didn't talk about such things. "Okay, who are you and what have you done with my mother?"

Silvia laughed. "You make it sound like I shouldn't know how to say the word, much less know what it means."

"Well, I—"

"I do have two daughters, Angelina. How do you think you and Tess got here?"

"I know how we got here." And she didn't really want the picture that thought brought to mind. What child did want to imagine her mother and father having sex? "It's just that... Well, you never talk about stuff like that."

"Just because I don't talk about it doesn't mean that I don't see when it's happening with one of my daughters. Does he make you happy, sweetheart?"

Angelina hesitated. How did she tell her mother what she shared with Jason was just sex? "It's all so new, Mom," she said vaguely. "We've only known each other a couple of weeks and..."

"And he's already sending you roses and gifts."

The rose and the box wrapped in the adorable paper. She'd actually forgotten about them. God! She'd left them lying on the desk at the airport office. "How did you...?"

"Tess told me about them." Silvia walked to a cabinet by the desk, pulled a single red rose in a small vase and the box from a shelf inside. "And she brought them home after the explosion. She took the liberty of putting the rose in water," she said as she turned and handed the items to Angelina. "Is he a firefighter or a policeman? The wrapping paper is a bit of a giveaway."

"Firefighter."

Her mother nodded. "When a man gives a woman a gift, it isn't polite to simply toss it aside unopened."

Taking the hint, Angelina turned the package over, carefully ran her finger under the flap in the paper and separated it from the tape. She reached inside the end of the package, grasped the contents in her fingers, and pulled it free. When she pulled the book from the paper she couldn't hold back the laugh.

"Sex Games," her mother read the title, intrigue and amusement ringing in her voice.

Angelina felt her cheeks flame. "Oh, God." She moaned in embarrassment.

"Looks like he's got something in mind." Silvia reached out, ran a finger over the top of the book, separating the pages at a dog-eared chapter.

Angelina flipped the book open to the page, read the chapter title, and knew exactly what game Jason Graham wanted to play next.

* * * *

Jackson Graham merged into the moderate traffic on Highway 49 and settled more comfortably into the seat of his Ford Expedition for the drive. His thoughts wound around the events of the past couple of days. His boss, Adam Cooper, all but ordered him to take a couple weeks of leave. Things were slow around the bureau, and Jackson was well overdue for a vacation. Reluctantly, he'd agreed, thinking that it had been several years since he spent longer than a weekend with his father or his brother.

Then, as he was preparing to leave, the vacation turned assignment. "You know people in Silver Springs, right? You have family there?" Adam Cooper knew full well that Jackson's twin and father lived in the relatively small town on the Gulf Coast. He knew where every member of his team's family, their extended family and even *their* extended family lived. A stickler for perfection and details, Adam Cooper missed nothing.

Still, Jackson had replied with an affirmative, rather than the "You know good and dammed well I do" that crossed his mind. And just like that his much needed, practically forced time off turned into an assignment. A privately owned airport under obvious attack, Silver Springs Police Department and the Federal Aviation Administration coming up dry for leads, see if it's related to the others.

Jackson hadn't uttered a word in protest. In truth, though he experienced moments of guilt over it later, he felt relieved that he would have something to do while visiting his brother and father. Simply put, Silver Springs bored him to tears. He preferred the big city life, the constant rush from point A to point B, the noise and yes, even the stress. Silver Springs was too laid-back for his taste.

It suited his father though, he thought now. The consistently warm and humid climate, the waters, the beaches, the quiet. After years in the military, Clint Graham had found happiness in a town known for easy living while a mere hop, skip and a jump over the bridge from the larger tourist attraction and casino wrought city of Billings.

And Jason seemed happy there as well, Jackson continued to reflect, as he gained on the bumper of a slower moving car in front of him. He flicked on his blinker, signaling to the cars behind him of his intent to swap lanes, and eased over. Yes, his twin seemed to have made a happy and successful life for himself in Silver Springs as well. Of course, all it took was a fire department and an endless supply of hot and horny women to make his twin happy.

You're much too uptight lately, Jackson. Get laid while you're gone. Have a quick fling. Maybe it will do us both some good.

Mallory Stone's last words came back to him right along with a clear mental picture of her curvy-as-sin body in that barely there, ball-squeezing outfit. His dick stiffened at the memory, and he shifted in the seat, his comfortable position no longer comfortable. Quick flings with women were Jason's thing, not his. When he took a woman to bed, he looked for more than a few hours, a night or even a couple of nights of sex. Unfortunately, every relationship he ever had ended with a finality that mirrored a 32-caliber bullet to the temple.

Because none of those relationships had been with Mallory Stone.

Jackson wanted her. Forget that she was the sister of Cameron Stone, his best friend for well over a decade. Forget that Jackson watched her grow from a scrawny and shapeless teen with a head far too large for her body into a sexpot that would make the perfect Playboy centerfold. He still wanted her. But all she wanted was sex. Shouldn't it be the other way around? Wasn't the woman supposed to desire the husband, two point five kids and the white picket fence while the man dreamed only of getting between her legs?

Maybe if he took her advice, found someone to have a quick roll on the beach while in Silver Springs, he could manage to give her what she wanted without tossing his heart to the firing squad. Hell, now that his supposed vacation had turned assignment, he might be in town longer than planned. Maybe he could find a couple of someones to fill his needs.

With irritation, lust, and indecision mixing a deadly combination in his gut, he punched the on button of the stereo, turned the volume up to just short of blasting. Buckcherry's *Crazy Bitch* poured from the speakers. Yeah,

Mallory was a crazy bitch indeed, he thought with a sigh. He knew what he would do in Silver Springs. The same thing he always did. He would spend a bit of time with his brother and father, work the case he'd been assigned, and return home with balls still throbbing from the lack of release.

* * * *

Bailey heard the knock at the door and tried to ignore it. It worked last night, her attempts to ignore the pounding on her door at midnight, the phone calls until nearly 3 am. He'd given up only to start again a few hours later. Persistent bastard.

"Leave me alone, Tripp." She moaned and buried her face in the huge throw pillow on her over-stuffed sofa. Blindly, she reached with her right hand and slapped at the coffee table until she found the television remote. As though reading something in braille, she grazed the pad of her thumb over the buttons, found the volume, and pushed.

"Come on, Colonel, you've got to give me a Section 8," Klinger's voice boomed from the television speakers. "Look at me. I'm wearing women's clothing."

"You look mighty fine in them too," Colonel Potter said.

M*A*S*H. One of Bailey's favorite shows. Any other time she would be eager to watch even though she knew each episode by heart. Not today. Today the only eagerness she could find was gearing up to be directed at the front door, at Tripp Barrett to vacate her front step as quickly as possible.

Unfortunately, quick and possible didn't appear to be connecting today.

"Bailey, come on." Tripp's raised voice carried through the door, over the still rambling voices of Colonel Potter and the big-nosed Klinger.

Jesus! He was going to disturb her parents. Sure, they lived in the main house several yards in front of her cottage but a voice like his easily carried.

"Please, let me in."

Bailey made a sound she never heard from her own throat and rolled off the sofa. She landed on her knees between the sofa and the coffee table. The short threads of the rug felt rough on her flesh, reminding her that she'd slept last night in only a short T-shirt and thong panties. She turned the volume of the television down to a whisper, stood, and snagged a pair of workout pants from the back of a nearby chair. Since when had the man become so unrelenting she wondered as she stomped to the door and threw it open.

"Are you not getting the hint here?" she asked and let all the fury she was feeling ring in her tone.

"Oh, I'm getting the hint," he spat back. "I'm just not taking it. We have to talk about last night, and I'm not going to wait until we are both on shift at the station again to do it."

The kiss. God, she couldn't talk about that now, didn't want to even think about it or the consequences, what it meant. "I'm not talking about that right now," she said, her voice shrinking even though she tried to keep it insistent and loud. "As far as I'm concerned, last night never happened."

"You can't ignore it, Bailey," he said softly.

"Want to bet? It's best for both of us." She sighed and cupped the sides of her face in her hands, rubbing her temples with her middle fingers. She could feel a monster of a headache beginning behind her eyes. "Go home, Tripp."

"Fine. You don't want to talk about what happened between us, then we won't. But that isn't the only thing we need to talk about. Something is going on with you, something that is affecting your performance on the department, and I can't continue to pretend that I don't see it."

Bailey felt her blood grow cold in her veins. He was her lieutenant. He outranked her by a mile and with that rank he could do severe damage to her career if he wanted to.

"I want to help you, Bailey." He reached out to touch her but dropped his hand before it made contact, letting it fall back at his side. "But I can't help you if I don't know what is going on."

She didn't want to tell him, didn't want to admit such a weakness even to herself, much less to him. Yet she could feel the bottle of her emotions beginning to overfill. The cork that sealed it tight for so many years would pop soon and what would happen when it did? She didn't know, but she feared the outcome, possibly more than she feared opening herself to this man.

"Let me get my shoes," she told him. No way would she let him inside her house. No way would she allow herself to be alone with him in such a setting. Not after last night. "We'll go for a walk."

* * * *

Tripp had taken a chance coming to Bailey's home, but he couldn't stay away. He'd followed her from the bar last night, knocked until his knuckles ached. Then, when she wouldn't answer the door, he'd started calling. He finally gave up in the wee hours of the morning, telling himself he was being too pushy, too obnoxious. He should let it drop, let her come to him. But he'd been unable to do so. In the light of the morning, the burning need to talk to her, to see her, to get to the bottom of all that was happening turned into a fire he simply could not put out.

He knew he shouldn't have kissed her last night. Even when he pulled her into his arms, he knew he was making a huge mistake. His feelings for Bailey Lamont had been growing for a long time now, his need for her gaining in strength and intensity each time he was near her. He tried to stop it, reminding himself daily that she was a fellow firefighter, someone he had no business wanting much less having such carnal thoughts about.

Still, one fact remained. He was falling in love with Bailey Lamont.

As far as I'm concerned, last night never happened?

Could she really ignore it so easily? She'd felt it too. He knew she had. The pull between them, the shared hunger in their kiss. Could she really push it out of her mind, forget about it?

Tripp prided himself on being an intelligent man, and right now that intellect was telling him to let it ride. There would come a time when she wouldn't be able to push it away, wouldn't be able to ignore her own feelings for him. Because she felt something for him too. He knew she did, had felt it in her kiss, in the way her arms encircled his neck and clung to him as they drew on each other's very breath.

When she stepped out the door and stopped before him, he shoved his hands in the pockets of his blue jeans, the need to touch her, to pull her into his arms again so strong it made his arms ache. She wouldn't let him inside her home. He knew the reason why. She didn't want to be alone with him. If he had his guess, he would bet because she didn't trust herself to be alone with him. As encouraging as that thought was, it tore at his heart to know she would deny herself, deny him the happiness he felt certain they could find together.

One problem at a time Mr. Fix-it, he told himself as he turned and moved down the front step.

"There's a path that leads through the woods to the beach," she told him as she stepped around him and began to lead the way. "It's a pleasant walk, if you're up for it."

It was also a private walk, secluded and romantic, he mused but kept the thought to himself. He could think of one hundred and one things he could do with her, do *to* her in the isolation of the woods, things that made all the blood in his body head on a tumultuous rush south. Apparently, she felt more secure alone with him in the dense woods than in her little house though, and he was smart enough to realize that voicing the one hundred and one ways to get it on in the middle of the trees would do his cause no good right now.

They walked in a strained, yet oddly companionable silence through the narrow gap of trees into the woods. The trail looked beaten, well used.

"How often do you come out here to walk like this?"

Bailey shrugged. "Depends on my mood and time. I may go months when I don't come out here. Then, sometimes I come out here every day." She crossed her arms and seemed to hug herself. "The trees, the sounds of nature, they soothe me, comfort me."

Which explained why she brought him here rather than for a walk in the sizeable yard between her parents' house and her own. "Do your parents own this land too?" he asked, knowing the two houses sat on at least three acres of land. There was enough property for the Lamonts to raise cattle if they chose.

Bailey nodded. "To the line of trees at the end of the trail. I feel funny sometimes, living on my parents' land," she confessed. "I mean, I'm pushing thirty, and I live in a little cottage behind my parents' larger home, the place where I grew up. Seems like it should be time to move on, to get my own space, but I just can't get up the want to move, you know?"

"You have your own place. There's nothing wrong with it being on your parent's property. You pay your own bills, buy your own groceries and such, don't you? You probably even pay your parents rent for the cottage."

"I do. And someday all of this will be mine anyway." She glanced up at the sky, looked down at her feet then settled her gaze straight ahead. "I guess I feel like, why bother moving when I'll move home eventually anyway."

"It does sound pointless if you're happy here," Tripp agreed.

"I am. I'm not sure I would be this happy anywhere else. Sounds dopey, but I like being near my parents, knowing they are a short walk out my front door."

"It doesn't sound dopey." This was a side of Bailey Lamont he hadn't seen before. A softer side, the nature loving side of a woman who liked to be close to her parents while still enjoying her freedom.

"It's another sort of comfort in the dark of the night," she said more softly, as though she spoke only to herself.

And there was the opening he'd been looking for. Only he knew better than to simply jump through that opening feet first and start demanding answers. All that maneuver would earn him would probably be a stonewalled expression from a very secretive, very frightened, very pissed-off female.

Instead, he would creep closer to his goal, lead up to exactly what he wanted to know and, if he got lucky, she would spill whatever it was she was holding onto so desperately tight. He would approach the situation like he would a raging fire in danger of spreading, sneak up on it with a hose set to minimum PSI—pound-force per square inch—and douse the flame inch by inch until he reached the heart of the blaze, then attack with everything he had.

"I bet it's really gorgeous out here at night," he commented and tilted his head back to look through the canopy of trees to the clear blue sky above. "The slim ray of moonlight that surely peeks through the treetops, the pitch black darkness everywhere else that the silver ray of light can't reach..."

Tripp let his words trail off, inwardly kicking himself over and over again. Jesus! What a way to tiptoe through that opening. Could he sound more like a sappy idiot? Okay, so he sounded like a romantic, poetic sappy idiot, but come on.

Dweeb or not, the comment got him the response he'd hoped for. Beside him, Bailey followed his gaze to the sky and let out a heavy, wistful sounding sigh.

"I wouldn't know."

"You wouldn't?" he asked lamely.

"I never come out here at night," she admitted, her voice low and sad.

"Never?" Tripp asked and gave himself yet another mental kick. He sounded more and more ridiculous and lame with each word. Asking stupid questions, repeating her words, come on man. What happened to that wisdom he prided himself in possessing?

All smarts have left the building, he thought and rolled his eyes at the sky, *or in this case, the woods.* God, this so wasn't working the way he'd planned. Smooth moves. *Yeah right, Barrett. Your moves are as smooth as a fucking porcupine today, buddy.* Maybe he should have taken the blurt-it-out approach.

Apparently she didn't notice his sudden dopey syndrome because she kept talking. "I like light," she said. She ducked to avoid a particularly low tree branch on her side of the trail and continued to walk. "Nice bright, blinding sunlight."

"Yeah, I noticed you don't care much for the dark." He didn't have to be touching her to know she stiffened at his words. He sensed her body went rigid beside him, saw in his peripheral vision that she squared her shoulders, heard her steps become harder and more pronounced.

"Lots of people don't like the dark," she said at the same time he said, "Do you want to tell me why?"

"I don't know why."

Tripp looked at her, watched the muscle in her deliciously curved jaw jump. It couldn't be easy for her, a woman generally so strong and confident, to have what many would see as a childish weakness and to not even know why.

"I've watched you," he told her. "The brush fire a few weeks back, the elevator at the hotel. You change in such situations, where you're surrounded by the dark. Your breath quickens, you perspire more. You want to freak out, but you don't."

"Exactly. And don't forget that, Tripp." Bailey shot him a look as they reached the end of the trail and stepped onto a sparkling yellow strip of sand. "I didn't freak out. So why bother analyzing this? I can hold my own even when I'm sweaty and breathing hard." She stopped, shot him another look that he clearly interpreted as a warning not to interject a double entendre to her last sentence.

The look only made it worse. With the clarity of a triple digit zoom lens, he pictured her breathless and sweaty as she straddled his hips, rode his cock until he screamed her name and begged for mercy. Then he pictured a pair of hands, two sets of fingers gripping the top center of the erotic image and tearing it in half.

"And what happens the first time you can't?" Tripp demanded. He was getting angry, with her, with himself, with the whole dammed situation. "What will you do when the fear slams into you so unexpectedly and so violently that you can't stop it, can't control your reaction? What are you going to do, Bailey, when the claustrophobia grips you so hard, the darkness squeezes you so tight it feels suffocating and you do freak out? What's going to happen to the other firefighters around you?"

He knew he hit on her worst fear when she stopped walking again and buried her face in her hands. Endangering a fellow firefighter, causing injury or, God forbid, death, was every firefighter's worst nightmare and greatest caution. Still, he hadn't meant to make her cry.

Way to go Barrett. Definitely your smoothest move yet, you imbecile.

But when she finally looked up several heartbeats later, he saw she hadn't shed a tear. He didn't know if he felt relieved or concerned. He didn't want to see her cry, knew the sight would tear his heart in two. Yet, he thought it would be good for her to let out the emotions he felt certain she held in for far too long. When was the last time she allowed herself a good cry?

She fell silent as she walked midway between the woods and the surf and lowered herself to sit on the sand. This area of the beach was deserted, the closest signs of human life nearly a mile down the waterline.

That was good, Tripp decided, not wanting anything or anyone to disrupt the moment. He sat down next to her, stretched his long legs out in front of him, and waited.

"I don't know if it's claustrophobia," Bailey said after a time. "It comes and goes. Just like the dreams."

"Dreams? What dreams?"

"Thick, impenetrable darkness, gut-wrenching fear of loneliness..." She shook her head. "I can't remember much more. I never can. I wake up covered in sweat, my heart pounding so fast I think it might jump right out of my chest, but I don't know exactly why."

Alarm settled in Tripp's belly like a heavy weight of steel. "How do you feel? In the dream, do you remember anything about what you feel, what you think, anything?"

Again, she shook her head, sighed. "Just the fear and..."

"And?" he prompted when she stopped.

She wrinkled her forehead as if confused. "Pain. Not horrific pain, but a burning type of pain."

Tripp sat up straighter. "Pain where? What hurts?"

"I don't know. It isn't a specific spot. It's everywhere. I—I don't know."

Tripp thought he did, and it chilled him to the bone. "Have you ever talked with anyone about this? A counselor, anyone?"

"No. It's been years since I've had these dreams. I thought they had stopped, that they had simply been a product of some sick side of my imagination."

A child's imagination, he bet. Only not imaginary but real. Super, duper real.

"They will go away again. The dreams," she qualified. "They will stop again. And the rest... I'll get over that too." She turned to Tripp then, her eyes imploring and sad, so very sad. "Don't kick me off the department, Lieutenant. Fighting fire is all I know, all I've ever wanted to do. I will get through this and I won't do anything to endanger my crew."

God, the vulnerability in her expression, in her voice, broke his heart. How could she think he would kick her off the fire department because of this?

"I don't want to get rid of you, Bailey. I want to help you," he said and watched as that fear at least visibly seeped out of her as though it were a tangible thing. "Jason has a brother—"

"Jason knows too?" Her eyes widened in horror.

"He was in the room when Dean and I were discussing it after the elevator call."

"So the Captain knows," she whispered.

"It's okay, Bailey. I told Dean I would handle it."

"Who else, Tripp? God, how many of the guys know?"

"No one. That's all." She closed her eyes, shook her head, and he knew what bothered her most about people knowing. "You aren't the only one on the department with a fear of something, Bailey. Jason has a fear of sharks."

She snorted a laugh at that. "Yeah, and as a firefighter he comes across so many burning sharks."

Tripp laughed too. "Okay, so maybe his fear isn't job related. Magee's is though."

"Right." Bailey rolled her eyes. "Like God's gift to women is afraid of anything more than running out of single white females to fuck."

"Actually, he's afraid of heights. I think it has something to do with how he injured his knee, but I never got the full story. Karlston can't swim," Tripp continued, wanting to give her as many examples as possible. "You ever noticed how he stays as far away from the water end of an open hose as possible? He's afraid of water. And Kyle Shannon is terrified of snakes. Yeah, I know, how often do we run across snakes when putting out a fire? My point is, Bailey, you aren't the only one on the department that's afraid of something."

"What are you afraid of, Tripp?"

You, Tripp nearly said but stopped himself just in time. He was afraid of her, both of having her and of never having her, of being around her constantly and of never seeing her again. He sighed, looking into her eyes so full of sadness and confusion and knew he could never tell her that. "I'm afraid of being taken out before I'm ready to go."

"Taken out? You mean out of the action? Killed in the line of duty?"

"No, not killed. If I had my choice of deaths it would be to go out with a fire. What frightens me is being hurt, taken out, being forced to live the rest of my life without the fire department."

"I think we all fear that on some level," Bailey admitted. "At least those of us who live and breathe the job."

"Like you and I do."

"Yeah, like you and I do."

"Let me help you, Bailey. Let me talk to Jason, have him talk to his brother."

"Jackson? His twin brother's name is Jackson."

Tripp nodded. "Jason said he used to be claustrophobic. He's an FBI agent now. Maybe we can get Jason to call him, see what he suggests, how he managed to get over his fears." It was only one of the many ideas he had going through his mind right now, one of the things that could and needed to be done, and the only one he thought she would agree to at this moment. She would need more, he was sure. Counseling, possibly even a shrink, but for now Jackson Graham would do.

Chapter 6

Jackson Graham hit town at ten-fifteen on Wednesday morning. A quick stop by his bother's house and an even quicker glance at the rotation calendar on the refrigerator told him Jason was on duty at the fire station until five o'clock.

Jackson hadn't told his bother of his visit, choosing instead to make a surprise appearance. He dropped off his luggage in the spare bedroom, decided he would check in with the local blues to inform them of his arrival in town then pop in on Jason at the end of his shift at the station. Together, he and Jason could visit their father that evening and do some catching up.

It took Jackson all of three minutes to get the impression he wasn't wanted at the Silver Springs Police Department. Not that he'd expected differently. When did the local police ever want the FBI involved in their town? He came across it all the time, the attitude, the stony glares, the cold shoulders that told him in no uncertain terms that he was the outsider.

The detective currently glaring at him across her desk was no different. Detective Samantha Becket, she'd introduced herself with a firm handshake that rivaled any man's. She'd stood when he first entered her office and he'd been momentarily taken aback by her size. She had a good twelve inches on him and her body would easily put her in the running for Ms. Bodybuilder America, if there were such a title. Her hair was blond, long and tied in a tight ponytail at the nape of her neck. Her large, round hazel eyes were oddly pretty and he guessed they could be friendly when she found herself in the presence of one she considered a friend. Given their current hard, icy glare, he concluded she didn't consider him such a person.

She stared at him with contempt and resentment in those expressive eyes, and he was about to piss her off. He sighed. Such was his job.

"This is all you have so far?" He frowned down at the thin folder that lay open on the desktop before him. Police reports, a few documented interviews, and the fire marshal's findings. He'd hoped for more, expected there to be more to lead the way in the investigation of the occurrences at Keaton Aire. "There isn't much to go on here."

"There hasn't been much to find," the detective told him, her voice cold, each word as sharp as a splinter of ice. He could feel it as though it were a tangible thing, shards of it slicing into his flesh. She sat with posture stiff, her expression grim, and he wanted to tell her to loosen up. He wasn't such a bad guy after all, but somehow he didn't think she would appreciate being told so.

"The only thing we've managed to rule out is the possibility of terrorists. There are no known cells operating in this area or anywhere near here and the occurrences at Keaton Aire don't fit the general profile for a terrorist hit. We've talked to employees and the family. We've tested the photographs for prints and developing. This guy is careful, slick."

"Guy? Have you found something to substantiate that, or is it a hunch?" Jackson asked, knowing perpetrators were often referred to in the male sense but could just as easily be a female.

Samantha sighed and shook her head. "Not even a hunch," she admitted. "If you want hunches, Agent Graham, I think it's a female. Theresa Keaton, also known as Tess, seems like the most likely suspect we have so far."

The sister. Jackson leafed through the papers in the file until he found the transcript of the interview with Theresa Keaton. His eyes scanned the page, quickly reading parts and skimming over others. His hunch told him the detective was wrong, but he kept that feeling to himself. Everything he knew about the case, about the others before this one—if they were indeed related—told him the perp was a male. Keaton Aire wasn't the only private airport catching hell right now. Several others across the Southern states had been vandalized or burglarized in recent months. None of the others, however, reported any instances of warning photos being found. Whether the perp was indeed the same in each case, whether he was connected to the Keaton family or not, was still up for grabs.

"Have you talked to the cousin?" He shuffled through a few more pages. "This Marshall Keaton?"

"Out of town. Seems he took a trip to Aruba after his father's passing and hasn't been back. I talked with the authorities there, had them do a little checking up. He's staying at some exorbitant resort and hasn't left the premises since he arrived."

"Any clue when he plans to return?"

"The end of the week. I'd hoped the catastrophes at the airport would pull him back sooner, but he seems unconcerned. Says he's paid through the end of the week and intends to say there."

"I gather he isn't close to his cousin."

"Certainly doesn't appear to be."

"Are we sure it's him and not someone pretending to be him?"

"As sure as we can be without flying to Aruba ourselves."

"Which is not out of the realm of possibilities if it comes to that. I want to talk to this Theresa Keaton myself," Jackson said and watched the detective's hazel eyes darken as her temper flared. He'd expected as much. She wouldn't like him going over ground she'd already covered. "And the rest of the family too, of course."

A muscle jumped in Samantha Becket's jaw, but she nodded. "I figured you would. Although I doubt any of them will tell you anything different than they told me and the FAA official."

"Probably not," Jackson agreed, his tone placating for the sake of peace. "But just the same…" He shrugged and let his words trail off.

"I suppose you will want to catch up with Angelina Keaton first. She is the one who now owns Keaton Aire, after all."

"Actually, I would rather begin with the sister." Jackson placed Angelina's name farther down his mental list. He preferred to talk to the top person involved in a case after he'd spoken with other suspects. Begin to build an impression of said person before meeting them face-to-face. It proved to be a technique that had worked well for him in the past.

A brisk flash of surprise crossed Becket's expression, but she quickly hid it. She glanced at her wristwatch, one with a thick leather band with a wide silver plated face generally more suited for a man than a woman. "She'll be at the Keaton Estate. We can take a ride over there, talk to her, and hit the crime scene on the way back."

* * * *

She could do this, Angelina decided. She stared at the figures on the computer screen, compared them to those she'd jotted down on the scratch pad beside her keyboard. She could open the flight school she'd always dreamed of right here on Keaton Aire property. The fees would balance out the expenses of the classes, and the exposure would be good positive publicity for offsetting the damage done by the pest who seemed intent to shut her down.

That was how she'd come to think of the culprit who appeared hell-bent on harming her airport and, so far indirectly, harming her. A pest. Everything he'd done, while dangerous and frightening in its own way, turned out to be a complete aggravation to fix in the end. Not to mention costly to repair.

Still, she could make it. She *would* make it. The airport was open and operational once again. The tension she'd sensed in her employees had begun to fade with the addition of the twenty-four hour security. All in all, they were back in business and soon she would have the place ready to fly, in a manner of speaking.

She leaned back in her chair, rubbed the back of her neck and winced at the tension she felt in her muscles there. Her entire body felt like a rubber band twisted and wound tight, the stress of the last week weighing heavy in her bones. Maybe she should take a few hours to do some flying herself. She loved to fly and it had been so long since she'd taken a plane into the air, lost herself in the clouds and the serene blue sky.

She would soon, she promised herself. Until then, she could think of other ways to relieve a bit of tension. A night of hot, sweaty sex with a kidnapped stranger would do the trick, she mused as she picked up the copy of Sex Games that lay at the edge of the desk. She opened the book to the dog-eared page and read.

"Sex with a stranger can be the most arousing of erotic fantasies. Show up at your partner's house and sneak up on him/her. Pretend you have a gun. Be careful he/she doesn't think it's a real gun. A toy water pistol or banana works well. Blindfold your partner and take him/her back to your place where you've set the stage for a night of bed- burning sex."

Angelina closed the book, her finger between the pages to mark her place, and tapped a nail on her chin with her free hand. So Jason wanted to be kidnapped and taken home for bed-burning sex. How appropriate for a firefighter, she mused. She could do that. They would have to use his house, as she didn't have a private place of her own to act out such a fantasy. Her mother might be open to her daughter having sex, but she doubted Silvia would approve of Angelina bringing a blindfolded man through the front door of the Keaton Estate.

The thought made her laugh out loud. Nope, not a good idea. So Jason's house it would be. He was working today, but his shift ended at five. She'd checked with Veronica Wolcott on that one. A discrete stop into Romantic Illusions and a couple of seemingly idle questions had revealed B shift's rotation wouldn't begin again until forty-eight hours later.

She could do a lot in forty-eight hours, she thought, a sly grin unfolding across her lips. Ah yes, Jason Graham was in for some fun tonight, and she couldn't wait to get started.

* * * *

Tess's heart tripped at both the FBI badge in her line of vision and the man who held the slim black wallet that encased the brass shield. She felt a quick brush of recognition but pushed it aside, knowing there was no way she could have met this man and not fully remember him. Agent Jackson Graham, he'd introduced himself in the brisk, no-nonsense voice so often used by actors who portrayed the FBI in films. So their tone wasn't pure Hollywood after all. But Agent Graham, well, he was definitely directly from central casting. Tall, but not too tall, buzz-cut dark hair, awesome gray eyes the color of a stormy cloud and a jawline to die for. He wore the expected black suit and tie with a crisp white dress shirt and shiny black shoes. Tess guessed the black sunglasses were in a pocket somewhere.

Oh yeah, this man was definitely agent-licious from the tip of his spiky hair to the toes of those spit-shined shoes. Despite the no-frills voice and don't-mess-with-me expression, Tess felt her body's visceral response clean down in her panties.

"Tess, Agent Graham wants to talk to you about the recent incidents at Keaton Aire."

Tess pulled her attention from Mr. FBI Yummy to Silver Springs Detective Yuck. She scowled at Samantha Becket, not attempting to hide her dislike for the woman nor her disappointment that the agent hadn't come alone. The agent in question shot the detective a look, the quickest glance out of the corner of his eye, but it was enough to show Tess he didn't appreciate the detective speaking for him.

"Agent Graham is welcome to talk to me about anything he wants," Tess told the detective with a sliding gaze down the length of the FBI agent. She did it on purpose, played the honeyed Southern belle for no other reason then because she knew it would piss off Samantha Becket.

"Oh, please," Becket muttered under her breath.

Bingo! Tess bit the inside of her lip to keep from grinning and, wait, was that a slight smirk on Agent Graham's lips too? Yeah, she definitely liked him already.

"Please, come in." She led them into the front parlor, glad to find it empty. Her mother must be in her gardens, she guessed. It would stress her, Tess knew, to find the police at the Keaton Estate again and this time accompanied by the FBI. The woman was already wound tighter than a spool of thread.

"Can I get you something to drink, Agent Graham?" she asked sweetly over her shoulder. At Becket's quick eye roll, she added, "It's a hot day out. Perhaps something cool and smooth to awaken the taste buds?"

"A glass of water would be fine, thanks," Jackson Graham responded in that same passive, tone that only FBI agents did so well but under that Tess thought for sure she heard a bit of amusement.

That would do for now, she decided, as she walked to the wet bar on the far wall, making sure to add a little extra sway to her hips with each step. She would rather hear lust, heat, need in his tone, but amusement was a good start.

"You don't mind if I have something a bit stiffer do you, Agent?" she asked as she fixed his water and poured two fingers of bourbon for herself. She turned, swayed back to him, and held out the water as she took a long sip from her own glass. The bite of the room-temperature bourbon burned all the way down her throat. God, but she loved the stuff.

"Suit yourself, Ms. Keaton," the agent said and took his glass, sipped.

"Isn't it a bit early for alcohol?" Becket asked, pure disdain in her voice.

"It's never too early for a good, stiff drink," Tess told her, putting extra emphasis on the word stiff. "Sorry, Detective. I didn't offer you a drink. Would you like a glass of water too? I'm sure I can find some nails around here somewhere to substitute for the ice cubes, since you seem to enjoy chewing on them so much."

Anger flashed red and rapid in the detective's eyes, but before she could retort, Jackson cleared his throat.

"Ms. Keaton—"

"It's Tess. Please call me Tess." She gestured to a narrow settee and lowered herself to sit on one end as he accepted her invitation to occupy the opposite end. Although she didn't offer the detective a place to sit, not thirty-seconds passed before Samantha Becket took a seat in an armchair adjacent to the sofa.

"Ms. Keaton sounds so impersonal. May I call you Jackson, Agent Graham?" Tess asked but went on before he could answer. "I assume, Jackson, that you wish to question me about the accidents at my sister's airport."

"I know that Detective Becket spoke with you already, Tess," Jackson began.

Tess watched him and wished he would relax. He may be yummy-licious but he was way too uptight, she decided. She wanted to see him loosen his tie, unfasten the top buttons of his shirt, lean back on the settee with his drink resting on one thick, muscular thigh, an arm draped lazily over the armrest.

She could picture herself too. Sashaying toward him wearing a pair of six-inch heels and a smile. She would wiggle her hips enticingly as she crawled onto his lap and straddled him. Her hand moved between them and grasped the flap of his pants, unfastened them and...

"I hoped you might be able to tell me a bit more about what has been happening around Keaton Aire these past few months."

The agent's words jarred Tess from her daydream and just in time too. Though, on second thought, the daydream had been headed to a far more interesting place than his conversation. She sighed. Same ole' questions, and she would give the same ole' answers. She knew nothing. Why was it that everyone suddenly seemed to believe otherwise? She was the sister usually ignored, the one thought too stupid to understand anything that didn't involve the latest fashions in Hollywood or what role Orlando Bloom would play next.

No, it was Angelina people looked to for answers, Angelina people looked to when they wanted something taken care of. It was Angelina people left their life's business, their life's savings to.

Because no one possessed even a single ounce of faith in Tess. Until now, it seemed. Yet, the faith she received now came in the darkest and most unwanted form. This faith held the shape of suspicion, if suspicion could have a tangible shape, the belief that she was either somehow behind the problems at Keaton Aire or that, at the very least, she knew who was.

She had nothing to do with it, of course. Sure, she often felt bitter toward her older sister and definitely envious, but to do something to harm Angelina, physically or otherwise. No way! She wished with everything inside her that she knew who was behind the photos, the vandalism, and the fire. She wished for once she could be the one with the answer.

Tess sighed. The best answer she could give would be that Mr. Green did it with the rope in the study. Somehow, she doubted that would be good enough for anyone.

* * * *

Jason hit a homer. The big one. The winning one. The ball went sailing through the air at warp speed. It flew over the fence and disappeared into the trees.

"Say goodbye to kitchen duty, boys," he said to the members of Engine Co. 1 and Ladder 12 as he ran a pass around the makeshift bases for form's sake. "Oh, and lady," he added as he caught up with Bailey Lamont, who had decided to walk her point to home plate from second base. His comment and half bow earned him a playful slap on the head, as he'd suspected it would. She hated to be singled out from the guys that way.

"At least we know we won't be eating burnt spaghetti for a while," EMT Terri Vega—part of the losing team comprised of the Rescue Squad, Hazmat, and Pumper Truck crews along with Captain Dean Wolcott—called out.

Jason hung his head as he reached home plate. Would he ever learn? More, would he ever live it down? Thankfully, no one but he realized the reason he'd burned the spaghetti, that his attention had been more focused on Angelina Keaton. If they knew that, oh boy, would there be hell to pay.

"First round of drinks is on me," Ryan Magee proclaimed. "I figure the least I can do is provide a beer for the losers to sulk in." That comment got him a universally understood finger sign from said losers and a whoop from the winning team.

Jason checked his watch. He'd intended to head straight home after his shift but got coerced into a game of baseball instead. The stakes? No kitchen duty for the winners for two rotations each. They never played without some sort of bet. The last game had been played against C shift. The stakes for that game had been an hour early off rotation. It was how B shift came to end their rotation today at four o'clock rather than five.

He'd intended to go straight home in hopes of hooking up with Angelina. Maybe even become a kidnap victim, he mused, and chuckled out loud as he removed his batting glove, shoved it in his pocket. Surely she'd opened the present by now and read the page with the top corner folded down. Then again, he'd delivered it mere hours before the explosion at Keaton Aire. Was it possible it had gotten lost in the shuffle that day?

"You're coming, aren't you?" Magee shot him a quick glance. He grimaced as he knelt and began to gather the baseball equipment off the sidelines, his bummed knee giving him troubles.

Jason considered. What would the ex-Navy SEAL and number one playboy in Silver Springs say if he knew Jason actually mulled over a cold beer with the guys instead of steaming hot sex with Angelina Keaton or any other woman for that matter? Magee would order him to have his head examined.

And maybe he should, Jason reflected. Maybe a head doctor could explain the malfunction going on in his pea brain because, for the life of him, he couldn't figure it out on his own. He'd never thought of a woman day in and day out, hour-by-hour, minute-by-minute, hell, second by fucking second. Until Angelina Keaton. Rich, so out of his league, so completely hot and ready Angelina Keaton. She'd been fire in his arms and now, God help him, but he couldn't *stop* thinking about the woman, and wanting the woman, and picturing the woman naked in his pool with her eyes heavy-lidded by desire, her legs spread wide.

"Yeah," he snapped, putting a definite end to his hemming and hawing. "I'm going." Even though a cold beer with the guys in no way compared to sex, going home would break his number one rule. Never, ever sit around and wait for a woman to show or call or come kidnap his horny ass. He would go for the beer.

"Are you coming?"

Jason heard the Lieutenant's quiet question and realized just in time that it was directed at Lamont rather than himself. He sat down on a nearby bench and started to remove his cleats. He shouldn't eavesdrop. He should move to a different bench, one farther away from the Lieutenant and female firefighter. Yet, temptation won out. Though she was always invited, Bailey Lamont seldom tagged along to the Paradise Lounge after a baseball game or any other time for that matter. It was the underlying sound of hopefulness Jason heard in the Lieutenant's question that piqued his interest.

Lamont didn't answer, but rather, Jason saw out of the corner of his eye, looked back at the Lieutenant as though he were suddenly the number one candidate in the county for residence at the funny farm. Jason would have laughed, if he hadn't been doing his damnedest to pretend he wasn't listening.

"I don't think that's such a good idea," Lamont finally said, her voice equally quiet but rather than an underlining hopefulness as had been in the Lieutenant's tone, hers sounded despondent, even embarrassed. "We both know what a disaster my last visit to the lounge turned out to be."

"The other night was a lot of things, Bailey, but a disaster isn't one of them."

The other night? *Hell*o. What happened the other night? Jason slowed down his act of exchanging his cleats for the regular tennis shoes he kept in his duffle bag. The fire department grapevine had been growing in the direction that something was sparking between the Lieutenant and Bailey Lamont for some time now. Anyone could see the way the L.T. looked at the female firefighter and, yeah, the woman was pretty in a tomboyish Helen Hunt way. Yet, Jason never saw anything more than respect and adoration in Lamont's eyes when she looked at the L.T. Maybe he'd missed something.

"And the next morning at your house, on the beach," the Lieutenant continued. "That certainly wasn't a disaster."

The next morning at her house! On the beach! Oh yeah, Jason had definitely missed something.

Lamont sighed, a loud gush of exasperated air. "Tripp…"

Tripp? *Tripp*? Jason had never heard Lamont call the L.T. by his first name. Few people on the department did aside from Captain Dean Wolcott. Everyone called Tripp Barrett Lieutenant or L.T. and, on a very, *very* rare occasion, someone might call him Barrett but never Tripp.

"I thought we could use the time to talk to Jason," the Lieutenant said.

It was all Jason could do not to look at the L.T. at the sound of his name. If he looked, it would be a dead giveaway that he'd been listening all along. Talk to him about what? What had he done?

"I'm tired, Tripp. I'm going home," Lamont said, and now her voice rang with every ounce of exhaustion she claimed. "Thanks, again, for everything. I'll see you Saturday."

Saturday. When B shift would begin their next rotation. Ooo, that stung. Nothing like telling the L.T. in a not-so-subtle way she had no desire to see him outside of work, Jason thought, and felt a quick pang of sympathy for the other man.

"You can run from me, Bailey," the Lieutenant said softly as Bailey Lamont walked off the baseball field and to the parking lot. "But sooner or later, I'm going to catch you."

* * * *

Jackson Graham felt the barrel of a gun poke in the center of his back and froze. His first instinct was to go for his own weapon. A weapon he'd placed in a lockbox at his brother's house when he'd stopped by earlier to change. He'd dressed way down in a pair of worn-out jeans and a T-shirt that proclaimed he had his faults but being wrong wasn't one of them—a gift from Mallory on his last birthday—with an even more worn-out pair of tennis shoes. And no weapon.

His gaze darted wildly around him, looking for some reflection of his assailant in a nearby mirror or piece of metal. How big was the guy? Could Jackson take him? He'd learned more in the academy than how to shoot a gun. They taught him how to fight too. A single quick sweep of the leg as he spun, a quick blow to the assailant's arm and the fucker would go down, sending the gun flying.

"Don't move."

Jackson didn't move. It wasn't hard. Surprise had rendered him motionless. Holy shit! This guy was a woman! Shock had him trying to turn to face her, but the barrel of the gun poked harder into his back.

"Don't turn around."

Yes, definitely a woman. So okay, he thought and reassessed the situation. A woman would be far easier to disarm. Assuming, of course, that she wasn't some Xena, Warrior Princess bitch.

But no, a voice like that belonged to a slim brunette with long legs and shapely curves. It belonged to a woman more like Mallory Stone, not some man-slaughtering bitch headed straight for the state penitentiary.

"Okay, lady, you have my attention," he said slowly, his mind still going over his options. He could disarm her fairly easily. But he didn't want to hurt her and something in her tone told him she had no intentions of harming him. He'd quickly earned the reputation at the bureau for being one to choose talk over force when at all possible. He'd negotiated his way out of jams before. He could do it again. "Let's talk about this first. What's this about?"

"I don't want to talk," the woman said briskly. "Turn slowly and walk to the silver Mazda in the parking lot.

Jackson did and, okay, this was getting stranger by the second. He'd spotted the car when he pulled in but this was no ordinary Mazda. "You drive a Miata?" He didn't attempt to hide the surprise in his tone.

"Yeah," she said hesitantly. "I thought you knew that."

"How would I know what you drive?"

"Oh, right. Strangers. I forgot."

She forgot? What did that mean?

"Let's move," she said quickly and shoved the barrel of the gun a bit more forcefully into his back. "I have a water pistol here, and I'm not afraid to get you wet."

A water pistol? What the fuck?

She chuckled then. "Although, with all I have planned for tonight, you're going to get wet anyway."

Okay, this was no doubt turning out to be the strangest thing that ever happened to him. Sweet Jesus! Exactly what did she have planned? Jackson didn't know if he should play along—this was so obviously a game, wasn't it—or say something. Should he pray the C shift radio operator for the

Silver Springs Fire Department would come out of his little office to make a pass through the station's bays or hope this mysterious woman didn't get caught in whatever game she was playing?

Jackson had arrived at the SSFD a couple minutes before five o'clock, just in time to discover that his brother, along with all other personnel of B shift, had cut out early, and C shift had already taken over. Mere minutes later, the station had cleared except for the C shift radio operator as two separate alarms came through. He had been walking through one of the station's bays when this voice of an angel, want-to-be criminal with a water pistol—no doubt about it, he had to give her credit for creativity—had approached him from behind. Apparently, she'd been hiding somewhere inside the bay.

"Do you do this often?" He had to ask because, my God, what kind of a woman hid in the bay of a fire station and attempted to kidnap the first man who walked by with a toy gun?

She chuckled again, such a sweet, melodious sound that he expected a choir of angels to join in the fun. "Would it ruin it if I admitted this is a first for me?"

Jackson wasn't sure how to answer that one. It was comforting to know this woman wasn't some cuckoo-coo clock who went around kidnapping men. On the other hand, what drove her to start now? And why him? He decided to let her question hang and ask another one of his own. "Are you planning to take me for a swim?"

"Nah, we did that already. What I have in mind will be a bit more of a sticky kind of wet."

Sticky wet? The possibilities of that one made his dick stiffen behind the zipper of his jeans. "Exactly what do you have planned for tonight?"

"Uah, uah, uah, that's for me to know and for you to find out, handsome. This may be your fantasy but it's my night, my game, and my rules. Now walk, please."

His fantasy? How did she know what his fantasies were? Jackson wondered as he slowly began to walk toward her car. They already did that. What did she think they already did?

His gaze darted around the parking lot and the street that ran in front of the station as they approached her car. All seemed deserted. Still, he had to give the woman credit for bravery. The day was bright and sunny, and here she was abducting him, as it were, out in the open in front of the city fire station for all to see.

Then, in a sudden rush of clarity that made him laugh out loud, he understood. This wasn't some lunatic woman out to get kicks by kidnapping a stranger. This woman thought he was Jason.

Oh brother, what kind of games are you up to these days?

Jackson could easily see how she could mistaken him for Jason. They were identical twins, after all. And he had been walking out of the fire station when Jason should have been ending his shift. Was it possible she didn't even know Jason had a twin brother?

"There's something you should know. I'm not who you think I am."

"Of course you aren't. You're a stranger, and I'm kidnapping you. Stop and put your hands on the roof," she told him when they reached the passenger side of her car.

She obviously thought he was getting into the role, playing the game. Jackson turned and put his hands on the warm metal above the passenger door. "No. You don't understand," he tried again.

"Do you see anyone around?"

"I—no," he said and couldn't help but chuckle. "Aren't you supposed to be watching for people, making sure you don't get caught?"

"So I'm a novice at this." He couldn't see her shrug but it was there in her voice. "You're too tall. Will you bend your knees, please?"

"Are you going to pat me down now?" he asked, becoming amused by the entire situation. He needed to make her listen, to make her understand she got the wrong brother and yet, a part of him couldn't help but wonder what tonight would be like if she carried out her plans on him.

You're much too uptight lately, Jackson. Mallory Stone's words spoken before he left the bureau echoed in his head. *Get laid while you're gone. Have a quick fling.*

Would there ever be a better chance than this one? Yet, what if Jason really cared for this woman? What if he loved her?

The thought of that nearly made him laugh out loud again. Jason, in love? Yeah, right! Hadn't his brother often told him over the years how they should play a few games together, share a woman? Jackson had never considered it before. He didn't go for quick flings and sex games the way Jason did.

"No, silly, I'm going to tie this on."

Jackson snapped out of his thoughts in time to see a strip of black cloth moving in front of his face. Reflexes had him catching her wrists before she could cover his eyes. He heard her quick, surprised intake of breath and forced himself to loosen his grip. "What are you doing?"

"I'm going to blindfold you," she answered, her voice a little uncertain now.

"Is it necessary?"

"A kidnap victim isn't supposed to see where he is being taken. Besides, I have a few things to set up when we get there."

"Where are you taking me?"

"We'll have to use your place," she said on a soft laugh. "There's no privacy at mine."

His place? She intended to drive all the way to Waterston tonight?

But no, she meant Jason's house. Because he was supposed to be Jason. And when they got there, Jason would be home and this whole charade would end.

Reluctantly, he let go of her wrists and allowed her to tie the silky black cloth over his eyes. He fought to not panic as everything went dark.

Chapter 7

"Where are your keys?" Angelina asked as she led Jason up the walkway to the front door of his house.

"Front right pocket."

She laughed when he just stood there, obviously expecting her to get them out of his pocket herself. Smiling, she reached around him, inched her hand into his pants and smiled even wider at his quick intake of breath. She took her time fingering his pocket, searching for the key ring, all the while making sure to rub her breasts against his back, caressing his upper thigh through the lining of his pocket.

"Can you take this thing off now?" he asked, his voice husky. "I want to see you."

"Not yet." She slowly pulled her hand free of his pocket but took a second to reach farther around him, to brush her palm over his crotch before she stepped away. He moaned and blindly stuck a hand out to catch her, but she moved out of his reach.

She pushed her tote bag, heavy with goodies she purchased for tonight's fun, farther onto her shoulder and fumbled with the key ring. Jeez, the man had a lot of keys. Her father and Uncle Edward had carried only the bare essentials—house key, car key, trunk key. Not Jason. He seemed to possess a key to every lock in town.

"Which key is it?" she finally had to ask because, Jesus, they would be out here until the sun went down if she tried them all.

"The silver one with the three holes. Should be the fourth or fifth key. If you would let me take this—"

"I found it," she spoke over him as the silver key, fifth one on the ring, slid into the lock and turned with the ease of a knife sliding through melting butter. "Watch your step," she told him as she led him through the open door. She supposed the warning was probably unnecessary. It was his house, after all. He knew the layout far better than she. Including where to find the bedroom.

Angelina waited until he was inside the house and then closed the door, flicking on the nearest light switch. She shrugged the tote bag off her shoulder and began to rifle through its contents. She pulled out the passion berry scented votive candles first. She'd brought a half dozen complete with glass holders.

"Stay here," she said to Jason and made her way down the hall to the only open door at the end. There she set out the candles. One on the dresser, a bookcase, a small shelf in one corner, the nightstand and two on the floor on either side of the doorway. She lit them with a long fireplace lighter she snagged from the front parlor of the estate then returned to her tote for the rest of the goodies she'd brought.

The king-sized bed in the center of the room made her smile. She hadn't slept over the other night, nor had she taken a tour of the rest of the house. She'd expected to find a decidedly male bedroom much like the other rooms she'd been in, decorated sparingly in neutral colors. She figured she would find strewn clothes and open dresser drawers and she wasn't disappointed. But the bed, oh my, it was definitely a pleasant surprise. It looked like something taken out of her own sexual fantasy. Red silk sheets crumpled by the previous night's sleep covered the cherry wood framed mattress with close to a dozen red, black, and white pillows of various shapes and sizes. A row of wrought iron bars lined the wall behind the bed, serving as a headboard, and six-by-six square mirrors covered the complete expanse of the ceiling over the bed.

"Hey! Where did you go?" Jason's voice carried through the house from where she'd left him standing at the front door. He sounded odd though, she noted, almost frightened. Just the slightest tremor in his tone.

No, she decided, as she quickly stripped out of the oversize T-shirt and jeans she wore to reveal the black, fishnet stockings, garter belt, black crotchless panties and barely there negligee. She exchanged her slip-on tennis shoes for a pair of black high heels and did a quick spin in the room in search of a mirror to check her appearance. It took her all of a second and a half to give up. Apparently, if she wanted to know how she looked in this room, she had to be on her back atop the bed.

"I'm on my way," she told Jason as she made her way back down the hall to him. God, she hated high heels. It was all she could do not to break her neck in the dammed things. But, for some stupidly testosterone reason, men loved naked women —or in her case at the moment, nearly naked woman—in high heels.

Said heels made a clack, clack, clacking sound on the hardwood floor, and she watched Jason's eyebrows rise above the blindfold as she neared him.

"High heels?"

No. He didn't sound frightened anymore.

* * * *

Jackson let her take his hand and followed as she led him through the small living room of his brother's house, down the hallway to Jason's bedroom. Even with the blindfold, Jackson remembered the layout of the house. He could also tell by the lack of sounds that it was empty. Where in the hell was Jason?

"Are we alone?"

She sounded a bit startled by his question when she answered, "Yes, of course."

That confirmed it, Jackson thought. He was toast. He'd been expecting, hell, even half hoping for his brother to save his ass. Jackson had been so sure Jason would be home. Only he wasn't, and that left Jackson alone with his brother's woman. A woman who, though he couldn't yet see for certain, he guessed had stripped down to a pair of high heels and probably not much, if anything, else.

Holy God.

"Were you expecting company?" she asked as she moved in front of him. She splayed her hands flat on his chest and let them slide down to the hem of his T-shirt.

"My br—" he started to say, but when her hands contacted with his flesh as she pulled up his T-shirt he felt something short circuit in his brain. It had been too long since he'd felt a woman's touch. His body absorbed the warmth of her hands, registered the softness of her palm and the faint sharp edge of her nails as she caressed her way up his torso, pulling the shirt up and, mindful of the blindfold, over his head.

Cool air met his heated flesh, and he shivered involuntarily. This dammed darkness fucked with his senses, made him nervous and at the same time heightened his awareness of every sound, every feel. It was both frightening and arousing. His hands were at his side, and he fought not to reach up, to remove the blindfold.

"Are you cold?"

"I don't like the dark," he admitted.

"Really? I didn't know that about you."

"That's because—" I'm not Jason. I'm Jackson, he started to say, but she was already talking over him.

"Because we're strangers. Sorry, I keep forgetting that part."

Jesus! He was starting to think he wasn't meant to tell her the truth. Every time he tried, she interrupted him with this stranger stuff. Fantasy or not, if he didn't tell her, she was going to get one hell of an awakening when it was all over. Both of them would when Jason found out.

"How about I make you forget the dark?" she said, her voice dropping to one of pure sex and honey. Her hands returned to him, this time moving down his torso to the waistband of his jeans. "Kick off your tennis shoes. I want you naked."

And Holy Mother of God, when she said things like that all thoughts of the truth left his brain right along with his sanity. Jackson kicked off his shoes, said a quick and silent apology to Jason because he was going too far with this to stop now, and pushed all thoughts but those about the woman in front of him out of his head.

She helped him out of his pants, his briefs and then he stood there naked but for the dammed blindfold she simply refused to remove. The dark wasn't bothering him so much anymore though, he realized. Arousal and adrenaline won over the fear.

He felt her kneeling in front of him, felt her hands skim up the outside of his legs, felt her slight hesitation when her hand grazed over the scar tissue midway up his left thigh. But when he expected her to stop, to realize something wasn't quite right—Jason didn't have a scar like that on his left thigh—she kept going instead. Her hand snaked between his legs to his inner thigh and continued up. She fingered his balls, rolled them in his hand

and Jackson heard the boom inside his head. It was the sound of the final bullet of his senses being fired into oblivion.

Jackson let his head roll back on his shoulders as a quiet moan escaped his lips. Then, Jesus, she took his dick in her mouth and he forgot everything including his own name.

* * * *

"Chip Wrigley is retiring next year."

Jason stopped, his beer bottle halfway to his lips. Wrigley was retiring? He hadn't heard anything about that. He polished off the last of his beer, motioned with the bottle for another from the bartender and listened to the conversation between the Captain and Lieutenant on the bar stools next to him. Apparently it was his evening for eavesdropping.

"I half expected that," the Lieutenant said. He sat half-turned on his stool toward the Captain but he spoke loudly enough for Jason to easily overhear. "He's been having health problems, hasn't he?"

"Seems so," the Captain answered. "High cholesterol, blood pressure, and who knows what else."

"Who's taking his place?"

The Captain sighed, and Jason knew what was coming. The bartender set his beer on the bar in front of him, and he snatched it up, taking a long pull to cushion the blow before the Captain said the words.

"He wants me to."

And there it came. Though it was exactly what he'd expected to hear, the swallow of beer went sour in Jason's throat. Oh man. Chip Wrigley was the battalion chief for the district. If the Captain took Chip's place, he would no longer be in direct command of B shift. Not B shift alone, at least. With four other stations in the district, the battalion chief juggled his time between them all. It would be a promotion for the Captain, sure, but, as childish as it sounded, Jason didn't want to share him with the other stations. He also didn't want anyone else as his direct Captain.

"Are you going to do it?" the Lieutenant asked the question that was on the tip of Jason's tongue.

Jason couldn't help it. He no longer cared if the Lieutenant and Captain knew he was listening. He turned slightly on his stool, leaned over the bar so he could look around the Lieutenant. The Captain saw him and nodded, a hardly noticeable movement of his head.

"I don't know." Dean Wolcott sighed again. He picked up his own bottle of beer and gulped down half before dropping the bottle back to the bar again. "It's the next step. I've been working my way up the ladder since I joined the department. Battalion Chief is the next rank up."

"Are you looking to get out of the action?" Jason asked, inviting himself into the conversation. He couldn't simply sit there and listen. Not this time. Not when the outcome of this conversation could be his Captain deciding to leave B shift. "Because you know that's what will happen. Battalion Chiefs rarely see as much action as what you're used to."

"Six months or so ago, maybe," Wolcott answered. "If I'd been offered this position before I convinced Veronica to marry me, yeah, I probably would have taken it."

Jason knew it had taken the Captain some fast talking and charisma to convince Veronica Abbott to marry him. After her first husband had been killed in the line of duty, Veronica had been leery of marrying a man who put his life on the line for his job.

"Does she still want you out of the action?" the Lieutenant asked.

"She wants her husband to do whatever makes him happy," Veronica answered, appearing out of nowhere behind the Captain. She slid her arms around his neck as he turned his head and leaned in for a long kiss that had both Jason and the Lieutenant squirming on their stools and picking up their drinks.

Jason had to give the Captain credit, his wife was hot. A leggy blond with a curvaceous body dressed in the most flattering and often revealing clothes that raised men's blood pressure for miles around. Yeah, he thought, he probably would have given up a position as Captain for the woman too.

Veronica broke the kiss, then leaned over to plant a quick peck on the Lieutenant's cheek. "How's it going, Tripp?"

"Another day in paradise, beautiful." the Lieutenant said in a slow, lazy drawl. He smiled, but it seemed forced, halfhearted.

It was obvious, to Jason at least, that the Lieutenant had more on his mind than the Captain's possible promotion dilemma. If Jason had a guess, he would bet all his money the Lieutenant's thoughts walked off the baseball field with Bailey Lamont.

"Where's mine?" He feigned a pout and held out an arm.

Veronica laughed as she moved to him and kissed him lightly on the cheek. "Sorry, handsome. I'm surprised to see you here."

"I always tag along for a beer after our little games, especially when Magee is buying the first round."

"Yeah, I know. I figured you would be decked in purple fluffs and be covered in chocolate and strawberries by now."

What the—?

"Chocolate, strawberries, and purple fluff," the Captain repeated with a hoot of laughter. "You been holding out on us, Graham?"

Jason laughed. "Apparently, I've been holding out on myself, Captain. What are you talking about?" he asked Veronica.

"Ooo, I probably shouldn't say anything." Veronica covered her mouth with her hand, but her smile was too wide to hide. "Aren't you seeing Angelina Keaton?"

"We've…talked," Jason answered slowly. It wasn't entirely a lie. They had talked the night she came to his house. Among other things, he thought. Other things that simply remembering kept his dick hard for days afterward, *still* made his dick hard when he thought about them.

"Oh, well, she came in the store today and bought a few items."

Items that no doubt included chocolate and strawberry flavoring and purple fluff. Purple fluff? What in the hell could that be?

"I just assumed, after the little display the two of you put on in my store a couple of weeks ago and after you came in and bought that book, that things were meant for you."

"What book did you buy?" the Lieutenant asked, his eyes now alive with amusement.

"Sex Games," Veronica answered before Jason could say anything.

Jason grimaced and shot her a grim look. "Thanks." He glanced around. No one else at the bar seemed to be paying them any attention. But if anyone else had heard, the news would be all over the department by next rotation. Well, he thought with a resigned sigh, at least the guys would stop ragging him about the burnt spaghetti.

Veronica bit her bottom lip. "Sorry."

"Sex games, chocolate, strawberries, and purple fluff," the Captain said reflectively.

"Sounds like our bedroom, doesn't it?" Veronica said and Jason had the pleasure of watching the Captain's face turn so red it put a fire engine to shame.

"*Honey*," the Captain groaned.

"Sounds like Angelina has got plans for you, Ace," the Lieutenant told Jason. He tipped his glass of Southern Comfort and Coke at Jason's beer bottle. "Should I buy you another one of those, or are you out of here?"

"What do you think?" Jason asked and picked up his beer, drained it. He could make it home in less than five minutes, but what if she'd already been there? What if she'd come by the station, missed him there, checked his house to find he wasn't there either, and given up for the night?

He stood, pulled a couple of bills from his wallet, and tossed them on the bar. For the first time in his life, Jason cursed his number one rule.

* * * *

Angelina liked being in control. She hadn't thought she would. She'd always been more submissive in the bedroom. Maybe it was the blindfold that boosted her courage, knowing that Jason couldn't see what she planned, couldn't watch her as she did it.

She tightened her fingers around the shaft of his dick, just enough to draw a low grown from deep in his throat. She smiled around the thickness of the meat in her mouth. He seemed wider than she remembered. Then again, he hadn't given her the chance to give him a blow job the last time. He'd been in control then, doing to her and with her what he wanted. But she was in control tonight and what she wanted at that moment was to use her mouth to make his knees weak.

She pulled back until his cock nearly fell out of her mouth, sucked him down her throat again in one quick motion, and felt his legs tremble. Yeah, those knees were getting weak all right. He tasted warm, sweet and she could feel the vein in the underside of his cock pulse beneath her tongue. She moved her hand from his shaft to his balls, took more of his cock into her mouth, down her throat as she fondled and played with his jewels. She loved the way they tightened in her hand, rolled between her fingers.

"Oh God, yes."

His quiet cry gave her encouragement, empowered her as she devoured him. She felt his hand move over the top of her head, his fingers burying themselves in her hair. She reached around him with her free hand, found his ass cheek and caressed it with her palm, applying the gentlest of pressure to pull him closer still.

"Oh baby," he moaned as she began to suck him faster, harder. She licked him, used her tongue to trace the underside of his cock and marveled at his quick intake of breath when she let her teeth graze over his tender, sensitized flesh.

She pulled back, let his dick fall from her mouth and angled her head. She found the smooth strip of skin between his cock and balls with her tongue and licked him slowly all the way to the head of his dick, lapped at the beads of pre-cum she discovered there. Then she sucked his cock down her throat once more and felt his knees tremble even as his hips began to move.

His hand tightened in her hair as he started to pump, to fuck her mouth, dammit, to take control. He held her head still as he thrust into her mouth, rapid and unmeasured strokes that sent his dick impossibly deep down her throat. Her gag reflexes wanted to kick in, but she forced her throat to relax, to swallow as much of him as she could and then some. Then his hand suddenly released her hair, and she could move again.

"You have to stop," he said on ragged breaths of pleasure as he tried to step back from her. With her hand still on his ass, she held him in place. She'd allowed him a moment of control, but she would give him no more. This was her time, and it would end when she wanted it to. "Jesus! You have to stop or I'm going to—"

Angelina tightened her grip on his balls, quickened the pace of her mouth and felt his cock began to spasm as his cum, hot, thick and sticky sweet, shot down her throat. She drank his seed as it spewed into her mouth, tightened her lips and continued to suck, to pump, to milk his cock with her lips until she drained him to the last drop. Then she slowly released him, his dick, his balls and sat back on her heels to look up at him. He looked so gorgeous standing there with a sheen of sweat glossing his tanned skin, his chest heaving in spent breaths, his expression serene even with the blindfold.

"Well damn, I don't know whether to laugh my ass off or be pissed as hell."

Angelina whipped her head around at the sound of the voice. She felt her eyes grow wide, her mouth falling open as a quiet gasp of surprise escaped her lips. She looked at the man standing blindfolded in front of her, then back at the man who stood in the doorway of the bedroom, and knew her eyes had to be playing tricks on her. No way could she being seeing fucking double. Could she?

* * * *

Jason leaned a shoulder against the doorframe, crossed his arms over his chest and smirked. At least he hoped Angelina would take the tilt of his lips as a smirk and not some sign of anger. He wasn't angry. Actually, he wasn't exactly sure what these emotions surging through his veins at the moment were.

He'd rushed out of the Paradise Lounge and sped through the waning rush hour traffic, surprised and elated to find Angelina's silver Miata parked in his driveway. Only she wasn't waiting for him in the car, or in the yard, or on the front step. He'd even checked the backyard thinking maybe he'd left the side gate unlocked and she'd decided to wait for him out back, in the pool, naked. But no, she hadn't been there either.

He'd returned to the front of the house where, surprise, he found the front door unlocked. How had she gotten inside? She didn't have a key, and he was not in the habit of hiding one under an outside flowerpot or beneath the welcome mat at the front door. Had she picked the lock? Could she even pick a lock? Would she know how? He honestly didn't know her well enough yet to be sure where her talents lay. He knew she could kiss like a dream, knew she could make his dick hard with the simplest touch, knew she could fuck with the vigorous enthusiasm of the Energizer Bunny. But could she pick a lock? Who knew?

Silence, thick and somewhat unexpected, greeted him as he stepped inside the house. He'd half anticipated her to jump out at him from a dark corner somewhere or come up behind him, pretend to be a burglar or rapist or something and play a new game with him. She'd done none of that. He'd nearly called out her name when a strange sound stopped him.

He froze, his ears all but spiking like a dog's as he strained to listen more closely. He heard it again. A moan, low and guttural and almost painful sounding. Had Angelina somehow hurt herself? He'd taken a couple of silent steps farther into the living room and there it was again. Yes, definitely a moan.

Wait a minute. That moan was deep, husky, male. And that wasn't pain that laced the sound but sheer pleasure. But no, that couldn't be right. Could it?

"Oh, baby."

Shock twisted with confusion in Jason's mind at the breathy exclamation by, yes, a decidedly male voice. A male voice he recognized in an instant. Jackson's voice.

Jason had crept through the living room, silently followed the sounds of ragged breathing and quiet noises of pleasure that grew louder as he neared the end of the hall. And at his own bedroom door, he met the surprise of his life. The moans belonged to Jackson all right. A Jackson that stood bare-ass naked a few feet inside the room with his dick shoved down Angelina's throat.

Jason had watched them, shock and amazement rendering him speechless. He could see enough of Angelina to know she was dressed, though from what he could tell there wasn't much to the lingerie she'd chosen. Sweet Jesus! She looked like a Goth version of an angel in all that black. Her hand slipped between Jackson's legs, found his balls as she sucked him and dammed if Jason didn't feel his own dick growing hard from the sight.

Jackson said something too softly for Jason to make out, but he guessed it to be a warning because his brother began thrusting hard and quick, fucking Angelina's mouth. It wasn't until then that Jason realized his brother wore a makeshift blindfold. Jackson. Claustrophobic, don't-leave-me-alone-in-a-small-place, I-can't-stand-the-dark Jackson, blindfolded!

And with that, Jason knew exactly what happened. It wasn't hard to figure out. Angelina had decided to act out his kidnap fantasy but unknowingly got the wrong brother. She'd probably intercepted him at the station. It wouldn't be the first time Jackson popped into town unannounced and showed up at the department at the end of Jason's shift. She'd been there, Jason guessed, waiting for him, blindfolded Jackson and brought him here.

Jason had waited until they were through, until Jackson blew his wad down Angelina's throat, until she leaned back on her heels to look up at him, until his own dick throbbed in painful jealously, before he spoke. Now, Angelina stared at him, her eyes huge in her face, confusion her paramount expression. Jackson's hand flew to the blindfold, jerked it up and off his head as he shot a look over his shoulder. His eyes closed on a shaky breath then he opened them as he turned to face Jason.

"Oh, God." Angelina gasped and fell back on her rump. The move was definitely not graceful and Jason got one hell of a view of bare pussy lips— thank you crotchless panties—as her legs spread on her way down. Her gaze danced wildly from Jason to Jackson, back and forth, back and forth so quickly she reminded Jason of a cartoon character watching a ball ping-pong bouncing around wildly. "Shit," she breathed, the curse low and full of exasperation. "There *are* two of you."

"You didn't know we were twins?" Jackson asked, and the look he shot Jason was filled with accusation.

"No. I had no idea."

What could Jason say? It hadn't been an important factor to mention at the time? Jackson lived a good three hundred miles from Silver Springs and visited only once or twice a year for a day or so at most. Those visits generally coincided with Christmas and their father's birthday in March. They were in the middle of August, nearly smack dab in between Jackson's usual visiting months. Besides, how could he have guessed she would decide to turn criminal and end up with the wrong brother?

"And you aren't Jason, are you?" she asked and looked up at Jackson. Hope and a deep perception swirled in her so expressive eyes.

He slowly shook his head. "I'm Jackson."

Angelina nodded. "That's what you meant when you said I had the wrong guy." She winced and rubbed her forehead. "God, I thought you were just getting into the role."

"I take it you got the book?" Jason said and couldn't hide a grin. Dammit, he was jealous as hell that Jackson got to play out even half of Jason's fantasy with this incredible woman Jason couldn't get out of his mind. Jason's dick was pouting because Jackson got the first blow job, and yet Jason felt this insane urge to laugh.

Angelina glared at him through long lashes. "Wipe that smirk off your face, buddy. You are so not in a position to be smiling about anything right now, funny man."

Yet, was that a faint twitch Jason saw tug at the corner of her lips? He looked closer. Yes. Yes, she was definitely holding back a grin of her own. He looked at Jackson and, well what do you know, he was so obviously biting back a smile too. Was it possible the three of them could turn this into something to laugh about?

"Oh my God," Angelina groaned and covered her face with her hands.

Jason's heart leapt to his throat. Oh no, please don't let her start to cry. Let her scream, rage at him and Jackson, throw a few punches even, anything but cry. Jason couldn't stand to see a woman cry.

"I'm so embarrassed," she said into her hands.

He could see that much was true. Her skin was turning a pretty remarkable shade of red. And not just her face, or what he could see of her face around her hands. No. This blush began at the roots of her hair and quickly washed over her all the way to her ankles. He bet if he could see her toes inside those glossy black heels he would find them blushing too.

"I'm sorry," Jackson said, his voice soft as he knelt beside her. "I shouldn't have let it go this far."

She sighed, dropped her hands, and looked at him. No. She hadn't been crying, wasn't even about to. Her eyes were dry even if they did seem darkened by a cloud of self-recrimination. "You tried to tell me. I'm the one who wouldn't listen."

"I should have made you listen." He reached out, tentatively at first as though he expected her to slap at his hand, but when she didn't, he laid that hand gently on her bare shoulder. "I really am sorry."

And this was why Jackson was the twin that the women always went for? Jackson knew how to talk to a woman, knew how to show emotions that were so often too lost inside Jason to make a surface appearance. Jealousy curled in his gut, a familiar feeling he'd known most of his life. Jealousy because Jackson could show so easily things that he could not, and Jackson never felt embarrassed, or ashamed, or wrong about his emotions.

Still, it was a form of jealousy he could deal with. He'd lived with it for this long after all. This jealousy wasn't some new feeling, some new form that developed from watching Jackson with Angelina. No. As long as he got to join in next time, he would be satisfied. Wouldn't he? His relationship with Angelina was sexual. Wasn't it?

Just like that, Jason knew what to do. Provided, of course, that Angelina liked this sex game stuff as much as he thought. He pushed himself off the door frame, walked to her side opposite Jackson, and knelt. He didn't touch her, not yet. Instead, he rested one hand on his thigh and balled the other into a fist, placing it on the floor for balance.

"I'm responsible for at least half of what happened here," he told Angelina. She slowly turned her head to look at him, her eyes curious. "I told you I have a brother. What I didn't tell you is that he's my identical twin."

* * * *

That would have been a piece of useful information earlier, Angelina thought as she studied Jason. God, she couldn't believe this, couldn't believe the things she'd done to the wrong twin, the things she'd been about to do. She should be angry, furious as hell at both of them. Yet, as she watched the mischief move behind Jason's gray eyes, thought of the look that was both apology and desire she'd seen in Jackson's equally gray eyes, what she felt was inspired.

How many women could claim possession of two incredibly sexy men like Jason and Jackson even if for a short time? She'd begun her little fling, as it were, with Jason for fun, used it as an escape from the horrors happening in her life. Why couldn't she continue that fun now with both twins? She'd always fantasized about being with two men at once. What woman didn't? So why not turn this fiasco into a fantasy fulfillment of her own?

"I should be pissed at you," she said, but she knew the smile on her lips told a different story.

"Yes, you should." Jason touched her then, a gentle caress of his palm on her cheek, and she leaned into that touch, encouraging more. "But you aren't, are you?"

"I'm thinking there is a way you can make it up to me." She cast a furtive glance at Jackson. He'd sat down beside her, still gloriously naked and unabashed by it. He silently watched her. His gaze fell to her mouth, her breasts, and lower before rising again to meet her eyes, and she knew even though his dick lay soft between his legs, even though Jason was now there with them, he still wanted her.

"Actually." She licked her lips and reached out to trail the tip of her fingernail down the flat plane of Jackson's chest. "I know a way you can both make it up to me."

Jackson stared at her, a myriad of emotions alive in his expression. He knew exactly what she had in mind. That much was clear. He seemed to consider it, to test it against something she knew nothing about. Was it possible he was involved with someone? Dear God, she hadn't even considered that!

Angelina looked down at Jackson's left hand. No wedding ring. Of course, in this day and age and with his job as an FBI agent, that didn't necessarily mean anything. She opened her mouth to speak, to ask if he had a wife or girlfriend or some sort of significant other but stopped when he glanced at Jason, gave his brother the smallest of nods.

She glanced at Jason too, saw the quick flash of surprise pass over his expression before he nodded in return. An understanding passed between the two brothers, silent but clear, and it made her heart race in anticipation.

Still not saying a word, Jason stood and began to strip. Angelina watched him, let him see the lust she felt in her eyes. How could she not? Sheer male perfection such as Jason's demanded attention. In record time, he kicked off his shoes, shucked off his pants and—yep, he was going commando again—then pulled his shirt over his head. Then there he was, gloriously naked, his cock hard and jutting out from his body like a toy handle.

Angelina pointedly let her gaze linger on his cock for several heartbeats before she looked up, met his gaze, and licked her lips. She sat up straighter, and the change in her height brought her mouth nearly level with his cock. She started to move more, to curl her legs under her to get the last bit of height she needed to reach him, but he chuckled and stepped back.

"My, you are a dick-hungry girl tonight."

Angelina felt herself blush at the crudeness of that proclamation but, okay, it was true. She loved to suck a man's dick, to feel that hard length of flesh between her lips and down her throat. More, she loved the sounds she could pull from a man with such an act. Men were so often silent in the course of sex, but when a man's dick was in a woman's mouth, if she did it right, the woman could cause him to make all sorts of sounds.

"I want to taste you," she admitted and wiggled onto her knees, sat back on her heels.

"Maybe later." Jason held his hands out for her, waited for her to put her hands in his, and then pulled her gently to her feet. "I heard you bought some interesting supplies for your kidnap victim."

Angelina wrinkled her forehead at him. Interesting supplies? What was he talking about?

"You know, I've always been a big fan of chocolate, and Jackson, he's always leaned more toward the fruits. I believe strawberries were always your favorite. Is that right, Jackson?" Jason asked with a look to his brother over her shoulder.

And she understood, but then again, she didn't. "How did you—?"

"I stopped in the Paradise Lounge with the guys before coming home," Jason explained. "Veronica stopped in to meet the Captain. She sort of, how would you say it, spilled the beans. Anyway, since I've yet to have dinner tonight I'm pretty hungry and you know how much I like dessert before the main course."

Oh yeah, she knew. Memories of him eating her as the appetizer against the front door and later devouring her for dessert in the pool sprang to mind.

"And I'm dying to know exactly what you bought that have purple fluffs."

As if on cue, Angelina spotted a deep purple object dangling in her peripheral vision. The handcuffs, padded with fluffy purple material to prevent pain to the wrists. Jackson had found them and held one set of them up now for Jason to see.

"Well, well, well. I bet as an FBI agent you would know better what to do with those than I would."

Angelina turned, saw Jackson look at the cuffs then look at her. She saw the brief hesitation cross his expression before he quickly masked it. He seemed to change right before her eyes. The timid, seemingly frightened man she'd kidnapped had morphed into a bold, in-control agent. She guessed this was the side he used in his career, the hard-edged, tough-as-nails aspect of his personality.

Jackson moved behind her, so close she felt the heat from his chest on the back of her shoulders, but he didn't touch her. That fact alone made her tummy do all sorts of crazy twists and flips. He leaned in, still not touching her, his lips a mere breath from her ear. "Did you plan to use these on me tonight?"

His voice was a decibel higher than a whisper with an undertone that sounded brusque and unassailable. His cop voice, she thought as the sound slid over her, seeped into her skin, warming her blood to the consistency of molten lava. This was the voice he used for interrogations, the one he used to get what he wanted out of a person, to make that person do what he wanted.

She nearly said no. She hadn't intended to use the cuffs on him tonight. She'd intended them for Jason. Yet, she would have used them on Jackson if she'd had a chance, even if he did turn out to be the wrong twin. So yeah, she supposed she had planned to use them on him.

Angelina rolled her head to one side as she felt his moist tongue lick at her earlobe. "Yes," she breathed and couldn't say for sure if she meant that yes to be in answer to the question or answer of pleasure to the kiss. Her eyes closed on an involuntary gasp that quickly turned to a moan as Jason stepped forward, leaned in and licked at her other ear.

"You look beautiful tonight," Jason whispered. "Like a Goth angel, sweet and pure yet dangerous and exotic. I wonder, would wings be an appropriate accessory or would devil horns be better?"

Angelina smiled at that. She wanted to be the devil tonight. She felt a dark side emerging, a part of her that longed for the thrill and seedy satisfaction of dirty play and submission swimming to the surface of her soul. She wanted to be taken places she'd visited only in her fantasies, and she knew with a deep certainty that made her intimate lips slick with need that these men would take her there.

* * * *

If Jackson didn't know better, he would swear he was having an out-of-body experience. Only he was decidedly still in his body because all of these thoughts, these surges of carnal lust and desire, while alien to him until now, were far too strong for him not to be experiencing them firsthand. He felt as though an animal paced inside him, waiting to claw itself free. The tenderness, the conservative caution that was so much a part of his nature seemed to vanish, to cower terrified in the corner in the presence of this animal inside him.

He cast Jason a quick glance over the woman's head. Jesus! He didn't even know her name, hadn't even thought to ask. He tried to remember if Jason had called her by name, but if his brother did Jackson hadn't heard it. Oddly, he found her name didn't matter to him. At least not right now, not even until this night ended. The façade of strangers engaged in a night of heart-pounding sex was arousing. The realization that until he asked, tonight wouldn't be merely a façade but a well and true reality made his dick twitch with elation.

Jason returned his look with a quick smile and a wink. Yeah, Jackson had been pretty certain his brother was okay with what was about to happen here, in his bedroom, with his woman. He also didn't miss the swirl of confusion and surprise in his brother's eyes despite his playful expression. Jason didn't have to say a word for Jackson to know his thoughts. He could hear them now.

Holy shit! My straight-laced brother is about to get down and dirty with a woman.

Yes, he was. A woman who continued to be a complete stranger to him, whom he would share with his brother and no doubt walk away from when the sun came up tomorrow.

Are you feeling okay, Bro?

Yes. No. Hell, Jackson didn't know how he would answer that one if Jason were to voice the question aloud. So he wouldn't think about it, wouldn't even attempt to answer it even in his head, he decided. Instead, he returned his brother's wink and smile with one of his own. He knew in going through with this tonight several fantasies would be fulfilled. No doubt this woman fantasized about two men taking her at once. He knew Jason, on far more than one occasion, voiced a desire to share a woman with Jackson.

And yeah, okay, so maybe the whole ménage idea was a secret fantasy of Jackson's too.

He looked down to find the woman staring expectantly up at him. She was beautiful in an unconventional sort of way. Her nose was just a bit too large, her face a bit too long and narrow but her eyes, that amazing shade of brown with green flecks that sparkled with promise and mischief, made her almost breathtaking.

Jackson realized that she and Jason were waiting to see what he would do next. He shot a quick glance at the bed, at the wrought iron bars on the wall behind it, interesting that Jason had such a perfect setup for this, and knew what to do next. Wow! But how to tell it to her, to tell Jason? This open playmate thing wasn't as easy as he might have thought. He was almost embarrassed by some of the thoughts, the requests—or would that be orders—going through his mind.

Jackson reached down inside himself and pulled out his courage, found that toughened and adventure-seeking part of him that made him one of the top FBI agents in the Waterston office, and put it to use once more. But Jason seemed to think he needed saving. His brother spoke first in a voice roughened by escalating desire and harsh with authority. Jackson had often thought his brother would make a damned good FBI agent if he ever got tired of playing with fire.

He looked down at the woman again, this time putting a hand on her shoulder and letting it slide down her arm. Her skin felt like silk and warmed beneath his palm even as tiny goose pimples popped up in its wake. And he could forget that because this woman was solid, exotically amazing proof that Jason would never tire of playing with fire.

"Move to the bed."

Chapter 8

Lieutenant Tripp Barrett was decidedly the most hardheaded man Bailey ever met. When the knock sounded on her front door at a little after seven p.m., she had no doubt as to the identity of her visitor. She didn't attempt to ignore it this time, to ignore him. What good did it do her last time? Instead, she fitted the odd-shaped puzzle piece in her fingers into the open space among the others of the same color and rose from the small kitchen table.

She didn't speak as she swung the front door open to find the Lieutenant once again on her doorstep. Lust lodged in her throat, left her unable to speak, unable to do more than stare at him. He'd taken the time to change from the baggy jogging pants and uniform Tee he'd worn at the baseball field, exchanging them for a pair of olive drab cargo shorts and a slate gray tank. He had amazing legs. Bailey had always loved his legs, strong, sturdy, perfectly proportioned to easily support the one hundred and eighty plus pounds of muscle that was Lieutenant Tripp Barrett. The tank stretched across his hard chest and broad shoulders in a way that made her mouth water and her hands itch to touch.

"Hi," he said after several long breaths, breaking the silence that settled between them. "Mind if I come in?"

Yes. Yes, she did mind. God, didn't he realize they shouldn't be alone together? "I really don't think that's a good idea, Lieutenant." She purposely used his rank on the department hoping to remind him they worked together, he was her superior, and anything else between them simply wasn't acceptable.

A muscle jumped in his jaw and anger filled his eyes but when he spoke his voice was calm if a bit too low and controlled. "Are you going to let one kiss ruin a solid friendship?"

It was a good question. She valued the friendship they built since she joined the department. She liked him, as a man, as a lieutenant. He taught her so much about fighting fires that, without his tutorage, would have taken her years to learn. Yet, the undercurrent of more between them bothered her. As did the knowledge that she wanted more from this man, more that she couldn't allow herself to take even if he offered. And hadn't that kiss been an offer of sorts? Hadn't it proved that he too felt the undercurrent of passion between them?

"I thought you said we should forget the other night happened, forget those moments outside the Paradise Lounge."

She had said that. She thought it best for both of them, for their friendship as well as their relationship as Lieutenant and firefighter. Yet, she couldn't forget about that night, that kiss, couldn't push is out of her mind. Every time she saw Tripp Barrett now, all she could do was remember. The way his strong arms encircled her waist, the way their bodies seemed to fit so perfectly together, the way his tongue swept inside her mouth as he tasted and explored her. How could she expect to file away forever in her mind something that felt so wonderful and perfect?

"Is this how you intend to forget, Bailey, by pushing me away, by dissolving our friendship, by backtracking us so far that we end up nothing more than firefighters on the same fucking department?" He said it all in one breath, in a tone that no longer hid the anger she saw in his eyes. She'd pissed him off, and he decided to let her know it. That didn't happen often with this well-controlled man.

"You outrank me," she said. It was a stupid thing to say, and she knew it. At least it sounded stupid at that moment, but a part of her knew it really wasn't. His rank was the reason she couldn't have him. The fact that he was a firefighter on the same department, the same *shift* as she, was bad enough. Add to that his rank as Lieutenant, and it turned a bad situation impossible and forbidden.

She turned her back on him and walked to her tiny kitchen, leaving the door standing wide open. She heard the door close softly as he too walked inside, following her. She stopped at the table covered in puzzle pieces, but she saw none of the four hundred and some odd pieces left to fit together. Her gaze blurred for an instant and she closed her eyes, swallowing as she ruthlessly stomped out the urge to cry.

"Yes, I do." He stopped behind her, gripped her shoulders and turned her around. Still, she didn't look at him until he hooked a finger under her chin and tugged her face up.

She lifted her gaze, met his dead-on, and only then did he let his finger drop. He nodded, an almost imperceptible movement of his head, and stepped back enough to put a companionable distance between them.

"And because I outrank you," he continued. "You must follow my orders. The kiss was fantastic, Bailey, amazing even, but if that one kiss is going to cost me my friendship with you then it never happened. You were right to say we should forget about it. We. And by we, I'm not talking about me and the mouse in my pocket. I'm talking about you and me. I can put it in the past, but it won't work for us unless you do the same."

Could he really put that kiss in the past so easily? God! Maybe he really hadn't felt the same things as she in that kiss. Maybe she'd simply imagined the attraction she thought she saw in his eyes, felt in his touch, in that kiss.

Give the man a break, Lamont, he's giving you what you said you wanted. He's putting it in the past to salvage your friendship. And she would do the same. She had to. At least as far as anyone but she knew anyway.

"You have a mouse in your pocket?" she asked, and he laughed as she hoped he would. Yes, she could do this. As long as she didn't allow herself to dwell on those lines that appeared in his cheeks when he smiled, or the way his eyes brightened, or the way those broad shoulders shook when he laughed, or oh, hell, she just wouldn't allow herself to think when he was around.

"Yeah, he's white with black polka dots. I figured since we can't have a Dalmatian at the station because Terri is allergic, I would get a mouse. I can't show him to you though. Sorry."

"Shy little guy, is he?" Bailey cocked a brow, thoroughly amused.

Tripp shook his head and tsked. "Terribly shy. Terribly."

Bailey couldn't help but laugh, and just like that they were back. They were friends. They were coworkers. Could it really be that easy?

* * * *

Angelina felt both men's gazes on her as she walked to the bed, stopped beside it, and waited for the next order. Anticipation was a raging fire inside her, sending flaming embers of need through her bloodstream, quickening her heart. She'd lost control of tonight's little game. She was the pawn now, Jason and Jackson her kings, but she found no disappointment in the loss. She wanted this, wanted to be at the command of these men.

"Crawl onto the bed," Jason told her. His firm tone left no room for argument.

She did, positioning herself on her hands and knees on the side of the bed.

"Move to the center and lie on your back, hands over your head."

She crawled to the center of the mattress, making sure to add a seductive sway to her hips for the men's benefit. Her heart hammering in her chest, she lay on her back and stretched her arms above her head. She watched them as they walked to the head of the bed, Jason on her right and Jackson on her left. The mattress gave under their weight as they climbed onto the bed, each reaching for her arms, each snapping a cuff around her wrists. She heard the faint click of metal as they snapped the opposite ends of the cuffs to the bars on the wall behind the bed. Reflex had her tugging on the cuffs, checking the resistance. There wasn't much.

"You aren't trying to get free already, are you?" Jason asked, sheer amusement lining his words.

"No. Just testing the limits."

"Leave that to us, baby. Jackson and I will be happy to test your limits tonight."

Sharp slivers of desire shot straight to her pussy at his words. Trouble. Yeah, no doubt she could be in real trouble here and the thrill of that held a level of power she'd never felt before.

Jackson's hand slid lower, inching its way under the lace, pulling it down to expose her breasts. He made a low, appreciative sound that did amazing things to her ego. Then he touched her with a tenderness she'd come to expect from this gentle twin. His hand was easy, soothing, as his palm grazed lightly over her left nipple. Her nipple responded to the faint contact, hardened and sent pulse points of pleasure straight to her pussy.

Her eyes closed from the sensuality of the caress only to open half a heartbeat later at Jason's next command. "Spread your legs for me."

She did, letting her knees fall as closely to the mattress as they would go, opening herself for him. He'd moved to the foot of the bed, perched on his knees at the edge and stared at her now with lust and hunger swirling in his eyes. The crotchless underwear covered nothing, and she felt the cool breeze of the air conditioner flutter over her exposed feminine lips, chilling the fiery juices that made her tender flesh slick as glass.

"Have I told you yet how much I love this negligee?" he asked and reached out, skimming a finger down the outside of her pussy lips.

"No," Angelina breathed and arched her hips, searched for more of that touch but he'd pulled back.

"I'm proud of you too," he told her, his palms now gliding up and down her inner thighs.

She lifted her hips when his hands neared the aching heat at her center and again, he pulled back. She growled in frustration and saw satisfied grins unfold on both twins' faces.

"I'm proud of you because you listened to me when I told you to wear easily accessible clothing when you came to me again." One of his hands skimmed over her thigh and up her hip to the thin strap of elastic that held the crotchless panties in place. He slipped a finger under the elastic, pulled, and let it snap back into place with a smack.

The light sting drew a gasp of surprise from her throat and made her writhe on the bed. His request for more accessible clothing, as he put it, had been at the top of her requirement list when she chose what to wear tonight. Tearing off each other's clothes had been a lot of fun and erotically arousing, but it would surely get expensive after a while if they kept it up.

"I hoped you would approve," she told him now and met his gaze, watched as he exchanged a silent but telling look with Jackson before he slid off the bed.

Jason walked around to the side of the bed all the while looking down at her as though she were the only item on an all-you-can-eat buffet table. "Oh, I definitely approve, baby."

"As do I." Jackson's voice at the foot of the bed surprised her.

They'd changed places, she realized, as she watched Jason toss a small squeeze bottle through the air to his brother before coming to sit on his knees beside her. The flavored gels, she saw as Jason popped the flip-top on the one labeled "Chocolate Delight". She heard the same little pop sound as the mattress dipped farther at the foot of the bed. Jackson had opened the "Sinfully Strawberry" and was positioning himself closer between her legs.

Ah yes, she was definitely about to discover what it felt like to serve as a buffet for two hungry, horny twins. Only, it wasn't fair. She wanted to eat too, but with her hands cuffed to the wall and Jackson between her legs she couldn't move, let alone get involved in the upcoming action.

"Jason," she said at the same time as he squirted her breasts with the chocolate delight, outlining her swollen nipple with the brown substance. He didn't answer. Instead, continuing to coat her breasts in the eatable concoction with a concentration that reminded her of an artist working on his latest masterpiece. She tugged on the handcuffs already knowing it would do her no good.

He leaned over her, his mouth stopping a fraction of an inch away from her nipple, looked up at her, and grinned. "Still trying to get loose? Those are some pretty sturdy cuffs. Bet you didn't anticipate them holding you down when you bought them."

Angelina narrowed her eyes at him. Oh, he was going to pay for this. Eventually, she would get her chance to be in control and when she did... Between her legs, she felt a warm dribble of thick liquid spread over the smoothly shaved flesh above the V of her pussy lips. Strawberries drifted to her on the air, mingled with the scent of chocolate and made her mouth water. She rolled her head to one side, her gaze fixing on the long, thick meat that was Jason's cock jutting out from his body at full attention.

"You want that, don't you?" he said, watching her.

"Yes." She lifted her head, tried to reach him but her cuffed hands prevented her from moving far enough. She squeezed her eyes shut and growled in frustration.

She heard them chuckle, Jackson's low and throaty laugh in unison with Jason's lighter, more playful one. Then she felt the warmth of their breath a half a second before their mouths claimed her. They didn't lick the fruit flavored gels from her body but rather sucked them away, tugging at her flesh as they feasted, Jason at her breast and Jackson at her pussy. Jason sucked her breast deeply into his mouth then slowly pulled back until only her nipple remained between his lips. Then he rolled it, nipped it with his teeth, sending slivers of pleasure laced lightly with pain straight to her pussy where Jackson laid a claim all his own.

Jackson's tongue slipped between her folds, his fingers moving to her lips to spread them as he lapped at her clit before he sucked it between his lips. She gasped, her hips coming up off the bed, her arms straining at the cuffs, as electric shocks pulsed through her clit. Dear God, the man had a mouth like a vacuum cleaner!

Jason's work-roughened hand covered her right breast, his thumb and forefinger twisting and rolling the nipple even as he continued to suck and gently bite at the left one. Between her legs, Jackson lifted his head but his fingers remained on her folds, caressing them, slipping along the surface of her soaked, sensitive flesh.

"So wet," he whispered as he played. "And so sweet." He looked up at her through long lashes as he pushed one finger inside her.

Her hips rose to meet that finger, driving it deeper and still wanting more. The feel of their hands on her, of Jason's mouth on her breast, of Jackson's finger inside her, drove her mindless. Too gentle was all she could think. She didn't want gentle. She didn't need gentle.

"Please." The plea left her lips on an involuntary cry.

"You want more?" Jackson asked as he wiggled his finger inside her, circled it inside her womb.

"Yes!"

"I'll give you more, but you can't cum until my mouth is on you again. I want to taste you, drink you as you did me earlier."

Angelina barely heard him over her pounding heart. Still, she nodded. Whatever he wanted, she would do it as long as he gave her more. Dear God, she wanted more!

He pulled out of her, paused until she opened her eyes and lifted her head to look at him, then he drove two fingers side by side into her as deep as they would go. Her hands balled into fists as her back arched off the bed, pushing her breast farther into Jason's mouth even as Jackson began to fuck her with his fingers. With each push of Jackson's fingers inside her, with each brush of Jason's teeth on her nipple, her breath caught, her inner muscles clenched, and when Jackson's thumb grazed her clitoris her legs shook around him. She was close, so excruciatingly close. A couple more thrusts of those wide, long fingers, a few more caresses from that slightly callused thumb on her clit, a few more sucks and pinches to her nipples and she would explode.

As if sensing how close to orgasm she was, Jason's hand stilled on her breast even as he gave the other one last soft kiss and lifted his head. She wanted to scream in protest, but couldn't find the strength as long as Jackson's fingers pounded inside her. But then his fingers stopped too and, as he pulled them out of her, she found her strength.

"Jackson!" She nearly squealed his name, her head lolling from side to side as her body thrashed uncontrollably on the bed. Neither man was touching her now and her body screamed from the lack of contact, burned for the feel of a tongue, a finger, a cock, anything! "Please!"

"Do you want to come, baby?" Jason asked. "Do you want Jackson to make you come?"

"God, yes!"

Jason shifted beside her, moving closer to her head. He reached down, buried his hand in her hair and held her head to the mattress facing him. "Suck me while he eats you."

The mere eroticism of that order made juices seep from her folds and run down her ass. She looked up at Jason, a smile playing on her lips, and opened her mouth for him, waiting.

He chuckled and shook his head. "My, but you really are dick-hungry tonight." He shifted his hips closer still, and then his dick was in her mouth.

Angelina sucked him down in one even swallow and forced her throat to relax to take his full length. Jason was a bit longer than Jackson but not as wide. Still, the longer length proved a challenge. Even more so when Jackson slid his hands under her ass, lifted her hips off the bed and licked the inside of her thigh. She couldn't concentrate with the torment going on between her legs, couldn't think for the raging fire that consumed her insides.

She moaned around Jason's cock and wiggled her ass in Jackson's hands, begging for more. They gave it to her. Without warning, Jackson plunged his tongue deep into her vagina as Jason tightened his grip on her hair, driving his cock farther down her throat. She went mindless. Jackson fucked her with his tongue, thrusting inside her in rapid strokes that brought her to the brink of orgasm. She went wild on Jason's dick, sucking and licking in time with the pace Jackson set between her legs until she heard both men groaning in pleasure.

"Oh yeah, baby. Suck it harder."

Jason's breathless encouragement came at the same time that Jackson reached around and rubbed a slightly work roughened thumb over her clit.

And she was instantly there. Come burst out of her in a heated rush as her body convulsed, her mouth tightening on Jason's cock as he too lost control. She drank Jason's come as, between her legs, Jackson's tongue delved inside her once more, slurping up the juices as they spewed out.

Angelina couldn't say how long she lay there fighting for breath and control of her quivering muscles before she felt Jason's hand slowly loosen in her hair, letting go. It wasn't until she felt a hand on her wrist, heard the faint click of metal and felt the release of the cuff that she managed to open her eyes. Jackson had moved to set her free. Her arms felt stiff and unmovable, her body used and sated, and yet she knew the night wasn't over.

No, she thought as Jackson moved onto the bed beside her and lay down, his cock still fully erect. The night was definitely not over yet.

* * * *

She put together puzzles in her free time. Tripp couldn't quite say why that surprised him so, except that Bailey Lamont simply didn't seem like the type to enjoy such a tedious activity. Apparently she didn't find it tedious at all, he decided as he looked around the small house, cottage really, that she lived in behind her parent's place. Rather than hanging paintings or family portraits to accent the cream colored walls, Bailey put together puzzles, glued and framed them, then hung them around the rooms of the cottage. There didn't seem to be a theme to the puzzles either but more of a chaotic collection to represent her different moods and tastes. Some depicted nature scenes, while others formed pictures of cities and landmarks and still more of abstract shapes and even a few of the animated variety. Each revealed a different side of Bailey Lamont, parts of her that Tripp longed to know.

"You look amazed."

"Baffled would probably be a better word," Tripp admitted on a laugh. He turned from the wall in her living room decorated in a staggered arrangement of the framed puzzles to find her standing beside him, a glass of lemonade held out for him. He took the glass, sipped and felt his bemusement deepen. He arched his brows as he looked at her. "Fresh squeezed lemonade. You are full of surprises, aren't you?"

"One of my guilty pleasures," she said with a shrug and took a sip from her own glass, turning and moving to the sofa.

Tripp followed her. "There's so much about you here, so much I would have never guessed."

"You expected something different from my home? More of a bachelor pad look, I suppose." She settled on the end of the sofa, curling her long legs clad in tight athletic pants beneath her. "Sports posters all over the walls and clothes cluttering every available surface. Milk crates for end tables and neon bar signs for lights."

"You have to admit you do tend to give off more of the tomboy impression." Tripp stopped and glanced around. An armchair, worn and discolored by years of use, sat across from the sofa. He didn't want to be that far away. A tall entertainment center occupied the center wall, the shelves containing the expected television, DVD/VCR combo and small stereo and the unexpected 3-D style puzzles of the Washington Monument, Taj Mahal and Empire State Building. A coffee table sat before the sofa with two end tables sat on either side. Given the choices of seating, he guessed she didn't have company often. Sit in the chair, on the sofa, or the floor. He picked the sofa.

"Why is it that a woman can't work what is considered by most to be a man's job and still be a woman? Female construction workers, cops, lawn care professionals, firefighters such as myself, because of our chosen career we are thought of as tomboys, butch, hell even dykes! God forbid if we paint our fingernails or have long hair that we put into a barrette or wear frills and lace."

"You have long hair," Tripp pointed out. No way was he going to let on how his blood pressure soared at the thought of seeing her in frills and lace. "You keep it in a ponytail most of the time with a simple rubber band, but I've seen you pull it into a barrette a time or two."

"Got me there." She smiled and toasted the air with her glass of lemonade.

"And for the record, I'm a bachelor and my pad is furnished with sturdy wooden pieces and soft white lights. No milk crates and neon signs for me." That made her laugh, as he hoped it would. God, but he loved the sound of her laugh.

"You didn't deny the sports posters and clothes cluttering that wooden furniture."

"Guilty on both counts," Tripp admitted with a wince. When was the last time he'd done laundry at his place?

"A house says a lot about a person. I bet I could learn a lot more about you by stepping one foot inside your place."

"You're welcome at my place any time. Though I would prefer you bring your whole body inside rather than just a foot."

The smile slowly faded from Bailey's lips, and Tripp realized how that must have sounded. Friends. They were friends. Nothing more. She made that perfectly clear. He had to keep things on a friendly level. No sexual innuendos allowed. No hinting around about how badly he wanted her to visit his house. How he longed to see her in his room, in his bed, naked with all that long blond hair spilling over his pillows.

He studied her. Yeah, he could definitely picture her spread-eagle in the middle of his bed wearing nothing but an inviting smile. Yet, he realized as he took in the strained lines in her expression, the circles that were quickly transforming to bags under her beautiful eyes. What he would rather see at that moment was a peaceful, sleeping Bailey. He wanted to see her relaxed in sleep, all worry and fear swept away if only for a little while.

"When was the last time you got any sleep?" The question was out of his mouth before he could stop it. It surprised her too. He saw the shock in the slight widening of her eyes. Then he watched her posture stiffen, her lips form a thin grim line. She pulled away. He felt it. Not a physical pull but more a cerebral retreat. Dammit. He didn't want her to pull away from him. He wanted her to talk, to open up to him. *Come on Bailey. Let me help you. Let me be your friend.*

Bailey sighed and the sound held so much frustration and anxiety he felt it like a knife to his heart. She set her nearly empty glass of lemonade on the end table, held her head in her hands, and rubbed her temples with the pads of her middle fingers.

"Am I looking that bad these days?"

"You look—" Great, he nearly said but the look she shot him stopped him in mid-sentence. Shit! This friends stuff wasn't going to be easy. Still, she did look great. Okay, maybe that wasn't exactly the truth. She looked tired, worn thin, strung out, and great. "You look like you could use a good night's rest," he finally said truthfully. "It's the dreams, isn't it? The dark? They're keeping you up at night."

He knew he was right, knew she hadn't slept much at the station last night and doubted she slept any better alone in her own home. He'd lay in his own bed, four bunks down from hers, and listened to her toss and turn throughout the night, listened to her fitful breathing when she did managed to fall asleep, listened as she startled awake mere minutes later. How long had this really been going on?

Bailey's gaze dropped to her lap, her fingers fidgeting with the hem of the Mississippi State University T-shirt she wore. With the sleeves torn off at the shoulder seams and a V-shaped cut in the neckline, the shirt looked as though it had been put through the wringer. Tripp guessed it was a favorite and he could relate. Most of his favorite wear around the house clothes looked as though he pulled them from the deepest depths of a dumpster, ran over them with a fire engine a few times then tossed them in the wash on super spin cycle before each use. Still, that didn't stop him from wishing she would have left that shirt buried in the deepest depths of that dumpster. Oh, and since he appeared to be on a major wish fest tonight, she could throw those pants she wore in with the shirt because, damn, even sitting down their tightness and the way they formed to that sweet body of hers put him in serious running for the need of blood pressure medication.

"So much for keeping it light," she said softly. "Right?"

"Friendship can't always be light. That's the point of a friend, isn't it? Someone to laugh and joke with when things are good and the same someone to lean on when times get tough."

She looked at him then, hope and suspicion raging a war in her eyes. "Can I lean on you, Lieutenant?"

He knew what she was really asking, knew why he was suddenly once again back to Lieutenant and not Tripp. It was a not-so-subtle reminder of their rank in their careers, of their boundaries as friends. She wanted to know if he could truly be that friend for her to turn to, to lean on without mixing his sexual needs and desires. In this, he did agree with her. No matter how badly he wanted to be sexually involved with this woman, those carnal emotions would only complicate things right now. She needed a confidant. That's what he would be.

"Talk to me, Bailey," he said by way of answer and hoped he sounded sincere enough to make her give in. "How long has it been since you've had a good night's sleep?"

"A couple of months at least," she admitted. She didn't hold his gaze. She looked at her lap again, continued to fidget with that damned tear-me-off-and-use-me-for-a-dust-rag T-shirt that, yeah okay, he would definitely rather see as a dust rag than covering those tantalizing breasts. "I was handling it pretty well, you know? For the last few years it's been a fear, yeah, but not that bad. Then..."

"Did something happen, something to make it worse again?" Tripp encouraged her after she let her words trail off.

"I haven't managed to sleep well since...well, that call. The one on the South Side."

Tripp nodded slowly. He remembered the call. Thinking back now, he realized it was after that night when he began to notice changes in Bailey. Her jitteriness in the dark, an acceleration of her breathing in tight spots, her restless nights in her bunk. They all stemmed back to that call. Some two and a half months before, the tones dropped in the middle of the night. Structure fire on the south side, victims still inside.

Upon arrival on scene, the firefighters of B shift learned that victims were children—a boy of twelve and a young girl of five. It was every firefighter's worst nightmare. Children trapped inside a fully engulfed building, all exits seemingly blocked by fiery blazes. Tripp and Bailey had been among the crew sent in to perform the search and rescue of those children and they had rescued them, but apparently not before the horror had the chance to leave a lasting mark in Bailey's mind.

Bailey sighed and shook her head. "I haven't slept too well since that night."

She'd gotten trapped for a time in one of the tiny bedrooms, Tripp remembered. He'd gone the other way, into the other bedroom where he'd found the boy. It wasn't standard operating procedure for firefighters to separate the way they had. If anything, it was a major no-no, one he got his ass reamed for later by Dean Wolcott. He hadn't sent Bailey in to save the little girl on her own. David Karlston had been with her acting as support on the hose. But Karlston had even less experience than Bailey in such a situation. No doubt, Tripp had made a bad call on that one. A call that he was discovering now had been even worse than he realized.

"You said the fear, the nightmares come and go. Are you saying that night, what happened on that call, was the trigger this time?"

"Don't blame yourself, Tripp," she said quickly, correctly reading the expression he knew must be on his face.

He did blame himself. Still, that was a problem he would now have to deal with. She had enough to face without concerning herself with his guilt. "I did some research," he confessed. "On claustrophobia, how to fight it. I still think we should talk to Jason Graham too. His twin could probably offer some advice but until then, there are ways we can confront these fears, things we can do to help you learn to get over them."

"We? Are you loaning me the mouse in your pocket now?" The corner of her lips curved in a small grin but it was so obviously forced.

"I'm offering to be the mouse in your pocket."

"I'm scared, Tripp." She said it so softly he had to strain his ears to hear her and, oh man, her bottom lip trembled with the admission.

The last thing he should do was touch her. He knew it, and yet he found himself reaching out for her, skimming his palm down her shoulder to her elbow and farther down to hold her hand. To his surprise, she turned her hand over in his, laced their fingers together and squeezed. She looked up at him, her eyes wide and luminous, and he couldn't stop himself from making yet another huge mistake. He slid closer to her on the sofa, pulled her into his arms, and held her head against his chest.

"It will be okay," he whispered as he held her, one hand sliding down the back of her hair, the other rubbing her shoulder as, Jesus, she began to cry. Her shoulders moved up and down in sudden, ragged breaths as she tried to hold back the tears but they came anyway. He felt the evidence of them soaking through his shirt. "We'll make it okay. I'll help you. Whatever we have to do, we'll get through this."

She said nothing. She simply cried in his arms, the soft, almost inaudible sound of her tears slicing away at his heart. Tripp didn't know how long he held her that way, how long she cried. He knew that some time had passed before her shoulders stilled, before her breath steadied, and he realized she had fallen asleep in his arms.

Chapter 9

Angelina felt exhilarated, ready to shout with happiness from the tallest mountain in the world, and holy cow, so unbelievably horny her body burned from head to toe. She should have been exhausted. After the earth-shattering orgasm these two incredibly, sex personified men boiled out of her only moments before, she should have rolled into a fetal position and drifted immediately off to la-la land. Instead, she felt ready to go again. She needed penetration, hard and fast, sweat-building, heart-hammering, breath-panting penetration. Now!

She turned her head, first to the left and then to her right. Jackson lay on her left flat on his back, one leg up and bent at the knee while the other lay straight. His hands were behind his head, elbows out. If she'd been even a fraction of an inch closer to him, she would have clocked herself on his elbow when she turned her head. She pushed herself up, rested her weight on her forearms, let her gaze travel down that wickedly tempting body. Who knew under those dark suits, crisp white shirts, and neckties the FBI's real weapon was rock hard body agents like Jackson Graham? And yes, she saw with a pleased smile, rock hard body did currently describe every single, long and wonderful inch of this particular FBI agent.

She looked to her right where Jason lay on his side facing her, his head propped on one hand, his gaze both blazing and bright with awareness. Yes, he knew exactly what she was thinking, what she wanted, and with the dead-on eye contact and the slightest movement of his head, gave her permission for exactly that.

Gave her permission. She hesitated for a quick moment as the reality of that thought fully sank in. That had been exactly what his nod was meant to do. He used that small, almost imperceptible gesture to let her know he was okay with her turning to his brother, that he knew her body craved to have a dick buried inside it more than it craved oxygen. He understood that because

she so recently sucked him off and he had not yet had time to recover, she
wanted to turn to Jackson for what she needed.

Yes, for an afternoon that started entirely under her control, each event
all but choreographed like a fucking stage show, the night had surely done
one hell of a massive flip-flop, straight into Jason's skillfully authoritative
command. She remembered how he acted at the airport the day of the
explosion, how he seemingly took command of the situation, barking out
orders to the other firefighters and taking the lead right into the danger. She
saw much of that same side of him in this bedroom tonight. It was a slightly
different side than he showed her the night out back at the pool, a side she
found just as amazingly arousing and she realized Jackson wasn't the only
twin with the split personality thing going on. Hell, when she thought about
it that way, she currently lay in a bed between four different men, not two.
And wasn't that one hell of an arousing discovery? Her own version of an
orgy, with two different sets of twins trapped in the same body.

She returned Jason's nod, hoping he would read in her eyes that she
understood a whole lot more than the obvious. Then she shifted, sat up
between them, and reached for Jackson. Her fingers wrapped around his
thick, stiff shaft, giving it a little squeeze, and she watched with satisfaction
as his eyes rolled back in his head.

"Jackson." She whispered his name, stroked him, and squeezed a bit
harder until he opened his eyes, meeting her gaze. "I want this inside me."
She watched as the initial haze of pleasure induced relaxation slowly faded
from his eyes and her words sank in.

He swallowed, nodded. "We need a condom."

Leave it to the FBI to be cautious above all else, she thought and bit
back a smirk. He was right of course. They were, after all, strangers—in
play as well as reality. Although she was on the pill, that didn't protect any
of them from sexually transmitted surprises.

"Heads up." Jason tossed a shiny blue packet over her head and it landed
squarely on Jackson's chest.

"Thanks, Bro." Jackson tore open the foil wrapping and started to sit up,
but Angelina stopped him with a firm hand on his shoulder.

"Allow me." She took the condom from his hands, swung one leg over
him until she straddled his thighs and began to cover his cock. "Jesus! Is it
going to fit?" She met his gaze and found him grinning.

"It'll fit." He reached down to help her and together they stretched the rubber over his engorged cock. "I take it you want to be on top."

She laughed. "You bet your sweet ass I do."

"Scoot to the center of the bed," Jason told them. "Give me some room to get to you."

Jackson gripped her hips and scooted them both, then Angelina walked forward on her knees. She glided up his body to straddle his waist, lowered herself in one brisk move onto his cock and then, oh yeah, he was inside her.

"Shit," he breathed, his grip tightening on her hips. "Hang on, baby. You were supposed to do that slowly."

Jason laughed behind them. "She doesn't do anything slowly unless you make her."

"I don't like it slow." She pushed her body up, digging her knees into the mattress, letting his cock slide almost fully out of her vagina before she dropped down again, jamming him inside her to the hilt.

"Christ! Keep that up and this won't last long," Jackson warned.

God, but she loved to bring a man to the edge of control this way. She repeated the move and laughed when his short nails dug into the flesh of her hips.

"Don't make me handcuff you again," Jackson growled.

"Promises. Promises. You're at a bit of a disadvantage now, Mr. Agent Man. I'm on top this time."

"Yes, but not as in control as you think." To prove his words, Jackson reached up, caught the back of her hair in his fist and pulled her down to lie on top of him.

He kissed her. His mouth ravaged hers and she couldn't stop him, couldn't move. Damn, but the man was strong. He had only one hand left on her hip, but his grip was firm and unyielding, holding her steady despite her attempts to move.

She felt a hand rub over her ass, Jason's hand. For the briefest of moments, she had forgotten he was there on the bed with them. Then she felt his breath on her butt cheek just before he licked the tender flesh and, oh yeah, no way could she forget him now. His calloused palm glided over her rear end, his mouth rotating a kiss and a lick to her cheek, even as Jackson's tongue continued to probe at her mouth. Then Jason slipped a finger between her butt cheeks, and her breath caught. No way. He didn't intend to.

Jason put his other hand on her ass, used it to spread her cheeks wider as his finger grazed over her anus. Sweet Jesus! He did intend to! The shock of that realization coupled with the eroticism of the thought and her pussy muscles convulsed around Jackson's cock still lodged inside her. She felt the finger retreat only to return seconds later bringing a chilled wet feel with it. Lubrication, her mind registered, as the finger inched its way inside her forbidden hole.

She tried to move, tried to pull away, tried to break the kiss with Jackson so she could tell Jason. What? Tell him to stop? She didn't know if she wanted him to stop. Tell him she didn't want this? She wasn't sure that she didn't. Jason had embarked on untouched territory. She'd dreamt of having that cavity of her body explored, but fear prevented her from allowing it in the past. Could she let him do it now?

"Relax, baby." Jason's soothing words came to her on a gentle breeze. "Let me play. You'll like it. I promise. I won't do more than play if you don't want me to."

Do more than play. He wanted to do more than play. Angelina's mind whirled with the implications of that. She knew what he meant by more than play. He wanted to fuck her there.

No way. No fucking way! Her mind rejected the thought without consideration. She knew how big Jason was. The cock inside her now, Jackson's cock, was large, thick and almost impossibly long. Though she hadn't broken out a tape measure, she knew Jason was even longer. Not quite as thick, but still too damn thick for her anus.

Jackson finally broke the suction he had on her mouth, pulling her head back with the grip he still had on her hair. She gasped, sucked in air, but before she could speak, Jason's finger slipped deeper into her anus. My God! The sensations that rocketed through her were both pleasure and pain. But it was an erotic sort of pain, an arousing pain that made her body burn and beg for more. Could she take more?

"You have such a beautiful ass," Jason whispered as his finger wiggled a little inside her, eased out a mere inch only to slither its way in again. "I really want to do more than play here, baby. Can I please do more than play?"

Her gaze locked with Jackson's. His grip on her hip loosened. The hand in her hair released and skimmed down her back to her waist. She could move now, but she was suddenly too afraid.

"Have you ever been touched here, baby?"

The mattress shifted behind her as Jason moved to straddle Jackson's legs. Then Jason's finger retreated once more only to be replaced by something much larger. The tip of his cock rubbed at the rim of her anus, and her body went rigid with fear.

"Jason!" His name burst from her lips, a cry of panic and surprise.

"It's okay, baby. I won't do it if you don't want me to. All you have to do is say no." To prove it to her, he didn't attempt to enter her. He simply continued to rub the tip of his cock over that sensitized hole, waiting for an answer.

Angelina knew he wouldn't do it. If she said no, he would back off and he wouldn't be angry or hurt. He would respect her wishes and find a different way for the three of them to pleasure one another. But she couldn't bring herself to say the word, couldn't make her lips form the word no. Was it possible she was going to let him do this?

Jackson correctly read the mixture of fear and indecision in her eyes. "You'll love it," he told her in a voice of utter certainty. "But he won't do it if you tell him not to."

"But you're still inside me." And wasn't that something she hadn't thought about until the words were out of her mouth? Yet, he was. Jackson's dick remained buried inside her vagina, and Jason wanted to put his cock in her ass! She'd heard about double penetration, read about it in books, even saw it in porn flicks. Okay, so that last was simply acting. She doubted those actors were really doing the full penetration thing for a television camera. Still, she knew it was possible but could her body take it?

Jackson simply smiled. Yes, he was still inside her and he obviously intended to remain there too.

"It's your call." Behind her, Jason caressed her back with a gentle palm, patiently waiting for her answer.

"Slow," she heard herself say and watched as a small part of her step to the side and raised her brows at that answer. "Take it slow."

"Oh, now she wants it slow." Jackson laughed.

Jason did take it slow, telling her to relax as he moved their bodies when necessary to make his dick fit inside her with Jackson's dick still in her vagina. It wasn't easy to relax when two large objects invaded her most intimate spots at once, but somehow she managed and she was glad for it. The spears of razor-sharp intensity that slashed through her body at the invasions made her mindless, drove her to the brink of orgasmic overload and beyond. Dear God! Was it possible to die from pleasure?

"Are you okay, baby?" Jackson asked. He was watching her, searching her face for any signs that they might be hurting her, that she wanted them to stop.

"Yes." She hissed the word and only then realized that it was true. She was okay. She was wonderful, fantastic, incredible! "It...feels...so..."

"Hold still, sweetheart. Let us do the work," Jason told her and began to move. He pushed his cock farther inside her anus, and her body fell down onto Jackson's dick, pushing him farther inside her pussy. The sensation of having them both inside her, filling her more than she could have ever imagined possible, was too much. They began to fuck her, Jason setting the pace with his thrusts into her ass, Jackson following with his pounding in her pussy.

Somehow during all the thrusting one of them, she couldn't tell which one and frankly no longer cared, managed to find her clit with the pad of his thumb and began a pressured massage. And she couldn't take it anymore. She exploded. There was no other word for it. She screamed, a sound of mind-blowing pleasure that left her body tingling, convulsing all over, heedless of any order she may have given it. She couldn't move a single muscle on her own. She was paralyzed.

Seconds later she heard Jackson's grunted release at nearly the same time that she felt Jason's thrusts slow into her anus as he reached his own climax. She fell on top of Jackson, the quick movement effectively dislodging Jason's dick from her ass. Jason fell too, breathless and exhausted on the bed beside her and Jackson. Minutes, hell, maybe even hours, passed before any of them attempted to move.

Jason's hand idly caressed her shoulder as Jackson's arms wrapped around her lower back. Her head lay on Jackson's chest facing Jason, and she slowly opened her eyes to find him staring at her, grinning from ear to ear. Damn him. She laughed.

* * * *

Tess instantly recognized the envelope. She had superb eyesight and, despite popular belief, a fairly quick brain. Even from the doorway of the large rectangular office that once belonged to her father, she could easily make out the legal size manila envelope that lay on the otherwise clean surface of the desktop as well as the ink scrawled across the front. Ink she knew would read Angelina Keaton. No. That was not an envelope her sister merely left behind. It was another one, another warning. Tess didn't need x-ray glasses to see the single photo that envelope contained. She knew it was in there. Just as she knew he—whoever he was—had been in this house, this office. Dear God!

Fear left a bitter taste in her mouth. Her breath became labored and quick as she shot a glance over her shoulder. Odd that the house seemed deserted at barely eight o'clock in the morning. The long hall, the stairs, the downstairs foyer, all were empty of both body and sound. The housekeeper, Carmilla, would be in the kitchen fixing breakfast and, yes, okay, if Tess strained her ears enough she could just hear the faint rustling of pots and pans and Carmilla's lowly whistled morning tune, *You Are My Sunshine*, drifting up the stairs. But where was her mother? Silvia Keaton liked to spend an hour or more playing the piano each morning. It was a tradition her mother began long before Tess' own birth and Tess couldn't remember the last time a morning passed when her mother hadn't played. Well, except for the days immediately following her father's and uncle's deaths. Still, her mother should be in the downstairs parlor by now. Yet, no matter how Tess strained her ears she heard nothing, no light tap of the keys, no soft melodic tune.

And Angelina, where was she? Why hadn't she found the envelope yet? She should have been up by now. She always rose at a quarter past sunrise. It was simply one of the many baffling mysteries of her sister. Tess knew even though the Feds, local P. D. and FAA cleared Keaton Aire to reopen for business, Angelina still did quite a bit of her paperwork and other things in this office. Hadn't it become a habit for her sister to drink her first cup of morning coffee at this desk?

Unless she simply hadn't come home last night, Tess considered. She took one shaky step and then another into the room, her arms crossed under her breasts, goose pimples from both the chill in the air and fear covering her flesh. Her bare feet made the softest of squeaking sounds on the marble floor and then even that whisper of sound stopped as she stepped onto the Italian rug covering the center of the office floor. Okay, so Angelina hadn't come home. Yeah, right. Where would she have gone?

Tess remembered the flower, a single red rose, the gift wrapped in such interesting paper, and the to-die-for hunk that'd made the delivery. She froze, the dread of opening the envelope temporarily forgotten. No way. No fucking way! The Mr. Licious FBI Agent! That's why he'd seemed so familiar. FBI Agent Jackson Graham was the super-duper hunk-a-licious who stopped by the airport to see Angelina.

"You little witch," Tess muttered aloud as admiration twisted with envy in her gut. "Thought you would keep your little affair with Mr. Sexy MIB a secret, huh?"

And didn't it figure? Tess had some really great fantasies going since her meeting with FBI Agent Jackson Graham. So great she'd even toyed with ideas for staging another meeting. A private meeting where she would coax him into loosening that tie, shrugging out of that stuffy white shirt, and using the concealed weapon inside those black trousers. She'd had a few moments of panty-wetting, imagination soaring fun thinking of the many things they could do with his handcuffs. The FBI did carry handcuffs, didn't they?

Tess reached the desk, and all thoughts of the handsome agent left her as she stared down at the envelope. Angelina's name was indeed scrawled on top as she'd known it would be, but there was another name beneath it, a name that had her breath catching in her throat. Her name along with the words: I've got her. Can you find her before she's dead?

* * * *

Bailey awoke to a bright ray of sunlight streaming through the open blinds covering her living room window. Disoriented, she blinked, rubbed her hands over her face, and sat up. She'd fallen asleep on the sofa. That wasn't all that unusual really. She often fell asleep there watching a movie, waiting to fall into a deep, dreamless state of unconsciousness. What *was* unusual, however, was the boat-sized tennis shoes that sat of the floor between the sofa and coffee table. Tripp's shoes, she suddenly realized with a rush of adrenaline that washed away all grogginess in an instant.

He'd slept here, at her house, on her sofa with her in his arms. She remembered that now, falling asleep in his arms. Crying herself to sleep was more like it, she thought with a grimace as she stood, smoothed down her shirt, ran a hand over her hair. She heard water running in the kitchen, smelled fresh coffee brewing and closed her eyes, sighed. This was going to be awkward. The morning after thing always was. No matter that this morning after didn't follow a night of steamy, sweaty sex in her bed. Just a night where she'd broken down, let all her inhibitions and fears out in the way of babyish tears that soaked the man's shirt for heaven's sake.

Not one to hide from her worries—except for her worries of the dark, the nightmares —she took a deep breath, squared her shoulders, and walked to the kitchen. He stood at the stove, his back to her, and a spatula in his hand. She leaned a shoulder against the doorframe and allowed herself a moment to simply watch him, the way the muscles in his shoulders and back flexed and rolled as he flipped whatever he had frying in the pan, the way he stood with his posture lax as though he were totally comfortable in his surroundings. *Her* surroundings. Her house!

He turned, his free hand outstretched to fetch a plate that sat on the countertop, and spotted her. "You're awake. Damn, I'd hoped you would sleep until I finished in here. You know, a breakfast in bed kind of thing." His gaze darted past her into the living room, and he rolled his eyes. "I guess it would be more like breakfast on couch, huh?"

"You slept over." It was a stupid thing to say. Of course he'd slept over. He was, after all, standing in her kitchen at a little past eight in the morning.

"Yeah, sorry about that." He picked up the plate, covered it with two paper towels to catch the grease and turned back to the stove, began scooping up crisp strips of bacon. "I didn't mean to stay over last night. I just—" He shot her a glance over his shoulder, his eyes full of apology, and shrugged. Was it possible his cheeks were blushing? "I sort of drifted off, and the next thing I knew it was morning."

If any other man had given her such a lame excuse, she wouldn't have bought it. She would have assumed that he'd taken advantage of the fact that she'd fallen asleep, that she wouldn't know he stayed until she woke. But she believed Tripp. She knew he simply *had* drifted off as he said because he would never take advantage of her or any situation that way.

"I didn't know how you like your eggs so I went for scrambled. Sort of the all- American compromise." He turned off the burners of the stove with a quick twist of his wrist, moved from the stove to set the plate of bacon on the counter. He turned back to her then, leaned against the counter, and crossed his feet at the ankles.

God, he looked like an exotic advertisement for Formica countertops with his hair all tousled from sleep, his feet bare, standing there surrounded by pans and plates. Oh yeah, no doubt all of the house fix-her-upper magazines on the market would sell quadruple the issues with him in their advertisements.

"Scrambled eggs are fine," she said at the same time he asked, "Are you mad?"

Bailey stared at him, forced herself to meet his gaze rather than to continue to admire all the rippling muscles and hard planes of his body. Mad wasn't exactly the word she would use. Nervous, conflicted, uneasy maybe but no, not mad. "This is weird. Don't you think?"

He shrugged again, his gaze never wavering from hers. "Yeah," he admitted on a soft laugh. "A little. But it doesn't have to be." He pushed himself off the counter, turned to load two plates with the bacon, eggs and toast he'd prepared, then took a step toward the small kitchen table before he stopped. "Umm…"

Bailey bit the inside of her cheek. She could see his dilemma. The pieces of the puzzle she was currently working on covered every available space on the table.

"I guess we could always sit on the floor," he suggested. "A bit of a kitchen picnic."

"The sofa would be more comfortable. We can use the coffee table. It's a bit less cluttered."

He nodded and carried their plates to the other room. "I gather you don't have company over for dinner often."

"More like never," she admitted as she watched him set down their plates then walk back to the kitchen.

"Coffee?"

"Of course."

"Let's see if I remember this correctly." He moved to the refrigerator, yanked it open and pulled out a container of cafe mocha Coffee-mate. "Two teaspoons of this, right?"

Bailey simply nodded. The guys at the station ragged her for months after she first started because she insisted on the flavored coffee creamer rather than simply drinking her coffee black or adding a bit of the powdered cream and sugar the guys used. Girly coffee, they called it and, unlike nearly everything else about her, it was the one thing she did allow to distinguish her from the men. Girly coffee or not, she couldn't live without her cafe mocha coffee in the mornings.

Tripp fixed their coffees, he took his black, and carried them into the living room. When she didn't follow, he shot her an amused glance. "I'll be happy to feed you too, if you want, but it will be kind of hard with you standing way off over there. Come on. It's getting cold."

Yeah, this was definitely weird, sharing breakfast on her sofa with Tripp Barrett. She'd dreamed of mornings like this. Okay, so in her dreams the breakfast had been in bed after a morning bout of hot, sweaty sex but still... She sat down on the edge of the sofa and tried not to think of her dreams, tried not to think about how much this felt like such a *couple* thing to do.

Obviously sensing her discomfort, he asked, "Didn't you ever have sleepovers when you were a kid?"

"Yes, but..."

"Only with other girls, right? Well, pretend I'm a girl if you must." He batted his eyelashes and covered his heart with his palm. "What did you think of the latest Brad Pitt movie? Don't you think he was too gorgeous?"

Bailey burst out laughing. She couldn't help it. Such a thing, such an act from a big, muscle-bound, decidedly straight man like Tripp Barrett was too dammed funny. And yeah, okay, so maybe this morning thing between friends wasn't so bad. After all, it wasn't like they had sex last night or anything.

Unfortunately.

No, no, no!

* * * *

He hadn't wanted to take her so soon. He still had other plans, other games he wanted to play. Keaton Aire remained in business. He'd altered his plans, figured out a way to get what should have been his by right. Force Angelina to close, to sell, and then he would take over. But she caught him in the office, leaving the latest envelope, and he had no choice. All his plans had to be sped up a notch, or ten. He'd quickly altered the outside of the package, added Tess's name for a bit more fun and his little message to the sisters, then he'd taken her.

The stupid bitch wasn't near as naïve or stupid as he'd always thought. Truth be told, she was pretty quick to figure out he'd been the one causing the problems at Keaton Aire. She hadn't been so quick to figure out why though. He thought that much should be obvious. She'd killed both his mother and his father, all but murdered them both personally with her dainty, lavishly jeweled hands. It was her fault that he'd lived most of his life as an outsider, unable to be close to his father, unable to have everything he so desperately wanted that should have been his at birth. It was her fault he turned to crime to get what he wanted, her fault he turned to the bottle when things didn't go as planned, her fault that his father always thought him a no-good loser.

And now she would pay, all three of them would pay. Divine justice. That's what it would be. Yeah, her death would definitely be divine justice, and he wouldn't bat an eye at committing a crime he'd yet to explore. Murder.

Chapter 10

Tess couldn't breathe, and then she was breathing too fast. Her head whirled, her vision blurred and she had to catch herself on the desktop to keep from falling. *I've got her. Can you find her before she's dead?*

Angelina.

The bastard had Angelina.

Dear God!

Tess jerked up the phone, her fingers shaking as she punched in the number for Keaton Aire. Maybe it was a warning, like the others. Maybe the message was telling them he planned to kidnap her, to, oh my God, *kill* her but he hadn't done it yet. Maybe it was meant to scare her and Angelina. But if that were the case, why wasn't Angelina home right now?

She's at the airport. Tess tried to convince herself as the phone began to ring. Her sister would pick up the receiver at any second. She'd gone into the office early. That was all. The bastard delivered the envelope too late. Or maybe she hadn't even stopped by the home office before leaving.

"Keaton Aire," a voice answered.

Shit! Not Angelina's voice. "Janie!" Tess shrieked. "Where's Angelina? Put my sister on the phone. It's an emergency."

"Gosh Tess, I'm sorry. Angelina isn't here."

Tess's blood turned to ice in her veins. He did have her. No. No!

"I can try to radio her if you want," Janie offered. "You said it's an emergency. Is there anything I can do to help?"

"Radio her? What are you talking about?" The other woman's words didn't make sense.

"Angelina took the Cessna in the air this morning," Janie explained. "She's been gone about a half an hour at most."

He didn't have her. Tess took a moment to breathe as Janie's words penetrated the fear in her heart. Angelina had simply decided to go flying this morning. Thank you, Jesus. "Janie, listen to me. There's been another delivery, another envelope here at the house."

"Another photo?" Janie's perky, little girly voice instantly turned frightened. "Of what?"

Christ, she hadn't even opened the envelope. Tess turned it over in her hands, tore open the flap, yanked the picture out and froze. "Jesus, Janie. It's the Cessna!"

* * * *

Angelina loved to fly. There was nothing else like it in the world. The feel of the controls at her fingertips, the knowledge that inside this piece of fine machinery she could cut through the air and the clouds experiencing something only birds could was exhilarating. She didn't know if she believed in reincarnation but, if it did exist she hoped to come back as one of those birds. She would spend her life in the air. A life without worry, without recriminations or regrets, a peaceful life all to herself. She had so many regrets in her life, so many things that could only be blamed on herself. Last night, for instance.

No. She didn't regret last night. No matter how strange she felt this morning, how embarrassed she felt, she would not be repentant about last night. Sex with Jason and Jackson—God had she really had sex with both men?—had been wonderful, amazing, fantastic! Yes, she did have sex with both of them. More than once throughout the night even. The morning after hadn't been so bad either. She'd awoken in the bed between them both, gotten up, dressed in the spare change of clothes she kept in the trunk of her car, and kissed them both goodbye before heading out for the airport.

Her desk was covered with paperwork. She could picture it now buried nearly an inch thick in work that needed her attention. Her father's office back at the house contained even more to bog down her time. Yet, instead of tackling any of it this morning, she'd taken to the air. She needed time to think, to put her life in perspective, to decide what to do about the airport, about the twins.

The twins, she supposed, should be the easiest part of her life to figure out. The quick resolution that came to mind was to enjoy them. She laughed out loud at that and pulled the shift control to the right, sending the plane for a forty-five-degree slant through a particularly large white cloud. Oh yeah, she'd enjoyed them last night and, if given the opportunity, would surely do so again. Still, as frustrating as it may be to admit, she couldn't have them both, not forever anyway.

And what was she doing thinking about forever anyway? She'd flipped through the pages of the book Jason gave her several times, read the subtitles of the fantasies and not a single one of them mentioned the word forever. Her relationship with Jason was sex. Fun, interesting, exploring sex but still sex nevertheless. As for Jackson, well that couldn't even be deemed a sexual relationship. Last night with Jackson had been a one-night stand, a game gone wrong that they'd turned into one of great fun. Did he even know her name? She tried to think of a time last night when either man spoke her name but couldn't remember one. Even Jason had called her baby all night.

She knew Jackson was an FBI agent, knew he lived three hundred miles away in Waterston. He would be leaving soon, going back home, and she would be left alone with Jason once more. Wouldn't she? The fear that squeezed her heart as she wondered if Jason would leave her too surprised her. So much so that her hand jerked on the control stick, causing the plane to do a quick level out that made her stomach lurch. Jesus! She couldn't be falling in love with him. No. No way. They'd had sex. Two incredible nights, one of which they'd shared with his brother. That was all.

Okay, so maybe not all exactly. They'd talked too. She'd gotten to know quite a bit about him that first night at his house and, yeah, she wanted to know more. A lot more. But that didn't mean she was falling in love with him. Did it?

Yes. Dammit, yes it did. She knew it did. She knew all the feelings and desires inside her manifested to more than just I-want-to-screw-you intensity nearly the moment he'd first touched her against the door of his house. They were fire in each other's arms, dynamite that required only a touch to detonate to explosion. Still, the question remained, did he feel it too? Was that a part of their relationship Jason would allow them to explore? Or did he simply want to fuck, to play games?

Angelina pushed the question from her thoughts for now because it was a question only Jason could answer. Speculating on what would happen next between them, beyond sex at least, would mostly likely do her no good. She switched her thoughts to the Keaton Aire instead. Nothing else happened at the airport since the explosion, but she wasn't stupid enough to believe it was over, that whoever was attempting to drive her out of business had simply stopped. No. He was waiting. For what, she couldn't be sure, but she knew in her gut it wasn't over yet. It wouldn't be over until the bastard was caught.

"Alpha-one-Zulu, this is the tower. Do you copy?"

Angelina instantly recognized Janie's voice over the CB radio, picked up on the strain in her generally perky tone a second later. "Copy tower. This is Alpha-one-Zulu. Is there a problem?"

"Angelina, land that plane now."

What? Land the plane? Angelina looked out her side window at the gulf of rushing water beneath her. Yeah, right. This little Cessna wasn't made for water landings.

"Tess called. She's found another photo. Angelina..." Janie paused, breathed, and rushed on. "This photo is of the Cessna."

As if on cue, the Cessna's engine lurched, sputtered, and died.

Oh shit!

* * * *

"You're really okay with what we did last night?" Jason watched his twin as he poured himself a cup of coffee from the pot on the counter and then sat down at the table across from Jason, the morning edition of the paper in Jackson's hand.

Jackson sipped his coffee and studied Jason over the rim of the cup. "You thought I wouldn't be?"

"Hell no," Jason admitted on a bark of laughter. "I expected you to be freaking out or something. At the very least, attempting to put a wedding ring on my woman's finger." His woman? Had he really just called Angelina his woman? "I mean, Angelina's finger."

"You've really got it bad for this one, don't you, Bro?" Amusement brightened Jackson's eyes as he set down his coffee cup. The corner of his lips twitched, but he managed to hold back the grin. "And my guess is you don't even know how bad yet. Or, at least, you've yet to admit to yourself how bad you've let her get to you."

"Hey, she's great in bed." Jason shrugged and attempted to sound nonchalant as he picked up his own cup, drank from it. The coffee was still hot despite the cold half and half he'd added to it, and it burned his throat all the way down. He welcomed the pain. Maybe it would jar him back to his senses. His woman. Christ on a pogo stick, how could he even think of her in such a possessive way?

Jackson laughed and shook his head. "That she is, man. Last night was amazing. She's beautiful. Adventurous too. I bet being around her is a lot of fun, in bed and out. I know I certainly wouldn't mind a repeat of last night. That mouth of hers—"

"When are you heading back to Waterston?"

Jackson laughed at that so hard he nearly fell out of his chair, and Jason knew he'd made a mistake. He should have kept his mouth shut, let his brother continue to ramble on about how wonderful and sexy he found Angelina. Jackson was needling him and he knew it but, damn, watching her with Jackson last night hadn't bothered him. If anything, he'd been even more aroused. Especially when they'd shared her, taking her at the same time. This morning, however, he couldn't stand the thought of her with any man but himself. Even if that man was Jackson.

Because Jackson always got the girl. It was the reason Jason hadn't mentioned Jackson to Angelina in the first place. Now she'd met him, had sex with him, and was no doubt head-over-her-four-inch heels in love with him.

And what did he care? He wondered with a growing sense of irritation. He'd decided from the beginning that he wanted nothing more from Angelina than a bit of sexual fun. That was something she'd already given him in spades. To want anything more with her would be like having elective heart surgery on a perfectly healthy organ. Yeah, if she had fallen for Jackson last night, all Jason had lost was a hot as hell sex toy.

"I'll be heading back as soon as I wrap up this case," Jackson answered.

"You're in town on business? I thought you'd just dropped in to say hi, see me and Dad for a few days."

"That was the original plan. Adam insisted I take two weeks leave while things were slow around the office. I'd thought I would spend them here with you and Dad. Then this case came up. You've probably heard something about it. Hell, you were probably there. Were you on the responding shift when that explosion happened at Keaton Aire?"

"You're here to find out who's behind the sabotage at Angelina's airport?" Jason hadn't realized the local blues had called in the FBI on the case. Damn, he'd known she was in danger.

And there they were again, those feelings of concern for her, the nearly overwhelming need to hold her and keep her safe forever. Jason didn't want to think about what those feelings truly meant. If he had fucked up and allowed her to get too close, allowed himself to actually fall.

"Angelina's airport?" Jackson's eyes widened. "You mean last night... She was... That was..."

"Angelina Keaton. The owner of Keaton Aire." Jason nodded and had to bit the inside of his cheek to keep from bursting into laughter. It didn't work. He started laughing so hard he all but doubled over. Oh, this was too good. "You didn't know?"

"I never asked her name," Jackson admitted quietly. Awestruck was Jason's guess. "The whole kidnap the stranger thing, you know. And then we were...and you showed up and...you never said her name either."

"Damn, and here I thought my brother was too uptight to have sex with a stranger. Way to go, bro!"

"Does everybody think I've gotten too uptight lately?" Jackson scowled.

"Lately? Hell man, you've always been uptight. Why? Did someone else call you on it recently?"

"Mallory."

Jason forced himself to get serious. He knew a little about his brother's thing for his best friend's sister and fellow FBI agent, Mallory Stone and suspected he knew only a small part of it. "Still hot for her, huh?"

Jackson drained his coffee cup and stood, walking to put the cup in the sink. He turned, straightening his tie as he did so. He was back to his uniform black suit and tie of the FBI. Apparently, the tidying of his tie brought back the FBI attitude and unreadable expression too, because Jason couldn't have read his brother's thoughts now if his life depended on it.

"Forget I mentioned her," Jackson said as he moved back to the table, removing his jacket from the back of his chair as it began to ring. He fished his cell phone out of the pocket and answered with a crisp, no-nonsense, "Graham."

Jason stood too and moved to the coffee pot for another cup. Unlike his brother, he was off for the day and had no intention of dressing unless he had to. Maybe, if Angelina decided to come back later, he wouldn't have to dress at all, he mused. He picked up the pot, refilled his cup, only half listening to his brother's end of the phone conversation. He caught the words "calm down,""shit," and "Tess." It was the last word that had him slamming the coffeepot back onto the burner and whirling around. Tess was Angelina's sister, and he knew of only one reason Angelina's sister would be calling the FBI.

"What's going on?" he demanded as soon as Jackson snapped his phone closed.

"Angelina's in trouble," Jackson told him as he hurriedly slipped into his jacket. "Get dressed. We may already be too late."

Get dressed hell. Jason slipped on the jeans he'd worn the night before. He ran to the closet in the hallway, snatched a sleeveless windbreaker off the hanger and put it on, simultaneously slipping his feet into the first pair of tennis shoes he saw. Too late? What the hell did Jackson mean too late?

He started to ask, but Jackson was already out the front door heading for Jason's truck because, oh yeah, Jackson's Ford Expedition was still at the fire station.

* * * *

She'd managed to get life back into the Cessna's engine but barely. She had to land before the plane did it for her. But where could she land a Cessna when her choices were the Gulf of Mexico and the jammed packed city of Billings? The highway she could see out her side window would have been a good option. Provided it hadn't been in the middle of morning rush hour traffic and chocked full of speeding motorists. No way could she land it there. The potential of taking out far too many other lives and her own was too great. She could say goodbye world, hope for that reincarnation thing, and plunge into the Gulf. Yeah, that seemed about her only choice, because there was no way she would ever make it back to Keaton Aire with this plane.

She knew of an airstrip about ten miles north in Billings but, with the way this plane was flying, she doubted she would make it that far either.

What had he done to the plane? Janie didn't know. Tess hadn't told her more than that the photo she'd found was of the Cessna. Obviously, it wasn't a bomb or she would have been blown to bits by now. Had he cut the fuel line? Put something in the oil to the engine? Dammit, she didn't know. Not that knowing would do her a hell of a lot of good right now anyway.

Then she spotted it, a landing strip to the side of one of the high-rise hotels belonging to the Paradise Casino. Of course! Why hadn't she thought of that? Several of the larger casinos had their own landing strips for VIP guests and such. She quickly glanced around, tried to spot one next to a closer casino, but the Paradise was her only hope. It was still a good three miles away, but if she could hold on that long, if the plane would hold on that long, she may have a prayer after all.

Angelina jerked the CB radio off its hook and put it to her mouth. "Alpha-one-Zulu, to tower 153. Come back."

"Copy Alpha-one-Zulu," Janie's voice came back instantly. "Angelina, are you still okay? What's going on up there? Where are you? Come back."

"I'm approaching the Paradise Casino Hotel. They have a landing strip there. Radio them and let them know I'm coming in for a landing."

And it isn't going to be a pretty one.

* * * *

"She's going to try to land it on the strip at the Paradise Casino Hotel," Jackson told Jason as he hung up his cell phone only to immediately punch in another number. "This is Agent Jackson Graham with the FBI," he identified himself. His tone was decisive, his words clipped. It was the tone Jason long ago associated with his brother's career persona. "I need a ladder truck and a Hazmat team at the Paradise Hotel ASAP."

Dammit! The Billings Fire Department would be called out on this one. Not that they weren't good firefighters. But this felt like a devil you know situation, and he didn't feel close enough to or comfortable enough with any members of the Billings F.D. to put Angelina's life in their hands.

"We have a single passenger airplane in trouble about to attempt a landing."

Attempt a landing, hell. Jason didn't know anything about Angelina's skill as a pilot, but he knew if she flew as well as she did everything else, she would make that landing. His grip tightened on the steering wheel as he sped through a stale yellow light before the bridge that would take them from Silver Springs to Billings. She would be okay, he told himself, repeating it like a mantra as he weaved through the rush hour traffic. She would land that plane and walk away without a scratch. He had to believe that. Then, when he was certain she was alive and safe, he would find the son of a bitch that did this and make him pay.

Jackson closed his cell phone, dropped it in his lap and grabbed for the handle above the passenger door as Jason whipped around a car moving at a snail's pace. He barely squeezed in front of an oncoming car in the other lane without taking off the car's front bumper. "Jeez man, slow down. Getting us smashed into pieces isn't going to help Angelina."

"I know how to drive," Jason said through gritted teeth. "What's happening with the plane?"

"Engine trouble. That's all I know. She's staying in touch with the tower back at Keaton Aire. The engine shut down on her over the Gulf, but she managed to get it restarted."

"The bastard sabotaged the plane this time." Jason saw Jackson looking at him with a mixture of bafflement and amusement in his eyes. Probably because he was clenching his teeth so hard the muscle in his jaw was about to explode out of his cheek.

"How much has she told you about what has been happening at that airport?"

Jason shook his head. "Not much. I know there was a break-in, some pretty expensive stuff stolen. Then there was the explosion. I was in command of the hose team on that one. I know it started by a remote-detonated bomb." He shrugged, and let out a string of curses. "Someone is trying to force her out of business, but this is going too far. Way too fucking far."

"Do you know about the photos?"

Jason shot his brother a quick look. "What photos?"

"Warning shots, apparently. Professional looking, hand delivered in a manila envelope, fingerprint free. Pictures of the stuff that was taken, of the bomb that blew up the chemical shed and now, Tess Keaton said she found another envelope on the desk in the office at the Keaton Estate this morning. It contained a picture of the Cessna Angelina is flying."

"Son of a bitch," Jason breathed.

"There's more," Jackson said slowly as if gauging Jason's temper before he told him the rest. "Tess said both her name and Angelina's were written on the outside of the envelope along with the words, 'I've got her. Can you find her before she's dead?'"

"Got her? Got who? Angelina?"

"I don't know," Jackson sighed. "Maybe that's what he wanted us to think but—"

"But what?" Jason slammed on the breaks as he hit a line of traffic backed up at a light. He glanced out his side window, checking his mirror. A line of cars blocked the other lane as well. There was nowhere to go. Legally that was. "Hold on," he told Jackson and took to the sidewalk.

"Might I remind you that you are driving a civilian vehicle right now, not a fire truck or police car?" Jackson said on a half laugh.

"So if we get in trouble you can flash that shiny gold badge of yours and tell them to fuck off." Jason said as he reached the end of the traffic jam and pulled back onto the highway. "But what?" he asked again. "You don't think he meant Angelina?"

Jackson hesitated but only for a minute. "It just doesn't make sense to me. I mean, okay, yeah, 'I've got her'. That could be interpreted like he's saying 'got ya' rather than meaning he physically has her, which we know he doesn't. But challenging us to find her before she's dead." He shook his head. "Even if he did mean got ya and plans to crash the plane, he has to know the moment that plane goes down we would know where she was. Dead or alive."

"So if the 'her' isn't referring to Angelina, then who?" Jason asked as he whipped into the parking lot of the Paradise Casino Hotel. He had the airstrip in sight. He saw the plane, saw the smoke and, Jesus, saw it bounce hard, fast, and sideways off of the landing strip.

* * * *

The bastard had her mother. Tess knew it with a certainty that turned her insides to stone. She'd searched the entire Keaton Estate before finding herself back where she started. Then she found the ring. Her mother's wedding ring. A ring her mother hadn't once taken off in over thirty years. It lay like a glistening golden beacon to the side of the office doorway floor. Where no doubt her mother had removed it and dropped it without her assailant's notice before he took her.

Dear God! She'd tried to call Jackson Graham, but got forwarded to his voice mail when he didn't answer. His full focus, she knew, would be on Angelina right now. Everyone's focus was on her sister. Was that what the assailant planned? Divert the attention of the authorities while he kidnapped Silvia Keaton? It didn't make sense. What would he want with her mother? How had he gotten in the house? Hell, how had he gotten into Keaton Aire?

Tess stood in the doorway of the office, her mother's ring in her fingers. Although she looked down at the ring, she didn't really see it. Her vision took on a blurry haze as her mind whirled with questions. Her sister had hired twenty-four hour surveillance for Keaton Aire shortly after the explosion. Tess knew Angelina gave those guards strict orders that no one was to receive admittance to the airport grounds who didn't own one of the planes parked in the hanger and even those who owned planes were not to be allowed in after dark.

Currently, Keaton Aire was home for only three planes aside from the Cessna. A Piper Comanche as old as its owner, Mr. Featerman. Tess often wondered how the plane remained intact much less in the air. A Beechcraft Baron 58 owned by a family friend, Mr. Harvard, who was nearly as old as Mr. Featerman. Then there was the Beechcraft B19 Sport that belonged to a younger couple who'd hit it big at one of the casinos across the bridge several months back. Tess simply couldn't see how any of the owners could be behind the sabotage at the airport and certainly not what any of them would want with her mother. Besides, surely the Feds had checked them out already. Still, it was obvious the Feds had missed something or someone.

What about family? Tess hated the suspicion that question made her feel. Jackson Graham questioned her. So did the local police and the guy with the FAA. She knew they'd question other members of the family too. And, yes, a family member could easily get onto the grounds of Keaton Aire without difficulty.

What was that first rule of law enforcement? She heard it referred to all the time on all the cop shows on television. Oh yeah, the most likely suspect is a family member or someone closest to the victim.

"A family member," Tess repeated aloud. "Sweet Jesus." She rushed back to the desk, jerking up the phone. She needed to know who had been granted admittance to the airport in the past twenty-four hours. She punched in the numbers, drumming her nails on the desktop in rapid fire as she waited for someone to pick up, all the while hoping, *praying* she was wrong.

Chapter 11

She'd done it. It had been a real test of her skills as a pilot but she'd successfully landed the Cessna and no one lost their life, not even her. Angelina moved on legs that shook far more than she would have liked anyone to see. She wanted to be viewed as brave, the woman who kept a cool head under tremendous, life-threatening pressure. She didn't want all the men surrounding her to see her as a shaking and panic-stricken female who needed to be coddled and fussed over now that the threat had passed. Still, she couldn't stop the soft whimper of relief that escaped when she stepped around the nose of the plane and spotted Jason.

She hesitated only a second, taking in the tight-fitting worn jeans, the tennis shoes, the sleeveless jacket over a bare chest that rippled with muscles, making sure that, yes, that was definitely Jason. Jackson, she saw with a quick glance, stood several feet away in a dark suit and tie talking wildly on his cell phone. He spotted her, shot her a quick thumbs-up, and she smiled albeit shakily. Then her gaze returned to Jason and suddenly, she didn't know how she reached him so quickly, she was in his arms.

"God, Angelina," he breathed, burying his face in her hair. "I was scared to death."

That admission from such a strong, steady man brought tears to her eyes. "Yeah, I was pretty scared myself. Nothing like a quick brush with death to add some excitement to the day." She tried to laugh, but it came out sounding more like a choked sob.

"Oh, baby." He squeezed her, his arms around her waist pulling her so close she could feel his heart pounding in his chest. "Are you okay? You aren't hurt anywhere? I saw you land, saw the way the plane jumped off the landing strip. Did you hit your head? Maybe jar something or—"

She lifted her head, pulled back just enough to see him and, oh wow, were those tears in his eyes too? "I'm okay." She forced her voice to sound normal, reassuring. Funny, she was the one who nearly went down with a plane in the Gulf of Mexico and yet she was trying to reassure him. She cleared her throat, because as hard as she tried she couldn't quite get that normal tone she searched for. "I'm not hurt. Just a little shaken."

"Jackson and I were in the kitchen when he got the call. He said you were in trouble, that the plane—God! I think it took ten years off my life."

She laughed, a quick burst of air, and this time it did sound a bit more like her usual self. "Well, aren't we a pair? I think I lost about ten years up there myself."

"At least we're keeping it close to the same age," he joked. "As long as we keep that up we'll never be left alone."

Angelina stared at him. He was joking. Wasn't he? But he gazed down at her with unabashed tears brimming his eyes, eyes that shown with comfort and concern, fear and relief, and something more. Something. They would never be left alone?

"Jason, I—"

"Angelina." Jackson's clipped bellow and rapidly approaching footsteps cut her off in mid-sentence. She turned in Jason's arms to find the FBI twin running toward them. "I just got a call from your sister on my voice mail. I couldn't make much sense out of it. She was babbling pretty fast and she sounded like she was scared out of her mind, but I did catch something about your mother being missing and something about a ring."

"A ring? My mother?" Angelina repeated dumbly as a fear worse than even that she'd experienced hundreds of feet in the air with a dead plane engine settled in the pit of her stomach.

"I can't find Tess," Jackson continued, talking over her in rapid fire. "I think she believes your mother has been kidnapped and she's gone to look for her herself."

I've got her. Can you find her before she's dead?

"He's got my mother," Angelina whispered as it all began to slowly sink in. He'd kidnapped her mother and planned to, Dear God, he planned to kill her.

"Angelina, there's more. I caught one other word in Tess's message. Well, more a name actually. Marshall. I believe she thinks you're cousin is behind all of this."

* * * *

"Why are you doing this?" Silvia Keaton sat with her hands tied behind the high back chair where he'd placed her, her feet bound tightly at the ankles and flat on the concrete floor. A concrete floor. Her mind made quick note of that the instant he shoved her into this dark, damp room. She knew she should look around, try to find other things that may offer some clue as to where he'd brought her, but she couldn't seem to pull her gaze off of him. God, never in a million years would she have guessed.

"I would think that should be obvious." He sat across the room, his side profile to her, his hands busily working on something she couldn't see. His voice sounded harsh, angry, almost psychotic.

No. Not psychotic. That was simply her imagination adding that wild, out of his mind undertone to his voice because she wanted it to be so. But no. As out of his mind as a stunt like this suggested, it was clear that he knew exactly what he was doing. Sanity had not left the building as Tess would have said and that fact, that knowledge, chilled her to the bone. And stunt? No. This was no stunt, no cry for help or play for attention. The photos, the theft, the explosion, they'd been stunts yes, but all intricately planned parts of this sadistic game he was playing with her daughter's life and now with hers.

"It was you all along. The photos, the sabotage, the bomb…you did it all."

"Brilliant wasn't it?" Pride filled his tone. "Bet you never knew I was so good with a camera."

"How did you get the bomb?"

"I have my connections. It wasn't hard to come by in this day and age, as they say. Stuff like that can be bought as easily as a bottle of liquor if you know where to go and have enough money."

"You were taunting her, taunting us."

"Of course I was. I was having fun too, and I wasn't done but you had to go and ruin it. You should have stayed at your piano this morning, *Silvia.*" He spat her name as if it brought a bad taste to his mouth that he was trying to get out. "It wasn't time for you. I wasn't going to involve you. Not yet."

"You fuck with my daughter, and you think it doesn't involve me?" That outburst earned her a quick glance and an amused smile.

"Well, well, well, the frail little lady of the house knows a nasty word after all. You should watch using such language, Silvia. A lady of your stature should know better."

Silvia's anger spiked, and she welcomed it, grabbed it and wrapped it around her like a security blanket. He planned to hurt her. She already knew that. And yeah, what he might do, what he could be capable of, scared her shitless. But her daughter, Angelina. "How could you not think that anything you do to my daughter would not hurt me as well?"

"You're right," he said in an admission that surprised her. "Poor choice of words, I suppose. You see, Silvia, I did know that hurting Angelina would in turn hurt you. It had. Oh, what is that old cliché? Ah yes, the benefit of killing two birds with one stone. I did, however, wish to watch you publicly grieve, to watch you reduced to the sniveling, heartbroken, ghost of your former perfect self I'm sure you would become after the loss of your daughter."

The loss of her daughter? Dear God! What was he planning to do to Angelina? "What are you talking about?" Silvia demanded. "What was in that envelope you put on the desk in the office?"

"But you had to ruin that for me too, of course," he continued as though he didn't hear her. "You've always ruined everything for me. You and that snotty half sister of mine. You've taken everything from me my whole life, and now I'm getting my revenge."

* * * *

Angelina was furious. Jason supposed she had every right to be. Somewhere out there the psycho who had been terrorizing her—had it really been her cousin Marshall all this time?—now had her mother, and her sister was also nowhere to be found. He knew she wanted to be out there too, a part of the active search to find her mother. Instead, she paced the glossy marble floor of the front parlor in the Keaton Estate and fumed. He could actually see the steam coming out of her ears! Someone needed to be at the estate in case either woman returned, Jackson told her and, after the terrifying brush with death in the plane, he thought it should be her. Angelina, on the other hand, thought he was wrong and didn't hesitate a moment in letting him know it.

It would have been funny had the situation not been so serious. The way she'd gone toe-to-toe with his brother, Jason wondered how often his twin ran into a female who so adamantly refused to back down, even from a big, bad FBI agent. He'd watched the two of them all but duke it out on the landing strip at the Paradise Casino Hotel, a part of him siding with his brother while the other half of him stood silently cheering her on. Damn but the woman was sexy as hell when she got pissed. In the end, Jackson won, threatening to have the local blues take her into custody if need be until her mother and sister were found. Angelina wasn't stupid enough to doubt Jackson's sincerity or clout. No one was when he got that all-powerful gleam in his eye. She had reluctantly backed off even if her mouth had continued to fight back. And fight back it did, all the way to the Keaton Estate. Wow, when the woman got fired up everyone within a hundred miles better watch out!

She was silent now. Silent and fuming, and Jason didn't know which was worse. In this state, her anger had more time to build, to solidify, and God help his brother if he returned to this house without both Silvia and Tess Keaton in one piece and completely unharmed.

Please God, make it soon. Jason couldn't help but cast frequent glances at the door, each time reciting that little prayer. For his sake as well as Angelina's, he needed his brother to return with Silvia and Tess Keaton. He would then know the women were safe and he could get the heck out of this house.

Uneasiness settled deep in his gut the instant he stepped inside the Keaton Estate as it always did when he found himself surrounded by such obvious wealth. Too many memories. Too much pain. God, but he wanted out of here!

"Maybe you should try to sit down for a while," he suggested in a low voice that cut through the silence of the room like a razor sharp knife.

"I don't want to sit down," she said briskly and with enough ice in her tone that he winced and tried to settle more deeply in the plush sofa.

The woman so obviously didn't want to talk, didn't even want him to be in the room, the *house*. Fine with him. He wanted to go. Yet, he couldn't leave her like this so, stupid him, he tried again. "Do you want me to get you something to drink? Maybe something—"

"I don't want a dammed drink either."

Jason felt his own temper spike, but he bit his tongue. Okay, be fair here. She's worried, stressed. She barely lived through one horrible experience only to be tossed right into another one. Still, she didn't have to take her anger with Jackson out on him. Yeah, they were brothers but hey, he wasn't the one throwing his FBI badge in her face.

Angelina stopped pacing to rub her temples with her fingers. She squeezed her eyes shut and let out a growl to rival any grizzly. It was definitely not a sound Jason would've ever expected to hear from such luscious, delicate lips. He gazed at her, lifted one brow in both surprise and question. Several seconds passed before she finally dropped her hands and turned to face him.

"I'm sorry." Her voice was barely a whisper, and she closed her eyes again, cleared her throat, and shook her head. "It's just that…"

Jason got to his feet and found himself standing in front of her before he even realized he'd moved. He took a gamble, quite possibly a big one after she'd cut him down so fiercely mere moments ago, and reached for her. Just like at the landing strip beside the Paradise Casino Hotel, she all but collapsed against him. He held her securely and oh-so tight, his arms around her slim waist, his face buried in her hair.

"You're pissed, worried, scared," he said, putting voice to his earlier thoughts about her mood. "I'm here, Angelina, for whatever emotion you want to let fly. Lash out at me, scream at me, talk to me, cry on my shoulder if that's what you need." *Please God, don't let her need to cry right now.* If she started to cry, really bawl her eyes out as he suspected she needed to do, he didn't know how he could take it. He could handle being a sponge to absorb her anger, her fear, but having to absorb her tears might very well kill him.

To his enormous relief, she didn't start to sob uncontrollably. Instead, her shoulders rose and fell in a deep sigh, and when she lifted her head to look at him she was actually smiling. Okay, so it was only a glint of the smile that usually brightened her face but even that was better than the alternative plunge of her lips that made her look so sad and tore at his heartstrings.

"I *am* sorry," she said again. She palmed his cheek, and her touch sent a vibration of heat straight to his groin. "You've been so wonderful today, so supportive, and I know you're only trying to offer me comfort now. And what do I do? I bite your head off."

Jason moved his head from side to side like a bobble head doll. "You're going to have to do better than that to dislodge this head from these shoulders."

She made a sound that could have been a laugh but came out sounding more like a sob. "Damn, no wonder I'm falling in love with you," she whispered. She kissed him, a quick, soft brush of her lips to his, then stepped back and began to pace once more. "I hate sitting around here not knowing what's going on, where my mother and sister are, how the search for them is going. It's driving me insane!"

Jason stared at her, only half listening. A part of him was back in the middle of the train wreck she'd just caused in his head. *Damn, no wonder I'm falling in love with you.* Holy shit! Did she really mean that? Was she really falling in love with him? He wanted to ask and yet, no. On second thought, maybe he didn't. Either way, the point was now moot because she'd moved on in the conversation and besides, now wasn't really the most opportune time to discuss something like that. Not with her mother and sister missing, possibly kidnapped and facing God only knew what.

Still, he'd thought what they had going was simply sex. Yeah, okay, so he woke up this morning unable to imagine her being with any other man but himself. And, okay, so maybe he'd been having these weird flutters in his gut since the moment he laid eyes on her in Romantic Illusions. Oh, and the fact that her nearly dying today, the thought of losing her, had nearly scared the life out of him. He'd even made that joke about them never finding themselves alone.

But he had been joking. Hadn't he? This thing they had going wasn't headed toward love and the happily ever after. Was it?

"Why hasn't Jackson called?" she demanded, breaking into his thoughts. "He promised he would call."

"He will," Jason told her and hoped he still sounded as convincing as he had before. With his stomach now in knots and his mind whirling out of control he wasn't so sure. "As soon as he finds out anything, he will call. What you should do is try to figure out where Marshall could have taken your mother. If he did indeed kidnap your mother, where do you think he would take her?"

"God, I don't know." She rubbed her hands over her face, shook her head. "I've been trying to figure that out and I—" She shook her head again, sighed. "I don't know."

"Does the family own any other property?" Maybe he was grasping at straws with that one and yet, where would a rich boy take someone he'd kidnapped? He'd take her to a familiar place, a place that belonged to him. At least that would be Jason's guess. An obvious one, yes, even to the authorities and he felt fairly certain Jackson already figured that one out. Still, what if he hadn't? "A hunting or fishing camp perhaps? Maybe a cabin in the woods or something?"

Angelina turned to him in horror movie time slow-mo. Jason didn't know that was possible to do in real life but she did it, complete with the color drained face and saucer wide eyes. Then she lunged for the end table by the sofa, snatched up the keys to his truck and ran.

"Angelina!" What the hell? He bolted after her. He was in good shape, great shape actually with all the physical training he did to stay fit for the fire department, but at that moment he bet she could have outrun him by a mile. She was out of the house and climbing into his truck before he reached the front porch. "Angelina, wait."

"I know where they are," she yelled.

"Then we have to call Jackson."

"You call Jackson. I'm going."

"Angelina, you can't just…"

She slammed the truck door, started the engine and peeled out of the driveway before he made it even halfway to the truck.

"Go after him on your own," Jason finished even though he was now talking to himself. Dammit! He turned in a circle in the middle of the empty drive. She'd taken his truck, and he didn't have the foggiest idea where. Worse, if she did find the bastard wherever it was she thought he had her mother, she would be walking straight into who knew what kind of danger.

Jason said a stream of curses that would have made his grandmother roll in her grave and snatched his cell phone from his pocket, punched the speed dial for Jackson's number. Maybe Jackson could save her, because he sure as hell had failed at the job.

* * * *

"How long have you known?" Silvia asked. She needed to keep him talking. Wasn't that what kidnap victims in the movies always did? They kept their captor talking until help could arrive?

"A long time. Years. My mother, did you know she kept a diary?" He hadn't moved from his seat across the room, hadn't abandoned whatever it was he worked so diligently on since he brought her into this foul smelling place.

"No. I didn't know that." Silvia watched him closely, still only looking away for no more than a second or two at a time. She'd managed to figure out that he'd brought her to some kind of hunting or fishing shack. The foul smell. She'd associated it with rotting fish and dead animals. The dampness would be attributed to the lake, or would that be a swamp or river? She didn't know. Could this be the shack her husband and Edward used when they were growing up? She'd thought it burned long ago when a fire destroyed this part of the woods. Had Marshall somehow rebuilt it?

"She knew too, you know? My father's betrayal is what killed her. Your betrayal. She thought you were her friend." He whipped his head around and pinned her with such a hard, stony glare that her blood froze in her veins. "She loved you, and you killed her."

"Your mother died in a car accident, Marshall," Silvia said, forcing a feigned calmness to her voice. A car accident in which Nora Keaton had been drunk behind the wheel, but she thought it best not to mention that fact right now. "You were so young and—"

"I wasn't too young to know what happened," Marshall yelled. His deep voice rang in the small room of the shack. "Then I found her diary, and that's when I knew. You broke up her marriage. My father wouldn't have left her if it hadn't been for you. She was devastated, heartbroken, betrayed by both you and my father, and she didn't know how to cope with it so she drank."

"Is that why you drink, Marshall? Because you don't know how to cope?" Silvia asked. Keep him talking, she thought again. She had to keep him talking, keep him distracted, keep him from noticing that all the while she was attempting to free her hands behind her back. Oh come on! They made it look so easy in the movies. A few twists and wiggles of the fingers, a few rope burns and voila they were free.

"I don't have to *cope* with anything. I'm in complete control of everything in my life. I drink because I want to. See?" He lifted a bottle of Jack Daniels from the floor by his chair to his lips, took a deep gulp. "Ahh, I drink because I like it, because it tastes good."

Because it keeps you from facing life, Silvia thought but knew she would only succeed in angering him more if she spoke the words aloud. Dear God. His life was so obviously more out of control than she'd realized. She knew he drank too much, knew he lost so much because of the alcohol, but she hadn't known he used the bottle to conceal a pain and deceit he believed to be true. A pain and deceit that never happened. At least, not in the way he claimed.

Only Silvia and Walter knew about the relationship she'd had with Edward Keaton after his divorce from Nora. A relationship that most would find sordid and embarrassing. Yet, in truth, it had been one of beauty and exploration, fun and excitement, and she refused to feel humiliated by it in any way.

"What I can't figure out is why you never told Angelina," Marshall said and took another gulp from the bottle. "Why is that Silvia? Why didn't you and Dad ever tell Angelina she is my sister?"

* * * *

Tess knew how to shoot. She and her father may have never been all that close but they had shared a love for one thing, guns. He'd taken her to the firing range when she became old enough to shoot. Later he even allowed her to tag along on weekend trips to the hunting shack with him and her Uncle Edward. Tess loved those weekends. It had been the only time she ever got her father to herself. The only time when Angelina hadn't been around because her sister hated guns, hated to kill helpless animals. Her sister never caught on to the sport of the hunt. But Tess had.

Yes, Tess knew the sport of the hunt. She also knew how to move silently through the woods, how to stay low and out of sight as not to alert anything—or in this case, anyone—to her presence. She did so now as she reached the clearing in the woods that was both familiar and new. The old hunting shack in which she'd spent more weekends than she could count when she was younger had burned about five years back. She knew it had because she'd come here with her father after the firefighters had extinguished the blaze that ravaged this area of the woods. There had been nothing left but the concrete slab on which the shack had stood.

Coming here had no doubt been a long shot and yet, it wasn't, she realized as her gaze fixed now on a new shack that covered that slab. Built of aging wood, it looked far older than she knew it to be. Some of the boards already rotting, others hanging at an angle as if they'd come dislodged from the support beam they had been nailed to. It was obviously the job of an amateur, no doubt built by someone who didn't know much about carpentry, built by someone like Marshall. How long had he been planning this?

Tess crept closer, banking on the slowly setting sun to keep her in the shadows of the trees. She moved in silence, approached the shack from the rear. She knew Marshall was inside. She'd found the place where he'd attempted to hide his car about a mile back in the woods along the battered path her father had made so many years ago. But he would be expecting intruders from the front if he expected them at all. The man was arrogant enough to believe he wouldn't be found.

"Should have picked a better hiding place." Tess mouthed the words though she didn't make a sound, not even a whisper. Her grip tightened on the handle of the 9 mm she held fully loaded, safety off at her side. Her finger twitched on the trigger, itched to pull. Not yet, she thought, though a part of her longed for the thrill of firing such a powerful weapon. She'd always felt a secret rush at the jolt of a bullet lowing through the barrel of a gun. She hadn't succeeded in much in her life, always fell short of her desires, but with a weapon in her hand, she felt empowered, like she could accomplish anything.

Oh, she wasn't stupid. She knew that firing a weapon at a human being would be far different than at an animal or a fixed target of any kind. Despite the amazing rush she felt every time she pulled the trigger of a gun, she harbored no desire to become a murderer. God, please don't let her have to shoot Marshall.

Maybe she was wrong, she thought suddenly, hope curling in her veins. Maybe she was wrong about all of it. Maybe Mr. Green—Marshall would fit the roll of Mr. Green best not because of a physical resemblance to the beefy character but because her cousin was always pure green with envy—hadn't done it with the revolver in the study. Maybe Marshall was in the shack alone, her mother somewhere else entirely, safe and sound.

Yeah, and maybe the tooth fairy, Santa Claus and, hell, why not bring the Easter Bunny too, would appear behind her any second to offer their assistance in rescuing her mother.

Tess rolled her eyes, flattened her back against the wall of the shack and took a second to breathe, just breathe. She'd auditioned for a role as a cop once. The part of the script used for the screen test had been that of a shootout, a standoff between the cop and an escaped con who'd taken a local convenience store clerk hostage. She hadn't gotten the part. The producers said she wasn't convincing enough. But hey, her mother hadn't been the hostage in question, her life in the hands of a madman.

Tess started to count to ten, made it to seven, and slowly peeked around the corner of the shack. Her heart hammered in her chest with such force that for a moment she feared it would give her away, that Marshall could actually hear her heart slamming against her ribcage through the walls of the shack. A narrow crack in the wall offered the smallest glimpse inside, but she saw nothing except darkness. She heard voices though—Marshall's voice and yes, her mother's.

She looked away, scanned the wall hoping for a larger opening to peer through and, oh God, a figure stepped into the clearing. Sweet baby Jesus, it was Angelina standing in full view of anyone who looked.

* * * *

Angelina burst through the trees in a full run and stopped short at the sight of the dilapidated shack. He was in there with her mother. God, had she gotten here in time? The door to the shack was closed, and there were no windows, no openings to peek through but for the few gaps in the boards that made up the rickety structure. Fallen tree limbs and leaves covered the ground between her and the front door. If she tried to approach, he would no doubt hear her. And what would she do if he didn't? Burst through the door and demand he let her mother go? Yeah, that would surely work like a dream.

She hadn't thought this out well, she realized as she slowly backtracked her steps to the tree line, ducked behind one particularly large tree trunk, and attempted to gain control of both her breathing and her racing heart. A plan. She needed a plan. Problem was, she brought no weapon and no cell phone, nothing to help her rescue her mother or prevent herself from becoming a hostage. Yep, this had been a great idea.

Maybe she could reason with him. Yeah, right. He'd already tried to kill her once today and left the threat that he would kill her mother. Did that sound like a man she could reason with? Hardly.

Angelina whirled around at the sound of a snapping twig behind her. A rabbit, a squirrel, heaven help her, a bear? But it was Jason—no, Jackson, her mind registered. Only an FBI agent would wear a suit and tie in the middle of the woods.

"Are you fucking nuts?" he demanded in a hushed whisper. Despite the fact that she knew it was Jackson, he sure did sound like Jason when he said things like that. "What the hell are you doing out here?"

"He's got my mother in there," Angelina whispered back, pointing around the tree at the shack.

"I know that. You're dammed lucky he doesn't have you too after the way you just walked out there in plain sight. Jesus. Angelina! You shouldn't be here. I told you, no, I *ordered* you to say at the Keaton Estate with Jason."

"Yeah, yeah, yeah, arrest me later, Mr. FBI. Right now we have more important things to worry about. Like getting my mother out of there." A thought occurred to her and her stomach did a revolting flip-flop. "Does he have Tess in there too? Did you ever find her?"

"No, we haven't found her. My men are setting up a perimeter around the area now. You need to head back, let me and the local blues handle this."

Angelina crossed her arms in defiance and stood her ground. "I'm not leaving until my mother is safely out of there."

Jackson shook his head, sighed. "Boy, my brother is going to have his hands full with you. I could order you out of here. This is a crime scene. You have no business here, and you know it."

"You've already ordered me once today, and that didn't work and you know it," she said, tossing his words back at him. "And I do have business here. That's my mother in there and possibly my sister too. Hell, if you want to get technical about it, that's my cousin in there too. Dammit, I'm not leaving Jackson!" She all but stomped her foot.

Jackson closed his eyes, let out another sigh. "Whatever happened to simple and compliant women?"

Though she knew it was meant as a rhetorical question, she answered him anyway. "Women's lib, babe. We don't have to bow at a man's feet anymore."

"Honey, I can't picture you bowing to any man," he said on a hushed laugh. "Fine. You can stay, but keep your sexy ass out of sight and let me and the local blues do our job."

Angelina nodded, all too happy to agree to that. She and her sexy ass, as he put it, would stay right here behind this tree, safe and compliant, at least for now.

* * * *

"What the hell do you think you're doing?"

It took everything Tess possessed not to scream at the barely audible whispered demand in her ear. She froze, her head the only moving part of her body as she slowly turned to look over her shoulder and meet the all too penetrating and cold stare of Police Detective Samantha Becket.

"Jesus! You scared the crap out of me," Tess breathed and all but collapsed against the shack wall. How had the woman snuck up on her like that? She hadn't even heard a twig snap!

"Are you trying to get yourself killed?"

Tess held a finger over her lips and motioned with her head at the shack. "He has my mother in there. I can hear them talking."

"We know that," the detective mouthed silently. Then Samantha grabbed her arm, jerked her back behind the shack, and began whispering again. "Stay put. Don't move from this spot."

"You can't cover both sides of the shack by yourself," Tess argued. Now that she looked, she could see other officers positioned in the trees to the left and right of the shack but they were still a good distance away.

"And what? You think you can do something with that handgun of yours? You are not a police officer, Tess. Stay out of the way and out of sight."

Tess opened her mouth to retort but a loud voice over a megaphone stopped her.

"Marshall Keaton," the voice yelled, and she knew what the next words would be. "This is the police. We have you surrounded. Come out with your hands up."

* * * *

Silvia Keaton jolted at the sound of the amplified voice coming from outside. The police. Hot damn, as Tess would say. They'd found her. Thank the heavens. But oh shit, Marshall bolted from his chair and, even in the dim light, she could see the wildness in his eyes. This was not a man that would be taken down without a fight.

She stilled herself, waiting for the gun he'd used to kidnap her to be pointed at her again. But that wasn't a gun in his hand as he stalked toward her, murder in his eyes. No, it was a syringe? Her fingers frantically went to work on the rope that still bound her hands together, but the knot wouldn't budge.

"It's too late, Marshall," she said quickly. All calmness left her voice as panic began to clog her throat. "You won't be able to get away now."

"It does seem as though the pigs are going to screw up my plans yet again." He continued toward her, the syringe positioned in his hand ready to plunge the needle into her flesh. What the hell was in that syringe? "But there's always a plan B, don't you know? I'd hoped to kill you exactly the way you killed my mother, but that won't work now." He sighed, but it sounded more resolute than defeated. "So, we'll have to do it this way. Have no fear though, my sweet aunt, I will get away."

"You can stop this all now, Marshall," Silvia said. She squirmed as much as her bindings would allow as he got closer and closer. She knew he saw her fear, could smell it, but she could do nothing about that now. Her moment of hiding that fear ended the second he began to advance on her with that needle.

"Oh, I do intend to stop this," he said as he reached her. He stopped behind her rather than beside her as she expected. She turned to look as far over her shoulder as she could, still squirming violently now, and saw him raise the needle to her arm. "Just as soon as I get you prepared."

Silvia felt the needle pierce the skin on the underside of her arm. Whatever the syringe contained, he shot it directly into a vein. She didn't know if it was the fear or the contents of the syringe or a combination of both that had her vision going blurry and black around the edges. The world seemed to spin around her and she barely felt it as he untied the knot, let the rope fall from her wrists. She couldn't have run now if she tried.

* * * *

"Oh my God!" Angelina gasped as Marshall appeared in the doorway of the shack with her mother slouched lax and unconscious against him, a gun pointed at her head. She felt a hand jerk her back and only then realized that she'd actually taken several steps out of the cover of the trees.

"Get back!" Jackson seethed through gritted teeth. "Dammit, Angelina. I told you to stay where you were."

"What have you done to her, you bastard?" Angelina screamed. She jerked at her arm, but Jackson's hold on her only tightened.

"Well, well, well, you actually survived the plane crash," Marshall yelled. "You must be a better pilot than I gave you credit for."

"I'm better at a lot of things than you give me credit for. Now let my mother go! This is between you and me. It has nothing do to with her."

"That's where you're wrong, dear sister. It has everything to do with her."

"You're pissed because Uncle Edward left the airport to me in his will. You think it should have been yours. Fine, you can have the dammed thing. Just let my mother go."

Marshall laughed at that, and it was so not a laugh of a sane man. "You think it's that easy, huh? I don't want that dammed airport. I want you to suffer the way I've suffered my whole life. I want this bitch..." He jerked Silvia Keaton in his arms. Her head lolled, seemingly boneless on her shoulders. "Dead."

"Surrender your weapon," the voice over the megaphone said, and Marshall only laughed again.

"Let her go!" Angelina screamed and managed another step toward him before Jackson yanked her back once more.

"Come any closer, sister, and I will blow her head off," Marshall warned. "You didn't know that, did you? That you're my sister? That this bitch fucked my father?"

* * * *

"Take him out."

Tess heard the command through Samantha Becket's police radio even as she strained to listen to the conversation going on at the front of the shack. Marshall had walked far enough away from the shack that she could see him clearly from her position at the corner of the small structure, could see her mother slumped against him. Dear God, what had he done to her? And what the hell was he talking about? Angelina was his sister? Their mother had slept with Uncle Edward? If she'd had any doubts as to Marshall's sanity, they were wiped away now. The man was certifiable!

"Dammit," Becket cursed. "I can't get a clean shot from here. He keeps moving. I'm afraid I'm going to hit her."

Tess raised her own gun, sighted down the barrel. "I've got a shot," she murmured.

"Don't you dare. It's too risky."

"I've got a clean shot, and I'm taking it." Tess took a deep breath, shut out everything around her, and pulled the trigger.

Chapter 12

Tess stopped at the foot of the long, winding staircase and listened. A beautiful, flowing piano melody she didn't recognize drifted to her on the air. The music moved over her flesh like a physical caress, encircled her like the smoothest of silk blankets. She'd feared she would never hear such lovely music in his house again. The morning a mere few days ago when she'd awakened to the smothering thickness of silence was still all too clear in her memory. She pushed that morning away now as she crept to the door of the parlor. Tess needed to see for herself her mother sitting at the grand piano, eyes closed as she lost herself in the melody she played. As Tess peered around the doorway, she saw that Angelina sat with their mother on the piano bench.

A short time ago, possibly even just the week before, such a sight would have made Tess turn green with envy. Now, seeing the two of them together that way simply made her happy. It filled her heart with a sense of rightness and contentment. Both had come so close to being taken from her. So close. Too dammed close. Her mother swayed to the beat of the melody as the song reached a crescendo and, beside her, Angelina jumped in with the accompanying part. And now Tess recognized the song. It had been a long time, so long since she'd heard it, since they'd played it.

As young girls, Angelina had sat on one side of their mother, Tess on the other, each with their own piece of the song to play. At the time, playing with her mother and Angelina had been more of a nuisance than a joy for Tess. She preferred to be out chasing boys or shooting animals or pretending to play the actress in a staring sit-com in her tree house. Now, she longed to take her place at her mother's side opposite Angelina and play her part but as she started to enter the parlor, her mother's eyes opened and her fingers stilled on the piano keys. Angelina stopped playing as well and the silence that followed was instantly thick and smothering.

"Tess, darling, I'd hoped you would come down soon," Silvia Keaton said with a smile that somehow managed to look both genuine and forced. "Come sit with us." She patted the bench beside her.

Tess knew the problem, knew that neither of them would ever feel completely comfortable in each other's company until they talked about what had happened. They'd yet to talk about it. They pretended as though that terrifying day never existed. But they couldn't continue to avoid it. Not if they expected to fully put the day behind them.

"I'm okay with what I did, you know?" Tess blurted. She didn't move to the piano bench. Instead, she remained just inside the doorway. She fisted her hands at her sides, squared her shoulders, made her posture stiffen, and held her head high. She was going for a look of confidence, not defiance and she hoped her mother, and Angelina too, would realize that. "I shot him. I killed him. My cousin," she clarified because she needed to hear it herself, to remind herself how close to her he'd truly been. "I killed him, and I'm okay with it. I don't see myself as a murderer. The cops, they didn't have a clear shot. I did. If I hadn't done it he might have shot you. I couldn't let him shoot you, Mom."

"Oh Tess," her mother breathed and, dammit, Tess realized as her mother rushed to her, pulled her into her arms that she had tears running down her cheeks. So much for appearing confident. "Baby. Oh my baby. My brave Tess, you saved my life. I know that. It was you who realized he'd taken me, you who found me, you who saved me. I know all of that sweetheart but that doesn't mean that I'm not worried about you."

"We're both concerned about you Tess," Angelina chimed in, walking to stand with Tess and their mother. "What you had to do Tess," She shook her head, sighed. "I can't imagine what it's like."

"Knowing that I killed a man, that I took his life, that I killed my own cousin," Tess said for her. She shrugged. "Honestly, he stopped being a man to me, stopped being my cousin, the minute he took my mother, the minute I realized it was him all along trying to hurt you," she said to Angelina. "I did what I had to do and I would do it again without a second's hesitation."

"Jackson said you aren't going to catch any flack from the police because you killed Marshall."

"No." And didn't Samantha Becket just hate that fact? Tess had been sure the detective would blow her top when she found out there would be no charges brought against Tess taking Marshall out. "Chief Stacey, he was there too, you know? He actually suggested I look into the Police Academy."

Silvia's eyes widened, and she covered her heart with one hand. "The Police Academy? You can't be serious?"

Tess fought not to bristle at her mother's question. It was fear rather than lack of faith in her daughter that made her act that way, Tess knew. "I told him I would think about it. I've always loved a good mystery and the thrill of the hunt. Well, you know."

"My sister, a police officer." Angelina shook her head and laughed. "I would have never dreamed."

* * * *

"It was morphine," Silvia said, and Angelina's laughter died. Apparently the time had come for each of them to talk about it, to let out their feelings and fears and come to terms with what had happened to them.

"We know," Angelina said softly. "The doctor told us shortly after you were admitted to the hospital. It wasn't difficult for them to determine what you'd been injected with."

"What they couldn't figure out was why morphine?" Tess interjected.

"I think because it was an alternative to alcohol. A faster way to achieve the same effect," she said thoughtfully. Her gaze took on a faraway look as she remembered. "He told me he wanted me to die like his mother."

"Aunt Nora?" Tess asked. "But she died in a car accident. Wasn't she—?"

"Drunk," Angelina finished when Tess broke off, her eyes growing wide with comprehension and shock.

"Yes. Your Aunt Nora was drunk when she got behind the wheel that night."

"So he intended to…what? Get you drunk, put you in the driver's seat of a car and make you wreck, hoping you killed yourself in the process the way Aunt Nora did?" Tess asked, incredulity ringing in her voice.

"I don't know for sure but, yes, I think that was his plan." Silvia nodded.

"He kept calling me his sister," Angelina whispered as she too remembered that day in the woods, those moments of sheer fear when she'd faced off with her cousin. She looked at her mother now, her gaze searching. "He never called me his sister before. Why did he do it that day? He said you never told me. He said that you..." Fucked his father. She couldn't repeat the shocking words that her cousin said that day and yet, what made him say such things?

Silvia sighed. "Come, please." She took both Angelina and Tess by the hand and pulled them to the sofa, but she didn't sit. She waited instead for both daughters to settle on the cushions before she gave a small nod that seemed both approving and accepting and turned to pace. Despite her straight posture, her squared shoulders and level chin, the nervousness that radiated from her was palpable. Still, she didn't fidget as Angelina expected. She merely paced, her gaze fixed straight ahead as if seeing something in the air only she could see.

"I promised myself long ago that I would never be embarrassed by my relationship with Edward," she said after several long moments.

"Oh my God, Mom, it's true? You really did f—" Tess cut herself off abruptly, her eyes wide, her mouth agape.

"You had an affair with Uncle Edward?" Angelina asked, her voice just above a whisper. She watched her mother and tried to make sense of all that she was telling her, tried to prepare herself for even more her mother hadn't yet said.

Silvia turned to her, shook her head. "No, Angelina. Not an affair."

"A one-night stand?" Tess supplied. She pushed herself forward until she perched on the edge of the cushion, her shocked expression morphed to one of adoration laced with a bit of humor.

Silvia actually smiled at that. "No, Tess. Not a one-night stand either. We were... Your father, your Uncle Edward and I were..." She couldn't seem to find the right words. "Wow! This is harder than I thought. Okay, so here goes. Well, the three of us were a..."

"Holy shit! A menage a trois?" Angelina tried not to gape at her mother but she couldn't help it. Her mother had a threesome with her father and her uncle? No fucking way!

"Yes."

"Go Mom," Tess piped up and Silvia laughed shakily.

"I believe at least one of you knows the pleasures of, shall we say, such an arrangement."

Angelina met her mother's gaze and knew that somehow *she* knew. She nodded, an almost indiscernible movement of her head, and couldn't stop the grin that tugged at the corners of her lips. Oh yeah, she knew the pleasures of such an arrangement all right. Still, her mother…her uncle…her father.

Her father. What did that mean about her father? Angelina narrowed her eyes at her mother, searched her unreadable expression for the answer but could not find it there. "Which man, Mom?" she asked slowly, quietly. "Which one was my father?"

"Honestly, they both were," Silvia answered.

"You don't know, do you?"

"Exactly whose sperm made you? No. I don't know for sure," her mother confessed. "I believe, as the three of us always believed, that it was a larger possibility that Walter was truly your father. I was married to him after all and Edward was a temporary addition to our bed every so often rather than a permanent fixture, so to speak. Besides, Edward was always satisfied being the uncle. It was the way he wanted it. The way we decided to keep it."

Angelina nodded. Okay, she could accept that. Because of the love her uncle gave her her whole life and that from her father as well, she could understand that. In a sense, they had both been her father and both treated her as their daughter.

"I still can't picture it." Tess shook her head and laughed.

"Do you not think me pretty enough to attract two men?" Silvia planted her hands on her hips and leveled a glare at her daughter. She was obviously going for an offended, even angered look but the corners of her lips twitched, giving her away.

"Oh, you're definitely pretty enough," Tess quickly backpedaled. "You're just so—"

"Prudish?" Silvia supplied.

"Well, yeah."

"Tess, my dear, I will tell you like I told your sister when I found out about that sexy firefighter of hers." Silvia stopped and angled a questioning look at Angelina. "Or was it the sexy FBI agent?"

"Firefighter." Angelina smirked. She was finding she liked watching her mother like this.

"Firefighter," Silvia nodded and returned her attention to Tess. "Anyway, as I told your sister when I found out about that sexy firefighter of hers, just because I don't talk about it doesn't mean I don't know how to pleasure a man, or in the case of your father and your uncle, two men."

"Oh my God!" Tess hooted with laughter.

"And, seeing that my oldest daughter has managed to get herself tangled with what appears to be a couple of extremely hot twins," Silvia spoke over Tess. "I'm wondering, is it the firefighter we will be seeing more of or the FBI agent?"

Angelina sighed, the humor fading fast from her lips and her mood. "I'm not real sure about that anymore. Jackson, the FBI twin," she said in case her mother hadn't managed to tell them apart with all that happened that horrible day and the days that followed. "I'm sure he'll be headed back to Waterston soon."

"So he is your Edward." Silvia nodded, a keen understanding in her eyes.

Angelina winced. "It's a bit funny, no, more like weird, to think of Jackson and my uncle in the same way but yeah, if you compare the situations, their role would be the same I suppose."

"And your firefighter?" her mother prompted.

"That would be Jason." Angelina sighed, shook her head, and let out a short laugh that, even to her own ears, sounded devoid of humor. "I'm pretty sure I managed to push him away." Very far away, she figured. After all, she'd scared the shit out of him one second by professing her growing love for him then, pissed him off royally the next second by storming out of the house and, Jesus, stealing his truck.

"So you intend to let them both walk away without a fight?" Tess asked, incredulity in her voice.

"Of course not. I needed a couple of days to set up the game board and get the pieces in line," Angelina said with a devious grin. Oh yes, she would come up with a plan for Jason Graham, and when she won this game she'd get more than a walk on the Boardwalk. She'd get forever in paradise.

"That's my girl," Silvia said and fell onto the sofa between her daughters making them all laugh.

* * * *

"He's avoiding me." Angelina leaned back on her elbows in the center of the bed and let her feet dangle over the edge.

Jackson took a dress shirt off a hanger in the closet. He was an unpacker, she noted as she watched him. Even though he knew he'd be in town only a short time, he'd unpacked everything, hung his top clothes neatly in the closet and even made use of the small dresser in the far corner of the spare bedroom. He neatly folded the shirt as he turned. "He's at work."

Angelina slanted him a duh look. "It has nothing to do with that night when the three of us—"

"Slept together," Jackson supplied briskly, and Angelina couldn't help but laugh.

"You know, for men who look, at first glance at least, absolutely identical, the two of you can be as different as mayonnaise and peanut butter."

"Yuck!" Jackson wrinkled his nose. "What an awful combination."

Angelina flipped over on her stomach so she could continue to watch him as he began to remove his underwear and socks from the dresser drawers. She quickly counted probably a dozen pairs of neatly folded white utilitarian briefs and an equal amount of neatly grouped together pairs of black socks. "Not much for variety, huh? I know exactly what to get you for Christmas."

"Please. No thongs with a giant sequined S over the crotch for super dick."

Angelina cracked up. She buried her face in the mattress and kicked her feet wildly behind her as fits of giggles overtook her body. "Oh my God," she barked when she could finally manage to speak. Then she looked up, and the lopsided grin on Jackson's face only made her laugh harder. "Oh baby…the picture…you just planted…in my mind…" she managed between gasps as she attempted to breathe.

"Sorry. It seemed like something you would do."

"I'm not sure even I would have thought of something like that." She dabbed at the tears in the corners of her eyes. Jeez. She'd laughed so hard she was crying! "Thank you though, for the idea. I'll be sure to write the request on my Christmas list."

"That wasn't a request—"

"But believe it or not, I'd actually been thinking more along the lines of some basic primary colored boxer briefs maybe. And yeah, okay, I would have probably gone for some wildly bright green and blue knee length socks with a Scooby-Doo print chasing behind the Mystery Machine or something."

"Cute, but Scooby-Doo is more Jason's style."

"Yeah, but see, you're the FBI agent, the detective. You and Scooby have a lot more in common. I mean, I've seen toys of Scooby dressed in turnout gear but I think that's more of a selling gimmick. I don't remember him ever actually fighting fires. He would have made a pretty pathetic firefighter anyway. Not that he made a much better detective when you think about it. Cool though he may be, the silly dog ran from everything including his own shadow."

"Do you think Scooby would have run from the woman he loved too?"

Angelina thought about that for a minute. Reruns of old Scooby-Doo cartoons ran in super fast forward through her memory. "Scooby did have a bitch but, no, I don't think he ran from her. I think he was all too willing to go tail over pointed ears for her."

"A bitch?" Jackson repeated, his brows arched in question.

"I mean that in terms of naming a female dog. Not as a euphemism for temperament. Female dogs are bitches." She shrugged. "And that brings us back to my original comparison, the mayo versus peanut butter combination. Okay, maybe those two condiments weren't the best example, but what I meant was that despite how alike the two of you are, your personalities and tolerances can be very different. Blunt language, for example, bothers you. You say we slept together. Jason would say we fucked."

Jackson nodded. "And what would you call it?"

Angelina rolled onto her back, closed her eyes, and smiled. "A fantasy come true."

Jackson laughed. "Okay, I can agree with your assessment."

"I thought Jason did too." Angelina stopped smiling and slowly opened her eyes. She bent her neck back, looking at Jackson upside down. "He *is* avoiding me, isn't he? I stole his truck, pissed him off, proved I'm not a helpless and dependant female, and now he's avoiding me."

"Is that what you were trying to prove? I thought you were trying to save your mother and sister and were too hardheaded to listen when I told you to stay at the estate. Quit lying like that," he added as he sat down on the bed beside her. "You're going to get a crick in your neck."

"I wasn't trying to prove anything that night. I believed I had figured out where the bastard took my mother, and I knew Jason wouldn't let me go. So I took his truck. We've already been through this." They had. She explained all of this to Jackson the day they found her mother and Tess. "But isn't that what makes a man run the most, a woman who is unafraid and capable of taking care of herself? Sort of shoots down the dependant damsel in distress thing, doesn't it?"

"Jason isn't avoiding you because you pissed him off," Jackson told her slowly. Angelina could tell by his expression that he didn't know how much he should say. How much could he reveal without betraying his brother's trust? "You've got him running scared, Angelina, and if you don't chase after him he will probably keep on running."

"Because I told him that I'm in love with him," she whispered.

"Jesus! You told him that?" Now Jackson looked totally floored.

Angelina nodded. "Just before I stole his truck. I said it as kind of a joke but..."

"Damn, you really did scare the shit out of him that day," Jackson said on a laugh. "The thing is, he loves you too."

"No shit? Why didn't you tell me that before? That explains everything. He loves me so he won't answer my calls, he won't talk to me, and he's made no attempt to see me. Now it all makes sense."

Jackson gave her an exasperated look and shook his head. "Put yourself in his shoes. Here's this woman that you've slept with—"

"Fucked," Angelina corrected and at Jackson's sideways glance she added, "You said to put myself in Jason's shoes."

"Fine." Jackson sighed. "Here's this woman that you fucked and now you're starting to realize that she's managed to grab hold of more than your cock."

"Ah, now you're sounding more like Jason."

"Yeah, well, only the last thing you want to do is fall for her. But it's happening anyway without warning. Then suddenly this woman is in danger. She's in the air, in a plane with serious engine problems and could very well crash, and there's nothing you can do to help her."

"She helps herself. Hence there is no damsel in distress."

"You watch the plane go down, and it bounces off the landing strip." Jackson steamrolled over her. "That part was pretty freaky to watch, Angelina."

Angelina laughed, but there was no humor in the tone. "You should have been inside the plane." She shivered. The memory, the fear and the squeal the tires had made as they contacted with first the asphalt of the landing strip and then skipped off into the grass still gave her chills.

"It scared him, Angelina. Hell, it scared me but Jason," He shook his head. "I've never seen him like that before. So okay, you're okay. Then you go back to the estate—"

"Only because you ordered me to," she interjected, but again he kept on talking.

"Where you proceed to tell him you're falling in love with him and, joking or not, that's a huge thing for any man to hear. Then all of a sudden you're rushing away after your psycho murderous cousin."

Angelina pushed herself to a seated position, crossed her legs Indian style and looked at Jackson. "So I managed to grab onto more than his cock, huh?"

"He's in love with you," Jackson said again with a nod.

"And he knows that he's in love with me? I mean, he's admitted it to himself?"

"That I don't know. He hasn't admitted it to me, but he doesn't have to. I can see it even if he won't talk to me about it. But Jason is the type to run from that too. He is afraid of love. He's afraid to love. Especially a woman like you, despite the fact that it's women like you that he's always been attracted to."

"What does that mean, women like me?"

"Rich, strong, independent, gutsy. Has he told you anything about our mother?"

Angelina shook her head. "Not much. He told me more about your father than your mother."

"Yeah, that's not something that's easy for him to talk about. She left us when we were pretty young. Dad raised us. Still, what happened with our mother more or less molded the way Jason looks at women. You should ask him about it."

"You aren't going to tell me?"

"He needs to be the one to do it."

"Well, that's going to be easy." Angelina snarled. "Especially when I can't even get him to talk to me about the color of the paint on the walls."

"Wow! Wouldn't that be a boring conversation?"

"Hardy har har." Angelina rolled her eyes. "Leave the smart-ass remarks to me wise guy."

"As you wish, princess." Jackson leaned in and brushed a feather light kiss over her lips. "I need to go. Tripp Barrett is setting up some kind of blackout maze at the fire station for one of the firefighters. Apparently, she has claustrophobia. I offered to lend her a few pointers before I leave town."

"Claustrophobia? You mean you? And I blindfolded you that night?" Angelina slapped a hand over her mouth. "Oh my God! Jackson, I'm so sorry!"

"You didn't know. Heck, at the time you thought I was Jason. Besides, I've learned how not to freak out in dark and enclosed situations. That's what I'm supposed to be helping this firefighter with today." He stood, reached out for her hands, and pulled her until she stood with him at the foot of the bed.

Jackson drew her into his arms, and for a moment she thought of nothing but her time with this man, with this twin. Jackson blindfolded and naked, her on her knees as she devoured his cock. Jackson laying on the bed beneath her, his cock so deep inside her. The memories made her wet, made her nipples tighten, made her want it all again.

But no, while she thoroughly enjoyed that night, this man, what she truly wanted was Jason. She knew it showed in her expression too because Jackson nodded, the smallest movement of his head, and smiled.

"My brother is a lucky man and he's an even stupider man if he doesn't realize it before it's too late." Jackson cupped her cheek with his palm and when he kissed her this time, it was with the passion of a man who knew he was kissing her for the last time.

Angelina poured herself into the kiss and mentally filed away the feel of his tongue in her mouth, his taste, his scent, his hard body pressed against hers, to hold it sacred in her memory forever. When at last she pulled away, they stared breathless at one another for several long moments before either of them could speak. Angelina found her voice first.

"Whoever she is, she doesn't know what she's missing," she whispered and grazed her thumb lightly over his bottom lip.

He gazed down at her, surprise sparkling in his eyes. "How did you—?"

Angelina shrugged. "Call it a hunch." She'd guessed in conversation with him that there was someone in his life, someone he desperately wanted, someone who was running from him as Jason was from her, perhaps.

Jackson didn't offer any further information, and Angelina didn't push other than to say, "You have my number. Call me if you ever need to talk."

"I will." He nodded and released her as he stepped back. "Jason's rotation ends in a few hours. You could stay, be here when he gets home tonight."

"Actually, I was thinking of something a little different." Her mind had already kicked into high planning gear halfway through their earlier conversation. "I could use your help with one little detail though."

* * * *

Bailey felt the darkness closing in around her and with it came the cold sweat, the racing heart, the rapid breaths. She cast a cursory glance over her shoulder even though she knew it would do her no good. Her arms began to shake. Her knees ached as she crawled her way through the maze of eerie black. She was surrounded by it, consumed with it. Not a sliver of light visible to offer comfort or sight. Yet, she knew that desperately wanted light was close. So very close. She only had to make it through this maze and she would be free of this terrifying darkness. Make it through or quit. Those were her options.

She stopped and sat back on her heels, her arms reaching for the bottom of her facemask. All she needed to do was lift the facemask. It would be dark, even without the blacked out shield of her helmet, but not so dark that she wouldn't be able to see her way out of the maze Jackson, Jason and Tripp built inside the station house bays.

Jackson, Jason and Tripp. Thinking about them made her drop her hands to the cool concrete, her helmet and shield still securely in place. They were out there waiting for her to pull through this, ready to come if she needed them, willing to help in any way they could. She couldn't let them down by giving up, by chickening out, by allowing the fear to get the best of her.

"Don't let yourself center on the fear." Jackson's instructions echoed through her mind. "Force yourself to think beyond it. Find something else to concentrate on, something that calms you."

Bailey thought of Tripp. His arms around her as she fell asleep, cuddled against him on her sofa. She fixated on that memory. So much so that she began to feel the heat of his body against hers, the strength of his arms around her, and her heartbeat slowed. It was only a marginally decrease in speed but she no longer felt as though a heart attack was only a few beats away.

Jackson's continued advice played in her head, his words delivered in the soft, kind, and understanding voice of a man who knew how she felt. "Sometimes it helps to say an incantation to yourself. You can even say it out loud if you need to."

An incantation. Okay, she could do that.

"I am not afraid," she said aloud, but her voice shook and drops of sweat rolled down her forehead to burn her eyes, ruining the positive effect the incantation should have had.

She'd picked the wrong thing to say anyway. Forcing herself to think of how not afraid she was only succeeded in making her *more* afraid. She paused, blinked until the stinging in her eyes subsided, then leaned forward on her hands and prepared to crawl.

"I am fully aware of the strength and abilities that are within me," she said, each word punctuated by a forward move of an arm and opposite leg as she crept her way toward the end of the maze. "I am strong enough to make it through. I am capable of conquering this task and any other set before me."

As she crawled, she focused on the words, on the memory of Tripp's body. She focused on, not the dark but the light that would set her free. Each move was a test of the strength her chant told her she possessed, each breath and heartbeat proof that the darkness she so feared hadn't taken her. Yet. And it wouldn't because she *was* strong. She could beat this.

"Do you hear me?" she said more defiantly into the darkness. "You aren't going to win. You aren't going to—"

Bailey heard the whoops, applause and cheers as she pushed her way through the last stage of the maze and knew she had done it. She made it. She didn't kid herself into believing that her fears were over but, as she stood and lifted the shield of her helmet, blinked as the sunlight blinded her, she felt the confidence rise inside her like a spell of empowerment. No. Her fears weren't completely gone but at least now she knew how to face and deal with them to make it through.

* * * *

"I know what to do now," Bailey told Jackson Graham, and for the first time in a long while Tripp heard an air of certainty in her voice.

Tripp wished he knew what the hell to do. He'd been playing the friends card just as she said she wanted, as he'd thought he'd be able too and it was driving him insane. Maybe if he'd never kissed her, never held that shapely body against his, never fallen asleep with her in his arms, it would be easier to simply play their relationship as friends. Maybe. But no, even before he'd done any of that his growing attraction for her already made the friendship route difficult to travel. Still, she'd made herself crystal clear. If he wanted any sort of relationship with her at all aside from the mere forced companionship between Lieutenant and a subordinate that he shared with some of the men, Tripp had to play the friends game.

No. Not play the game, he corrected himself and muttered a curse under his breath. He would have to make it real, accept that she would never give him anything more, actually *be* her friend and nothing more, not simply pretend. But damn, that sure wasn't easy to do when he lusted after the woman more than wanted to take his next breath and, oh yeah, watching her with another man was really helping too. Jesus! He never thought twice about her and any of the men on B shift. Okay, maybe at one point he'd wondered if she might hook up with Ryan Magee. The self-proclaimed ladies man had been relentless in his pursuit of her for several months. Yet, Bailey had surprisingly shot down Magee without so much as a hint of encouragement or mutual attraction.

Tripp gave Bailey credit for one thing, the woman's resolve was incredibly strong. Few women could even look at Ryan Magee without a steady stream of drool trickling out of the corner of their mouth. Yet, Tripp never saw the hint of a dribble on Bailey's lips when she looked at Magee. It made him think he was all the more stupid for entertaining the possibility that a woman like Bailey Lamont—beautiful, built, intelligent, gutsy Bailey

Lamont—would want anything intimate with a man like Tripp. Okay, so he wasn't an ogre or anything. Even as he rapidly approached his mid-thirties, he could still turn his share of female heads. Not as many as Ryan Magee.

Hell, even Ryan Magee's spot as top head turner appeared to be in jeopardy today because, man, look at how Bailey was looking at Jackson Graham. The FBI agent said something that Tripp couldn't hear over the roar of, yeah okay, admit it, over the roar of jealously in his ears, and she laughed that beautiful musical laugh that made his knees go weak. Oh drumming roar or not, he heard that laugh well enough. It was the laugh he heard in his sleep, when he was awake, when he sat daydreaming sometimes for hours on end and right now that laugh was directed at another man, at Jackson Graham. Whose bright idea had it been to ask the man for his help in the first place?

Oh yeah, that had been his bright idea. Tripp rolled his eyes and sighed almost wistfully as he watched the way Bailey met Jackson's gaze, the way her lips tilted in a killer smile that showed complete comfort with him and their conversation. Tripp never noticed her looking at Jason that way. The men were twins after all. If she found one attractive, wouldn't it stand to reason that she would think the same about the other brother?

Not necessarily, Tripp realized, his gaze raking down the other man, because Jackson Graham had one point in his favor that his bother did not. Jackson wasn't Bailey's coworker. He was FBI not fire department and in Bailey's no-fraternizing view that would make Jackson completely touchable, completely doable and that was so not something he wanted to think about now.

"I should get going," Tripp heard Jackson tell Bailey.

Yes. Yes he should. Tripp stomped down the urge to offer the man an escort straight out of town.

"I really appreciate your help," Bailey said as they began to walk through the open bay of the station house to the front parking lot.

"I don't really think I told you much that you hadn't figured out already," Jackson said on a laugh.

"Maybe not, but hearing it from someone who has battled it himself, someone who has made a successful career in a demanding job where he often finds himself in tight spaces is a big help in itself."

They reached the bay doorway and Bailey stopped, sighed, and turned back to look inside the station house. She could have been looking directly at Tripp—he stood right behind her, following at a fairly close distance—but he knew she didn't see him. He knew she was seeing the way the bay had been set up only a mere quarter of an hour ago. They'd emptied out the bays of trucks and gear, plunged them into darkness, painted the face shield of Bailey's helmet black, and set up obstacles to make it a bit of a challenge for her to maneuver through. She'd done it too, all on her own though he suspected that Jackson's voice and calm instructions had been with her in spirit along the way.

"Call me," Jackson told her as he pulled his keys from the pocket of his black slacks. "Any time you need a little voice of encouragement or an ear to listen."

"Thank you. I will."

Jackson leaned in and brushed his lips over her cheek. It was a sweet kiss, a friendly kiss with absolutely no heat or obvious intent of seduction involved and still, Tripp heard that jealous roar start up in his ears once more.

Friends, friends, *friends*! That word had become his new mantra over the past few weeks.

"And Bailey, I really hope you will consider my other piece of advice too."

Tripp could see only Bailey's back now but he didn't need to see her face to know her smile faded at those words. Her posture went slack and her head slumped just a bit. It wasn't much but it was enough to be a giveaway that, whatever his advice had been, it hadn't been something she wanted to hear or think about.

Still, she nodded and said a quiet, "I will."

Seemingly satisfied, Jackson flashed her a grin and, glancing over her shoulder, gave Tripp a quick wave before he turned to leave.

Tripp moved to Bailey's side. She waited until Jackson's Ford Expedition drove out of sight before she sighed and looked up at him. "He thinks I should see a shrink."

Tripp pursed his lips and rocked back on the heel of his boots. He was stalling for time, unsure exactly how to respond to that.

"You agree with him."

"I think there may be something more to this claustrophobia than a simple fear of the dark or tight places," Tripp admitted slowly. "The dreams. Did you tell him about the nightmares?"

Bailey nodded. "He thinks there's something there too, something that maybe I'm blocking out."

"I'll help you," Tripp blurted. "Whatever I can do, whatever you need."

"I know." She looked away, but not before he heard her say a soft, "Thank you."

Jesus! Did she actually think he meant—? Dammit, he wanted her to know she could call him anytime too. He wanted her to feel comfortable enough with him, close enough to him, to look to him for help and advice. Not that he knew exactly what advice to offer her, but he would go to the ends of the earth if need be to figure it out.

"Listen, our rotation ended a while ago," he pointed out unnecessarily. "How about we blow this place and go out for a—"

"Ice cream cone at the park?" Bailey interjected.

He had been about to suggest a burger and fries or something but, yeah, okay, an ice cream cone would do too. At least she was looking at him again, and she no longer seemed uncomfortable by the course of the conversation. *Keep it light. Keep it neutral. Keep it friends.*

"I'll meet you at the park," Tripp nodded and walked to his truck, all the while wondering if he wasn't the one who needed to go on a trip to see a shrink.

Friends, friends, *friends!*

Yeah, right.

* * * *

Jason needed a beer. Okay, so maybe *need* was much too strong a word. How about want? Yeah, want sounded better, he decided as he grabbed his gear bag and headed out of the station house to his truck. To need something implied a desire too strong to ignore, to be unable to go without that something a moment longer, to be unable to cope without that something in his life. No. A beer didn't fit any of those descriptions. He simply wanted that beer, but what he needed, what he was discovering was too strong to ignore or cope without in his life, was Angelina Keaton.

Dammit! He cursed under his breath, the full truth behind that definite need slamming into him like a wrecking ball in the middle of a demolition. Yeah, that was about right too because the demolition going on consisted of both his mind and his heart being pounded to bits. He'd hoped to put a stop to the destruction. After all, a man couldn't fall apart if the object of his destruction was no longer around. Could he?

Yes. Hell yes. Apparently a man could fall apart just fine with no help at all. He was living proof of that. He'd stayed away from her for... How long had it been now? Ah yes, one week, two days, six hours, Jason checked his wristwatch, and fourteen minutes. Give or take a few. And it had been the longest one week, two days, six hours and fourteen minutes of his life. God, but he missed her!

"You're running scared, Bro." Jackson didn't know how on the money he'd been with that observation. Then again, maybe he had because he'd also asked, "Are you going to push that amazing woman out of your life just because she pissed you off a bit?"

Pissed him off a bit? Hell, she'd infuriated him. She stole his truck, peeled out of the driveway without giving him the slightest clue where she was going, and leaving him to wonder if she would end up getting herself hurt or, worse, even killed. Pissed him off a bit? Yeah, he'd been pissed but that anger had instantly transformed into gut-wrenching fear for her safety. She'd scared the hell out of him all right, first by telling him that, holy shit, she was falling in love with him and then leaving him to wonder if he would ever see her alive again. She'd terrified him out of his mind and brought so many memories to the surface that he dammed near suffocated from them.

He couldn't take it. What began as fun play at great sex got way too complicated way too fast. He didn't need this shit, didn't want it. His life had been smooth sailing until he met Angelina Keaton, and it would be smooth sailing again without her.

Yeah, and who was he kidding? He stopped at the driver side back wheel well, tossed his gear bag in the bed of his truck and gave an absent wave to the Lieutenant as the man pulled out of the parking lot following Bailey Lamont. Hmmm, and wasn't that interesting? Jason thought. Apparently the time half of B shift spent this afternoon in the blacked out bays of the station house hadn't been enough for the L.T. Of course, the bulk of Bailey's focus had been on the training op, as Ryan Magee termed it in ex-Navy SEAL speak. Jackson managed to claim quite a bit of her attention as well.

Because his brother and Lamont shared a mutual fear, Jason reminded himself. He moved to the driver door and pulled up on the handle. Lamont's focus on Jackson had been purely one of a student looking to a teacher. It had nothing to do with attraction. He wondered if the Lieutenant realized that though. Jason knew something had been sizzling between Lamont and the L.T. for a while now. Yet, these days the Lieutenant seemed to be attempting to act more as the woman's savior than vying for top spot as her lover.

So okay, the L.T. had something freaky and really confusing going on with Bailey Lamont. More power to both of them, Jason thought as he slid behind the wheel. Jackson was headed back to Waterston, no doubt where he would pine after Mallory Stone for another five plus years, despite the amazing sex he'd had with Angelina that proved Jackson wasn't near as stuffy as everyone thought him to be. But that was a good thing. Both that Jackson knew how to loosen that FBI tie after all and that he was on his way back to Waterston. It meant that Jackson didn't have any plans of engaging in any more of those nights with Angelina. It meant that Jackson hadn't fallen for her.

No indeed, because Jackson was the smart twin, the one with the brain, the one with enough sense to keep that night of amazing, out-of-this-world sex exactly that. Sex. Jason knew his brother said his good-byes and drove away with fond memories and no regrets or longings of a continuous repeat. No. The longings for a continuous repeat all belonged to Jason because he was the twin without the brain, the twin who'd lost all senses and gone and fallen in love with the dammed woman.

There. He'd admitted it. He'd lost his ever-lovin' mind and fallen boots over turnout jacket for Angelina Keaton. Christ! Now he *needed* that beer. Make that a six-pack, he decided as he pushed the key into the ignition. The engine came to life with a soft purr. He would need at least a six-pack while he attempted to figure out what the hell to do next.

What to do next? That question made him laugh out loud, the sound more like that from a crazy person than one of true humor. He slammed the gearshift in reverse, and that's when he spotted it. A small folded piece of paper wedged between the gear stick on the floor and the cup holder, a Hershey's kiss perched beside it.

Jason stared dumbly at the paper for a long moment before he shifted back to park and picked up the note. It had to be a note, he decided, as he started to unfold it. He thought of the envelopes Marshall, Angelina's deranged and now dead cousin, left for her to find. Had she felt this perplexed when she discovered the first one, he wondered? Probably. Still, there was no comparison to those envelopes and this little note. This note wasn't a warning of danger to come. Was it?

He finished unfolding the paper and read. "Are you ready to play? If so, go to your house, to your bedroom for further instructions."

Jason read the note a second and third time before he shook his head and squeezed his eyes shut. No warning of danger to come? Bullshit! The instructions in this note would surely lead him to nothing but danger. No doubt playing this time would be playing with fire.

He said good-bye to the idea of the six-pack, shoved the unwrapped kiss in his mouth and slammed the truck into reverse once more. He peeled out of the station parking lot, grinning like an idiot as he headed for home. Playing with fire was, after all, his specialty.

Chapter 13

Angelina took a gamble. At least her instincts told her it was a gamble, leading Jason to the Keaton Estate with the notes and chocolate kisses she'd left for him to find. They needed to talk. Apparently about far more than she'd realized. Yes, she could have skipped the game with the letters and simply ambushed him at his place when he came home from work. But she wanted him on her turf. Even with all that had been on her mind, all that went on, she hadn't missed the way he'd looked so uncomfortable here the day her mother had been taken. He'd seemed so out of place, ill at ease and almost ready to run at the first given opportunity. Instead, she'd been the one to run, leaving him here where he no doubt felt like an alien from another planet intruding on her classy, lavish Earthly home.

It all stemmed from his mother. She managed to drag that much out of Jackson at least. Apparently, their mother had been a rich, headstrong woman who did what she pleased with little regard for her husband or children. She abandoned them—Jason, Jackson and their father when the twins were only five. Still, Angelina guessed that knowing about his mother, growing up without her somehow managed to warp Jason's sense of love and marriage, of family and, possibly worst of all, women.

Because she could, Angelina played the rich part to the max. She took another gamble with her clothes, choosing a no-nonsense, highly expensive Armani suit in a devilish red instead of the jeans and T-shirts or even the frilly lingerie Jason was used to seeing her wear. The outfit was designed to shine, to flaunt both her wealth and her beauty, to show Jason she could be both the woman he fell in love with and the classy rich girl she was born.

Angelina's heels made a soft clacking sound as she stepped onto the second floor balcony that overlooked the driveway. She tried not to notice how the sun was already setting in the distance, bathing the sky in a sea of purple, orange and pink as it slowly disappeared. Jason would be off work by now. Long before now, she amended with a sense of growing disappointment. She rested her forearms on the balcony rail and stared down the long, windy driveway that led back to the street, willing a truck to come into view. Not just any truck, of course, but a specific, solid black Toyota Tundra with chrome rims and a firefighter license plate. Jason's truck that did not come.

She took a gamble and she lost.

"If tonight's game is the one where the princess is held captive in the tallest tower awaiting her prince to come rescue her on a white horse, you probably should have chosen a more formal, frilly dress."

Angelina blinked back tears that suddenly filled her eyes as she glanced over her shoulder to see Tess step onto the balcony.

"Although," Tess continued as she moved to the rail, mirroring Angelina's pose. "I suppose a princess of the twenty-first century might wear an Armani suit instead. I don't remember the princess looking so nervous in any of her stories though."

"I'm not nervous so much as scared and becoming quickly disappointed," Angelina admitted.

"He'll show."

"I wish I had your confidence."

"You are waiting for Jason, right? I guess that would be a tough toss-up. I mean, the FBI-agent-to-the-rescue thing. Jackson's already done that. Then again, firefighters do have those trucks with the tall ladders that—"

"Jackson is on his way back to Waterston by now." Angelina spoke with just enough volume to cut Tess off in mid-sentence. "And Jason has apparently decided he no longer wants to play."

"Hey! What's up with this defeatist attitude all of a sudden? That's not the sister I know. You had two incredibly *hot* men. No way are you going to give up on both of them. Gosh! I still can't believe you slept with both of them. At the same time! Man, Sis, you rock!"

Tess playfully nudged Angelina with her shoulder, and Angelina couldn't help but laugh a little. "Where are you headed tonight?" She glanced down at her sister's simple mauve colored blouse and pleated tan slacks. She looked nice, adult, sophisticated in a so-not-trying-to-attract-attention sort of way.

"Just out to dinner," Tess answered with an attempt at a nonchalant shrug.

"You're going on a date dressed like that?" Angelina knew she sounded surprised, but she couldn't help it.

"I didn't say it was a date." Tess bristled slightly. "And what's wrong with the way I'm dressed?"

"Nothing," Angelina said quickly. "Absolutely nothing. You look beautiful. It's just that, well, I don't think I've seen Paris Hilton or Jessica Biel wear anything remotely like that lately."

"Yeah, well, I wasn't going for the Hollywood look tonight. I'm having dinner with Samantha Becket."

Angelina was suddenly grateful the balcony rail stood so high because she surely would have tumbled over it at that news. "You're having dinner with Samantha Becket, as in Silver Springs Police Detective Samantha Becket? As in the, oh what was that colorful name you gave her, pissy bitch of the police force Samantha Becket?"

Tess shrugged again. "We talked after that day and, well, she's not so bad. Believe it or not, she wants to help me. You know, with the whole getting into the police academy thing."

"Wow!"

"Yeah. I think she's realized I'm serious about becoming a cop. It won't be easy, of course. I know that. I don't expect to have Mahoney or even High Tower as instructors at the academy or anything. But I want to do it, Angelina. I really do. I think it will be a good career move for me. You know, until that big part in the next Grammy Award winning movie comes up."

"Wow. Tess, that's..." Definitely unexpected, Angelina thought. From aspiring actress to future police officer. Not a leap she would have anticipated out of her sister but hey, the past several weeks had been chock full of the unexpected. "Great."

A thin beam of headlights cut through the quickly dimming sunset as a car crept up the drive. No. Not a car but a truck, Angelina realized and her pulse leapt into double time. Jason's truck. Maybe she hadn't lost yet after all.

"Looks like your prince has arrived." Tess pushed herself away from the rail but not before she leaned over and gave Angelina a quick kiss on the cheek. "I'm out of here. Good luck with the Rapunzel thing."

And with that, she was gone. She appeared moments later in the driveway where she stopped to exchange a few words with Jason that Angelina couldn't hear. Tess pointed to the balcony where Angelina stood then waved good-bye, slid behind the wheel of her Corvette, and sped out of the drive.

* * * *

Jason regretted that he didn't stop for that beer. Not as an alternative to coming here. No. He knew from the moment he began to follow the little notes that led him to the Keaton Estate that he would come to Angelina wherever she wanted him. Still, a little liquid courage would have been nice right about now. He pocketed his keys and watched as the taillights of Tess's car faded out of the drive before he turned back to the house and looked up.

Angelina gazed down at him, a vision surrounded by the dim white light that streamed out through the door behind her. She left her hair down, the long chestnut strands falling over her shoulders like a curtain of shiny silk. He caught the glitter of diamonds in her ears through that curtain— diamonds that no doubt cost a small fortune, but he pushed that thought away. Through the bars of the balcony rail, he saw that she wore red. A stylish and equally expensive executive style suit. Still, the old Chris De Burgh song *Lady In Red* came to mind. God but she was beautiful! How had he thought he could ever stay away from her? Looking at her now, he wondered how he managed the last several days.

He felt the uneasiness try to settle in his gut and viciously stamped it out. The past, his reservations about her wealth, the memories of his mother, none of that mattered anymore. What mattered was having her, holding her, and never letting go.

"Should I be looking for another note?" he called up to her when it became obvious she wasn't coming down to meet him.

"No. Just come on up."

Jason hesitated, noting the slight quiver that accompanied her words. Jesus! Was she crying? He stared up at her, but with the distance between them he couldn't tell. Although, that quiver in her voice could be simply because she was nervous at seeing him again, he considered. Heaven knew he felt a bit jittery facing her after the way they'd left things.

Right here in this driveway, he thought. That memory made him pat his right front pocket, checking to be sure the keys to his truck remained safely buried there as he headed for the front door. The temperature change from the warm evening air to the crisp and slightly chilled air conditioning inside brought goose pimples to his flesh. Yeah it was the temperature difference that did it, he attempted to convince himself. No way were those goose bumps a visible product of this feeling borderline on sheer fear that came over him as he moved up the winding staircase to the second floor.

He expected to find her on the balcony outside a second floor parlor. Better, he hoped to find her on the balcony outside her bedroom. Instead, he found the light that spilled into the upstairs hallway came from two standing lamps arranged in the corner of a very impressive office that reminded him of the home office of an attorney or some corporate bigwig in the movies. A set of French doors was open across the office, and there she was.

Angelina turned, her hands gripping the rail behind her, one knee slightly bent causing the knee-length skirt to ride up her thigh just enough to kick his already racing pulse into triple time. Despite her own apparent nervousness, she looked incredible, richly exotic and way out of his league.

His step faltered as he slowly moved toward her, the out-of-place feeling in his belly growing with each step. The notes he'd followed to get here first led him home, to his bedroom where a change of clothes lay on his bed waiting for him. The same worn-out and ratty jeans he wore the first night they made love with a shirt of nearly equal condition.

He should have been comfortable in his favorite lounge-around clothes. Instead, he felt like lower-class scum in comparison to what Angelina wore. Christ! Was that an Armani suit? He didn't have anything in his closet with a top dog designer label but he did own nicer clothes than what she'd laid out for him.

"Did you uh, just come from a meeting or something?" he asked. There had to be some explanation for this wealthy-heiress-meets-little-orphan-boy scene. And that was it. He almost laughed as understanding dawned. This was another of their games, a little role-playing fun with the costumes to fit the parts. But Angelina nodded and, okay, maybe not.

"I did meet with Mr. Churchill this afternoon." She came inside but went straight to the wet bar in the corner. She tugged open a small icebox, pulled out two bottles—one beer, the other some soft of fruity wine cooler.

"Mr. Churchill?" Jason repeated dumbly. He was listening. Truly he was. Until his mouth started to water so much his ears began to fill. He couldn't say which started the overflow first, the sight of her bare legs in contrast to that red skirt and the way her muscles flexed and tightened when she walked in what had to be four-inch heels or the sound of the seal being broken as she twisted the top off the bottle of beer.

Angelina handed him the bottle of beer, then moved away so fast he almost sniffed his pits to make sure he'd remembered deodorant. She turned and walked back out onto the balcony as she continued talking. He checked anyway for good measure, bending his head for a quick sniff as he followed her out.

"The casino guru who has been so insistent on buying my airport even though I have told him repeatedly that I am in no way interested in selling." She said it all in one breath, her tone gaining a bit of heat at the end. "The man is like a freaking pit bull! A pit bull that, might I add, is now chasing after a different bone that I happened to throw in his direction." She upended her Smirnoff Twister—watermelon flavored, Jason saw now—and drank the level down below the neck of the bottle before she went on. "It seems that there is another private airport close by that is for sale. A few quick phone calls to confirm the fact and a couple of hints during my meeting with the vicious, teeth-bearing Mr. Churchill, and he is now growling up at that tree."

"Smart business woman." Jason tipped the neck of his beer bottle at her before taking a sip.

"Yeah, well, hopefully I've learned enough from my past failures and gained a bit of business smarts." She shrugged, sighed, took another pull from her Smirnoff and smacked her lips. "Tell me about your mother."

Jason blinked at her swift change of subject. He didn't want to talk about his mother. He didn't want to talk at all. He wanted to just be, to go back to that place with Angelina where it was all fun and games and no in-depth analysis into their feelings and souls. He walked to the rail, turning his back on her. "I've told you. She left when I was young. My father raised us. There's nothing more to tell."

"I think there is. I think there is a lot you aren't telling me, a lot I should know. I think that whatever happened with her is affecting what's happening between us now."

What's happening between them? What *was* happening between them? Things had gotten all screwed up. What began as something so simple, so carnal, had gotten so whacked out. All because he'd let himself fall in love with Angelina. He'd admitted that to himself, was ready to face it, to face her. That was why he'd come tonight. But why did facing that have to involve the past?

"Do I remind you of her? Is that why you ran from me?"

"I didn't run from you." He saw her sideways glance out of the corner of his eye and amended. "Okay, maybe I did. I have been. And yes, you do remind me a little of her. Not that I remember her well. I was only five when she—"

"When she left you," Angelina finished for him.

Jason shook his head, sighed, and closed his eyes. It amazed him how strong that little boy's pain still was inside him. It amazed him how clearly he could still remember that night when she'd run from the house never to return. "My mother was murdered, Angelina." At her gasp of surprise, he looked at her.

"Dear God. Jason, I'm so sorry. I thought—"

"That she simply ran off, abandoned us." He nodded. "Yeah, that's what I wanted you to think. It's easier that way, to tell people she just left us. She did, actually. She and my father were separated even though they still lived together. See, she was young and restless, not really cut out for family life. Jackson and I, well, we were a mistake, the products of a wild fling with a service man. She didn't want us, didn't want kids at all. When she found out she was pregnant—" He stopped and shook his head, a part of him wishing his grandparents had never told him the truth. It hurt more than he would have thought to know he'd been unwanted from the start. "Her family was loaded, well-known with a reputation to protect, and an illegitimate child— or in our case, children—simply wasn't socially acceptable. Neither was an abortion or divorce, for that matter. So she married my father."

"But she wasn't happy," Angelina said softly.

"She was never happy. She had Jackson and me and I think for a while she did try to be a wife and mother but I guess she got bored. Dad being military, he was gone a lot. She started getting into stuff. I don't really know what all she did. I just know she got into a lot of mischief. Then she started running around on my father. Dad put up with everything else, hoping she would settle down as she got older, but the infidelity was the last straw, I think.

"He came home on leave one night, caught her with some man she'd picked up in a bar. They argued, she refused to stop seeing other men, he threatened to divorce her. I don't really know the whole story. All I know is she stormed out of the house one night, presumably to go to one of the men she'd been seeing, and they found her the next morning dead, murdered by that man."

* * * *

Angelina didn't know what to say. Her heart broke for him, for that little boy left without a mother, even as a keen understanding of why the man had run from her took hold. She saw the similarities of those two nights so many years apart and understood the fear that gripped him so hard when she left him, the anger and turmoil that drove him away.

"When you took my truck that night, Angelina, God, I knew you weren't going to another man. I knew you were going to look for your mother and Tess and somehow that made it even worse because I knew that if you had figured out where they were you would be confronting a monster too. I was so afraid they would find you the next morning."

She reached for him. How could she not? She touched his shoulder, the side of his neck, his cheek, but still he didn't turn to her. His eyes glistened, Jesus, with unshed tears. He was crying. "Jason," she whispered, her own voice cracking with emotion. "I'm so sorry. I didn't think. I didn't know."

"I almost lost you twice that day." He spoke so softly now that she had to lean in to hear him. "Both times I felt so helpless, so scared. I was so afraid I was going to lose you."

"But you didn't. I'm okay. I walked away both times unscathed."

"And what about the next time?" he demanded, a trace of anger in his tone. He finally looked at her, his eyes luminous and filled with fear and pain.

Angelina dropped her hand, surprised by the heat in his question. "What next time? I hope nothing like that ever happens again. That day was no walk in the park for me either, Jason. I nearly lost my mother and my sister that day, not to mention my own life."

"Yet you didn't hesitate to go after them. You ignored Jackson when he ordered you to stay put here, to leave it to the authorities. You went after them without any regard for your own life."

"Isn't that what you do everyday? Every time you go to work, aren't you putting your life in danger?"

Jason shook his head. "It isn't the same. I'm trained to do what I do. It's my job."

"You're right that it isn't the same. Just like the things that happened that day aren't things that happen in my life everyday. Did I put myself in danger by going after my mother and sister? Yes, I did, and I would do it again without a moment's hesitation. If you're worried that I'm too young, too restless, and have to live on the edge of danger like your mother did to be happy you can rest assured that I'm not. If I never experience anything like what happened to me that day, I will be perfectly happy."

"Would you be perfectly happy with me?" He turned toward her, but he didn't reach for her. One hand remained on the rail, clenched around his beer bottle, while the other hung loose at his side.

Angelina's pose mirrored his and, while she did want to reach for him, she restrained the urge. "What are you asking me, Jason?"

He looked down at his feet, looked out at the night, and then finally met her gaze once more. "You told me before you ran off that night that you love me. Did you mean that?"

Unable to speak with her heart securely lodged in her throat, she nodded and watched as what could only be relief washed into his eyes.

He did reach for her then, his free hand gripping her waist as he pulled her against him. He leaned down, stopping only fraction of a breath from her lips as he whispered, "I'm asking you to be with me. I'm asking you to stay with me. I'm telling you that I need you, that I want you, that I—" He gulped, tried again. "That I—" He closed his eyes, his lips twitching in a nervous smile.

"You can say it," she whispered. She reached up to push her fingers through the short stubble that was his hair. "Is it really so hard to say?"

"You have no idea," he said on a laugh. Then he stopped laughing and looked at her, all humor gone from his eyes and his lips. "I love you, Angelina."

Angelina closed her eyes as the words drifted over her, around her, through her. Then he kissed her and, oh man, she melted in his arms. It wasn't like any other kiss she ever shared with this man. She felt him pour his heart and soul into her, felt him give himself completely to her and she gave him the same. His hand flattened on the small of her back, drawing her closer still as he kissed her so deeply she felt almost certain they would become one. Then he slowly eased back only to rest his forehead to hers as he gazed into her eyes.

"One more question," he said, his voice husky with need. "The suit. You look amazing. You always look amazing. But you aren't wearing that suit just because of the meeting you had with Mr. Churchill, are you?"

Angelina shook her head. "I wore jeans and a T-shirt to the meeting."

"Then you put this on for me? And left me to wear rags." He frowned, confusion evident in his eyes. "Did I miss a point to the game?"

"I thought it was a money thing. You know, me from a prominent family and you..."

"A middle-class man," he finished for her. "You thought your money intimidated me, that I thought you were out of my league."

"Well, yes."

"You weren't entirely off base with that one."

"I wanted to show you that no matter how I'm dressed I can still be me and that no matter what you wear I love you anyway." She pulled back enough to let her gaze slide down him, inching its way up again. "Personally, I *love* this look on you." That made him laugh. God, but she loved the way he laughed. "But if you will give me a couple of minutes, I'll be happy to get out of this suit for you."

"Getting you out of that suit is exactly what I had in mind." He started to walk her back to the French doors. "As a matter of fact, it works well for me." He backed her into the office then stopped to look around. "The whole setting works well for me. You know, the hard-working man taking the well-dressed woman in her office scenario."

Angelina laughed. "Is that the starting bell for another game I hear ringing in my head?"

"You bet ya. But this one is a bit more complicated." He kicked the French doors closed, upended his bottle, and guzzled down the remainder of his beer. He nodded at her bottle. "Drink up, sweetheart."

She did, and he took her now empty bottle, tossed both his and hers into the trashcan beside the desk where the bottles collided with a loud crash of glass on glass. She winced at the sound.

"We'll need both hands free for this," he told her with a mischievous grin as his hand returned to her waist, his other hand lifting to cup the side of her neck.

"How is this going to be more complicated?"

"I thought we would do a little role-playing. Well, not exactly role-playing. It's more like—" He seemed to search for the right word. "See, there's a whole script to this fantasy game."

Angelina raised her eyebrows. "Like lines that we have to say?"

"Yeah." He leaned in for another kiss, just a quick brush of his lips to hers before he stepped away smiling. "Is anyone else home?" he asked as if suddenly realizing the possibility that they weren't alone in the huge house.

"My mother." She laughed at the pouty expression that came to his face. "But she's in her room on the third floor way, *way* down the other end of the hall. Besides, she would love to know that we are in here like this together. You will never believe what I found out. My mother had a threesome thing going with my father and my uncle when I was a child."

"No way!" Jason laughed his surprise as he walked to the office door, closed and locked it. "Like mother like daughter perhaps."

"Apparently so. Is there some line I'm supposed to say here, something you're waiting for me to do?" she asked when he simply turned back to face her but stayed by the door.

"I'm thinking. I confess I don't really have this all planned out. Short notice, you know? I'm usually pretty good at thinking fast on my feet but trying to do that while looking at you," He shook his head. "It's not working out so well."

Angelina laughed. She was good at thinking fast on her feet too, and looking at him didn't make it hard for her at all. If anything, it made it easier because she knew exactly what she wanted him to do. She also knew exactly what to do to get the ball rolling.

She sauntered to the desk, looking at him over her shoulder as she put an extra sway in her hips. Her gaze never left him as she turned, perched on the edge of the desk, crossed her ankles. She put her hands beside her hips and leaned forward enough to make the low-cut opening of the suit jacket part. She saw his gaze drop to that opening, knew he could see the edges of her breasts. It would be enough to clue him in to the fact that she wasn't wearing a bra.

"Is it getting easier to think yet?" she asked, pure amusement in her tone. "Or harder?"

"Harder." He breathed. "Much, much harder."

"I've been watching you, Mr. Graham. The work you do is exceptional," she told him in her best professional sounding voice, pulling words from an imaginary hat inside her head. "I would like to repay you. Anything you want. All you have to do is ask."

"Anything?" He took two steps toward her and stopped again. God! The way he looked at her made her feel empowered, sexy, and just a bit slutty.

"Anything."

"Take off your jacket."

She did. Her fingers slowly freed the buttons that held the material together. She allowed her fingers to graze her skin as she opened the jacket, shrugged it off her shoulders, and let it fall onto the desktop behind her.

"Jesus!" He exhaled on a whoosh of heated air. "Touch yourself for me."

She slid her hands under her breasts, cupped them, and lifted them as she grazed the pads of her thumbs over her already taut nipples. She kept her gaze on him as she fondled her breasts, saw the fire that began in the depths of his eyes. Inspired, she bent her head to one lifted breast, licked the flesh with her tongue, and heard a low, barbaric growl tear from Jason's throat.

He took another step toward her but stopped yet again. "Tell me that you will be happy with me." His voice was quiet and all the more effective because of it. They were playing another game, acting out another fantasy, yes, but this was important to him. The look in his eyes and the sound of his voice left no doubt about that.

"I will be happy with you," Angelina told him, her gaze locked with his. She rolled her breasts in her palms, drawing his attention back to them for a half a heartbeat. "And I will make sure that you remain happy with me."

That made him smile. "Tell me you want to be with me, that you will stay with me and only me."

"I do want to be with you, and I will stay with you," she repeated and just to make sure he understood how serious she truly was, she added, "Forever."

He took the few remaining steps that brought him to stand in front of her, his step faltering only slightly as she added the word forever to the line he gave her. He seemed to ingest the word, then nodded slowly. "Take off my shirt."

Angelina pushed herself off the desk and gripped the hem of his T-shirt, slowly pulled it up and over his head. Unable to resist, she leaned in and licked her way over his pectoral muscle, rose to her tiptoes to taste his neck and jaw. His eyes closed and his head fell back, a soft moan escaping his lips. Then he caught her gently but firmly by the shoulders and pushed her back.

"Not yet," he told her on a ragged breath. "Take off my pants." When she grinned, he quickly added, "And no tasting."

She poked out her bottom lip in a pout as she freed the button of his jeans, pushed down the zipper and shucked his pants down his legs. His cock was gloriously hard and ready for her and she reached out to wrap her fingers around him but he caught her wrist, made a tsking sound with his tongue.

"No touching either."

"Then are you going to touch me soon because, God, seeing you like that is driving me mad! I want you inside me. I want you inside me. Now!"

Jason laughed. "I think you took care of about half the lines in the next part of the script in one breath."

"Good. I saved us some time. Now, *please.*"

"Turn around. Yes, like that," he said when she turned. His hands came around her, found her breasts and pulled at them until she was bent over the desk, her hands braced on the desktop. He skimmed his palms over her flesh, down her sides, her thighs, then slowly made his way back up, lifting her skirt as his hands climbed back to her hips. He made a low, appreciative sound at his discovery that she wore no underwear. "Where do you want me, Angelina?"

"In me," she gasped. God, but she was wet. Her pussy lips were slick with it. His orders to touch herself, the soft way he touched her now, drove her mindless with desire. She needed him inside her, wanted it hard and fast and so not gentle.

"Where? Tell me where you want me to fuck you tonight."

"My pussy." The words burst from her, a plea for his touch. She couldn't stand this, the erotic talk, the closeness without touch or even sight. She lifted her head, looked at the wall behind the desk and caught his reflection in the glass of the bookshelf. He was watching her there too. Their gazes met in the glass, and she half expected the glass to shatter from the heat that passed between them.

"Spread your legs. A little farther. Yeah, that's it." His hands moved between them and then, thank you Jesus, he was inside her.

Angelina gasped as he thrust his cock into her sopping-wet opening in one quick, vicious movement that had her rocking forward on the desktop. He slammed inside her, once, twice, three times before he suddenly stopped, buried deep inside her, their bodies all but molded together.

"It's time for me to say a few lines of the script."

"You're kidding, right?" Angelina tried to move, but he had her pinned between him and the desk. "Jason, please."

"Not yet." He laughed. "There are a couple of things I have to tell you."

"But can't it wait? I'm dying here!"

"I love you." He said it so easily this time, with such feeling and absolutely no hesitation that she stopped struggling. She met his gaze in the glass once more and he leaned over her, resting his chin on her shoulder. "I'm sorry for running away like I did, and I promise not to ever let anything you do scare me into running again."

She would have laughed at that, if he hadn't sounded so serious. "And I promise not to do something so dangerous and stupid that it will make you want to run away again."

He smiled, nodded. "Good enough. I want you to move in with me, Angelina. I want you to live with me, be there for me to come home to, be there with me forever."

She started to speak, but he pulled out of her almost all the way and then plunged back into her again effectively cutting off any response she might have said.

"The line you are supposed to say here is simple. One word. Yes." He moved inside her again, and the word spilled from her throat on a moan in answer to both moving in with him and the small taste of penetration he gave her before stopping yet again.

"Yes. Yes. *Yes*. I will move in with you. I want to live with you, be there for you to come home to forever. I also want to come dammit. Now please, fuck me!"

He laughed and, finally, *finally* gave her what she wanted. He pounded his cock inside her, their bodies slapping together from the force of his thrusts. The orgasm hit her without warning, exploding from her with such force that she could do nothing but collapse on the desktop as the spasms made her body jerk and quiver. She heard more than felt Jason's release, and then he folded himself over her as they both labored for breaths that seemed too far away.

"There are more lines left to the script, you know," Angelina panted.

"Say 'em if you know 'em, because my script just went up in flames, baby." His cock slipped out of her, and he kissed her lightly on the back of the shoulder before he pushed himself up and stepped back.

Angelina turned on legs that still shook from the aftermath of her orgasm. She pushed her skirt down and used her arms to pull herself to sit on the desktop. "Come here." She held out her arms for him.

He pulled up his pants before moving to her, all the while laughing. "I'm sorry. I can't stop smiling right now. I feel like an idiot!"

"You shouldn't. I love it." But she let her own smile fade from her lips as she gazed at him. "Just like I love you. Jason, I *am* the family type. I do want kids." She faltered then as his eyes widened, but she'd gone this far. Why stop now? "I lied a few minutes ago when I said I would move in with you and be happy. I will move in and, yes, I will be happy but not forever. I will be happy forever only if you marry me."

Jason looked like a guppy, his mouth opening and closing as he searched for something to say.

Angelina's laugh betrayed her, revealing all the nervousness his silence was starting to make her feel inside. "I guess I lied when I promised not to ever do anything that would make you want to run again too."

"I'm not running," he said quickly.

"You look like you want to."

"No. No. It's just that, wow, you were supposed to wait on me to ask."

"Oh." Relief surged through her.

"That is what you just did, isn't it? Asked me to marry you?"

"Well, yeah, I guess I did."

"Aren't you supposed to get on one knee or something?"

Angelina glanced down at his pants. He'd pulled them up but left them unbuttoned and unzipped. "Are you sure you're ready for me to get on one knee so soon?"

"Yes. No." He stopped, shook his head and laughed. "Yes, I will marry you. Yes, I *want* to marry you. No, I'm not ready yet. Give me about another ten minutes though and—" He waggled his brows suggestively.

"Sorry, but I don't have ten minutes. See, that's another game I want to play with you, and now is as good a time as any to get started." She hopped off the desk, dropped to her knees, and began to pull down his jeans.

"And that game would be?"

"To see how fast and how many times I can get you ready in a night. Do you want to play?"

"Oh baby, you know I do."

TWIN GAMES

The Heroes of Silver Springs 2

THE END

WWW.TONYARAMAGOS.COM

AUTHOR'S BIO

I began writing when I was in Junior High School. (We won't discuss how long ago that was :-) When my parents saw how serious I was about becoming a writer, they enrolled me in a mail course through the Institute for Children's Literature. It was there that I learned much of the ins and outs of the publishing world.

In 1999, my first young adult book (though no long available) was accepted for publication. And I was off! Six books later, I gave mysteries for adults a go. Writing under the pen name of Calley Moore, I had four books published. Meanwhile, my YA novels were still kicking butt. In 2002, I won the Best Author's award at the Book Review Cafe that same year.

As I continued to grow, so did my writing interest. In 2004, I expanded to adult romances, and in 2005, I turned erotic. <grin> I have several books that will be released in the upcoming months.

All writing aside, I am a native of South Mississippi, though I currently reside in Tampa, FL. I am a mother of two wonderful boys, and when I'm not writing, I'm reading. I also enjoy heavy metal music, various types of movies (anything with Matthew McConaughey is a sure winner with me) and dancing.

Check out Tonya's latest books at
www.sirenpublishing.com/tonyaramagos

Visit Tonya's website at
www.TonyaRamagos.com

Siren Publishing, Inc.
www.SirenPublishing.com

Printed in the United States
150285LV00004B/131/P